**David Wharton** grew up in Northumberland and lives in Leicester, where he has worked in education for many years. He now divides his time between writing fiction and training English teachers. *Finer Things* is his first novel.

# Finer Things

## DAVID WHARTON

SANDSTONE PRESS

First published in Great Britain by
Sandstone Press Ltd
Dochcarty Road
Dingwall
Ross-shire
IV15 9UG
Scotland

www.sandstonepress.com

Quotation from Allan Kaprow 1966 courtesy Allan
Kaprow Estate and Hauser and Wirth.
'Playwrights Against Apartheid' declaration reproduced by kind
permission of the Anti-Apartheid Movement Archives Committee.

The publisher acknowledges subsidy from Creative
Scotland towards publication of this volume.

ISBN: 978-1-912240-68-5
ISBNe: 978-1-912240-69-2

Cover design by Stuart Brill
Typeset by Biblichor Ltd, Edinburgh
Printed and bound by CPI Group (UK) Ltd, Croydon, CR0 4YY

For Frances

A happening is a game with a high, a ritual that no church would want because there's no religion for sale.

*Allan Kaprow*
*How to Make a Happening*

# MAY – NOVEMBER 1962

# 1

Sometimes Delia thought life might be easier on the game. Like the old joke said, at least you weren't on your feet all day, and hers ached from traipsing around stores. Selfridges Monday, Harrods Tuesday, Harvey Nichols Wednesday. Now it was Thursday, and Stella had asked her to take an apprentice round Barkers, show the girl how to go on.

Perhaps she should have said no. Stella would take no for an answer if you gave it to her reasonably – it was just that yes was often the wiser choice. So here Delia was, in Kensington Square at half past ten on a muggy May morning. Her scalp itched under a heavy brown wig, and the railings she was leaning against dug into her back. Teddy was supposed to have delivered the apprentice twenty minutes ago.

By quarter to eleven, Delia had taken three increasingly agitated turns around the square. Then, just as Teddy finally sauntered in at the Thackeray Street entrance with his arm around the girl's waist, a copper on the beat happened to enter from Derry Street, at the opposite corner. Luckily, Teddy saw him first, and steered the girl straight back out again.

Delia stayed where she was. On the inside she might feel like she didn't belong here, but nobody else could tell. She was dressed right. She knew how to make herself look to the rest of the world like Kensington Square was her sort of place. Teddy, on the other hand, stank of crime. If he'd been spotted near these genteel old houses in his too-small suit and greasy tweed overcoat, he'd most certainly have had to account for himself.

The copper strolled past, appraised Delia out of the corner of his eye, decided not to bother. Somebody's mistress, he'd be thinking, or the posh kind of brass. He toddled around the square to reassure anyone who cared to look down from an elegant window that the law was ready, should it be required. Then off he went, back the way he'd come.

Teddy reappeared with the girl. A fleshy little thing, London Irish most likely, eighteen or nineteen. Almost pretty. Not quite. Cherry red lipstick.

'You're late,' Delia said. 'I've been waiting the best part of an hour.'

Teddy tipped back his pork pie hat, and a bead of sweat dribbled down his face. 'Sorry darlin'. Got held up, if you know what I mean.' He gave Delia a conspiratorial little smirk. 'This here's Maureen.'

'Hello, Maureen,' Delia said.

'Hello, Miss.'

She fought off an impulse to pity this Maureen for her lumpen appearance and her *Miss*, like she was talking to a schoolteacher. Maybe it would work in the girl's favour, having so little to draw the eye.

'Now then, Maureen,' Teddy said. 'Delia's one of my best hoisters, so you listen to what she tells you. You'll just be reconnoitring to start with, but if things look promising, she'll teach you what's what, all right?' He gave the kid a squeeze around her waist, and she flinched, doubtless remembering where the dirty bastard's hands had been half an hour earlier.

'You all done now, Teddy?' Delia said.

'Certainly am.' He reprised his smirk to drive home the double entendre. No doubt he'd be even less subtle about it later on, telling the story to Tommy the Spade and Itchy Pete and the rest of those wankers in the Lamplighters.

'Well, then. I expect you've other business.'

Teddy stood a few moments longer, obviously not wanting to leave Maureen with the impression that Delia had dismissed him.

'Just bring the girl back to the Lamplighters after,' he said at last.

'Where else would I take her?' Delia said. And seeing he was too thick or too stubborn to understand that hint, she added, 'I work for your sister, not you, Teddy, so how about you clear off? You've already got me late starting.'

Teddy curled his lip and addressed himself to Maureen. 'Moody bitch, ain't she? On her rags, I expect.' Then he skulked away. Just before he rounded the corner, he turned and called back, 'Stella's got hopes for that one, Dee. Mind you take care of her properly.'

He was gone before she had a chance to reply. Back home in Fenfield, she might have yelled at him across the square – to tell him she was sure those hopes of Stella's for this girl didn't include a poke off Teddy in some backstreet by the bins. But she couldn't shout a thing like that here. Not in Kensington, where she had to pass for refined.

'Ignore him, darling,' she said. 'Especially all that about me being one of his best hoisters. *His* – like he's in charge of anything. Stella only keeps him in work out of pity, 'cause he's her little brother. He's nothing, Teddy Bilborough. Bleeding errand boy, that's all.'

Maureen was not the type who could conceal her thoughts. In quick succession, her face revealed understanding, then shame, then despondency. Obviously, Teddy had convinced her he was a person of influence, that if she gave in to him he'd look after her interests. Better try and make her think about something else.

'How'd you come to join our gang, darling?' Delia asked.

The girl cheered up at this jollier recollection. 'I used to work for the hairdresser who does Stella. Chantelle's on Robson Street. Trainee stylist I was.'

'She go there regular, does she?' The idea of the boss sitting in a hairdresser's, of her being anywhere other than the Lamplighters Arms, seemed unlikely somehow.

'Nah. Chantelle does her at the pub. Private. Anyway, I had to leave, 'cause I couldn't get the hang of the scissors. So Chantelle asks Stella if she's got a spot for me. That was nice of her, she could've just given me the sack. But Chantelle always liked me, even though I didn't have no aptitude for hairdressing.' Maureen hesitated a moment, then added, 'Is Stella all right to work for? I mean – she's a bit of a terror, ain't she?' The girl looked anxiously around her, as if at any second the boss herself might pop out from behind a corner or stick her head up from underneath a drain cover.

'Stella's fair. She'll look after you as long as you're straight with her.' That was the truth, mostly. The rest could wait for another time, if this Maureen shaped up right and needed to know.

They headed out of the square. On the brief walk to Barkers, Delia hit her usual brisk pace, while Maureen scuttled alongside, puffing and struggling, three short steps to each of the older woman's two long ones. Slow witted *and* slow moving, Delia thought. Not much hope for a hoister who could neither talk her way out of trouble nor run away from it.

'What was it Teddy said we'd be doing first?' the girl said between gasps. 'Recon—something?'

'Reconnoitring, love.'

'Yeah, that. What is it?'

'You've heard of casing a job? We're making sure it's safe to go to work. Reconnoitring – reconnaissance – that's what they call it in the army.'

Maureen frowned as she clumsily worked out the route between this new information and something she had already heard. 'Oh yes. Teddy told me he used to be a soldier.'

Delia snorted. 'I bet he mentioned that right off, didn't he?' Teddy liked to think himself a military man, on account of having stayed in for the whole of his national service and almost being promoted to corporal. Comparably speaking, it was an achievement. The rest of his lot had either dodged the call-up or brought dishonourable discharges on themselves. Teddy was always saying he shouldn't have left after his time finished. That he'd be a sergeant or even higher by now. Maybe he was right. He was useless at unregimented life.

Though she really didn't like Teddy, Delia felt a kind of sympathy for him. He was a victim of his own character, she supposed. Then again, other people were victims of Teddy's character too, like this girl he'd fucked that morning just because he could. Like Delia, who he'd kept waiting while he took advantage of the opportunity.

She was good at understanding other people, putting herself in their heads, seeing why they'd made their mistakes, but there was no use feeling sorry for them. When it came down to it, Teddy and Maureen were responsible for themselves, just like everyone else.

Approaching Barkers always gave her a thrill. The building's vast exterior surprised her every time. With its austere sheets of windows, its unexpected curves, its flattened towers, Barkers seemed an odd thing to discover on a London street – as if a chunk of 1930s Manhattan had lost its way and come to ground in quite the wrong city. Of all the stores to go hoisting, this was her favourite.

She took Maureen into the Food Halls first. There they strolled past slabs of cured beef; bright tubes of French biscuits; a stack of triangular tinned hams with windmills on their green and red labels – an intoxicating wash of colours and smells. All the other departments had wheeled out the summer stock: swimsuits, thin cotton dresses, lightweight bedding in sharp new season shades. Here it was Christmas all year round: spiced, hedonistic, excessive.

# Finer Things

Delia was sometimes tempted to slip a thing or two from the Food Halls into her bloomers. But there was no point, not when Tommy the Spade could nick the same stuff from any grocer and sell it for pennies. The valuable items – exotic meats, saffron, caviar, truffles – Barkers kept behind the counters, where fussy men in white jackets could dole them out by the quarter ounce. Too much trouble to thieve those in sale-able quantities, and anyway, Delia knew the interests of her clientele. Nice clothes you could flog easily but who'd buy shoplifted caviar? As for truffles, she had tried those once, mixed with butter on a cracker, at a party in Knightsbridge. She'd nearly thrown her guts up. For three days afterwards, she hadn't been able to rid herself of the taste of decay.

She picked up an onion, held it to her nose, dislodged some outer skin with her thumbnail, and let a crisp, papery fragment drift to the floor. Returning the vegetable to its display she told Maureen under her breath, 'We won't be nicking anything right now. First you've to learn how to look out for shopwalkers.'

'I ain't never been anywhere like this before,' Maureen said. 'Spensive, ain't it?'

'Overpriced for idiots. The sort who'll cough up double for digestive biscuits so they can take them home in a paper bag with *Barkers of Kensington* on it. Did you hear what I said about shopwalkers?'

Maureen nodded. 'I got to learn how to look out for them.'

'Good. Over there, by the fresh herbs,' Delia murmured. 'Blue coat. Just take a quick look. Tell me what you think.'

Maureen glanced at the woman clumsily, but briefly enough. 'Shopwalker?'

'Don't think so. But what do you notice about her? Why doesn't she fit in here?'

The apprentice gave the blue-coated woman another awkward look. 'Clothes?'

'Well done. What's wrong with them?'

'Too cheap.'

'That's right. Now keep an eye on her.'

Delia herself was dressed in items lifted from the best clothing departments in the city, and, because Stella had prepared her for the day's work, so was Maureen. Nothing flashy, but all high quality. Unlike the shoplifters they pursued, shopwalkers had to buy their own clothes, and they weren't paid well. They prowled about the stores in dumpy crap from Marks and Spencer, giving the alarm to any hoister who knew her business. But this woman's tat came from British Home Stores, or somewhere worse. She was a shoplifter. Some amateur.

It wasn't long before the woman confirmed Delia's assessment. She picked up a can of pilchards, pretended to scrutinise the label, took a swift look about, dropped the item into her open handbag and scurried off to another part of the store. The move was so crass, even Maureen saw it. 'She's a hoister,' the girl whispered excitedly. 'Same as us.'

Delia placed her hand in the small of Maureen's back and steered her out of the Food Halls. As they rode the escalator up to Soft Furnishings, she said, 'That wasn't any hoister. She was on her own. No gang behind her, and no skill. No sense either. If she isn't caught today, she will be tomorrow, or the day after. And for a can of bleeding pilchards! You see that one again, or one like her, you keep well away, Maureen.'

They toured the whole store, every department twice. Along the way, Delia pointed out important things for Maureen to remember. In Haberdashery, she bought three coat buttons and a bobble of black cotton thread.

'My niece here needs to learn to sew,' she told the assistant as she paid. Delia had listened carefully to the posh types slumming it in Finlay's Soho clubs. She could imitate their moneyed drawl impeccably. 'Her husband's coat has lost all of its buttons. Every single one! I can't imagine what they teach in school these days, but a girl ought to be able to darn a hole and stitch a button on, don't you think?'

'Certainly, Madam.' The assistant was a woman in late middle age wearing far too much make-up. She had tried to fill in all her wrinkles with powder. Close up like this she looked horrible.

'Tell me, what are the "in" colours this season?' Delia asked her.

'Fresh yellow,' the assistant said. 'And cornflower blue.'

'Oh yes, we've seen a lot of those up in the womenswear department, haven't we Charlotte?'

Maureen had been thoroughly briefed for this moment. She assented with a nod and a close-mouthed 'Mmmmm'.

'Just had her teeth done,' Delia explained in confidential tones. 'Won't let anyone see the braces. Well, thank you very much. Perhaps we'll take a look at those yellows and blues again. I could do with a new summer dress.'

They left the store then, and headed for Kensington Gardens. Delia dumped the buttons and cotton in the first bin they passed.

'Why'd you do that?' Maureen asked.

'Can't sew. Never sewed a thing in my life. I only bought them so we'd look like customers.'

Maureen looked alarmed. 'We wasn't being followed, was we? Not by one of them shopwalkers?'

'Course we weren't. That's not the point. Shopwalkers are the least of your worries, darling. I know every shopwalker in this store, pretty much every one in every store, actually. It's the rest of them who'll catch you out. There's all sorts of eyes in a place like Barkers. Assistants, porters, customers as well. You've got to be careful not to stick in anyone's memory.' She tapped her temple to reinforce the idea. 'See, when you go back next time, you don't want someone thinking, "Who's that over there? I'm sure I know her" – specially if it's right when you're popping something in your bloomers, because then—'

'What?'

Even saying it aloud could be unlucky. But Maureen was too dopey to put things together for herself. 'Well, then you'd be screwed, wouldn't you? That's why I bought the buttons.'

'Sorry Delia, I don't get it,' the girl said mournfully. 'I'm not very bright, am I?'

'You're fine. It's a lot to take in, all this. Think about it though, Maureen. We'd been walking round that store for more than a couple of hours, and not bought a thing. Maybe we were starting to send someone's radar bleeping.'

'Radar?'

The note of alarm in Maureen's voice made Delia smile. 'Not real radar, love. They haven't got that in shops. Not yet. I mean one of them might start feeling suspicious, that's all. But as soon as I picked up those buttons and paid for them, I turned into a customer. Not an important customer, mind you, just a person they can forget. Some run-of-the-mill old bird.'

'You ain't old, Delia,' Maureen protested.

'Nice of you to say.' And at thirty-eight still true, Delia thought, just about. 'But if you go back and ask that assistant what my age was, I bet she'll tell you forty-five at least. Fifty, maybe. 'Cause she'll be guessing. She won't remember much about me – not my eyes, not my hair, not my height. All I was to her was a customer, not a person. She looked at me, but she didn't see me.'

'Clever,' Maureen said, probably not getting the idea at all. Delia couldn't blame her. And in truth, she had bought those buttons for an entirely different reason. They were a present, a secret sacrifice, for her Imps.

They sang in the blood in her veins, in the air against her skin, in the nerves in her teeth the moment Delia walked into any store. Told her when she was safe, warned her when she wasn't. It was like dowsing.

When she'd arrived at Barkers that morning, they had told her this wasn't a day for recklessness, but if Delia took care, they said, she and the girl would be fine. Then that amateur had nicked the can of pilchards, and somehow that had knocked the balance off. She'd felt it all the way around the store afterwards, an increasing sense that something was not right after all. So she had bought those buttons for luck, to remind the Imps who protected the working shoplifter of her love for them. To keep them on her side.

More than likely that was all a load of old cobblers but everyone had their superstitions. Most hoisters got caught once in a while, and Delia hadn't, not ever. So she didn't care if her little rituals were meaningless. She'd bought those buttons for the Imps: she felt safe again. When she and this apprentice returned to Barkers that afternoon, they could set to work with confidence.

The walk across Kensington Gardens was clearly an enormous distance to Maureen. Delia had to slow down so as not to leave her behind. That had its compensations, though. The park wasn't especially beautiful, just a lot of lawns and trees planted with drab regularity, but it felt good to be surrounded by space rather than people for once. Here and there, young mothers, or nannies – it was hard to tell – played with their children, or their charges.

'Can we stop a minute?' Maureen said. 'My legs ain't half aching.'

'You'll need to get fitter than this if you want to be a hoister,' Delia told her. But they waited for a while, Maureen leaning against a tree with her eyes closed while Delia watched a kid in school uniform feed a pair of lurid green birds that had no place in any English landscape. Parrots or something like that.

They flew up to the boy with brazen confidence, landed on his wrist and shoulder and took peanuts directly from his hand.

'Who are we going to see?' Maureen asked, as she and Delia set off again.

'Lulu Everard.'

'Isn't she the one what went to bed with Al Capone?'

'I doubt it.' Delia had heard the Capone story, of course, but she had no interest in gossip. If the girl hung around the others, she'd soon hear all their nonsense about Lulu's American years. How between the wars she had consorted with slick-suited businessmen whose glossy names shimmered with violence. Dutch Schultz. Lucky Luciano. Meyer Lansky. And how, in 1934, Lulu was standing behind John Dillinger in the queue outside the Biograph movie house when Charles Winstead's bullet exploded out of the gangster's cheekbone. That same day, they said, still drenched in the blood of Public Enemy Number One, she had walked into a travel agency and booked her ticket back to England.

Three decades after she'd come home, Lulu's London accent was still peppered with Americana. Whatever she had done over there, whatever had been done to her, or for her, she was glad to keep her memories to herself. She certainly had no time for the likes of Tommy the Spade, Itchy Pete or Teddy Bilborough – grown-up boys still playing at Cagney and Bogart in the streets of Fenfield. They acted those parts no better now than when they'd been kids, despite the off-the-peg suits and trilby hats Stella's hoisters had nicked for them.

The afternoon was just beginning in Kensington Gardens. Shopgirls and office workers reaching the ends of their lunch breaks readied themselves to return to work. Delia and Maureen found Lulu near the Peter Pan statue, sitting alone on a bench by the Serpentine, surrounded by half a dozen well-stuffed shopping bags. They took seats either side of her.

# Finer Things

At sixty-three Lulu was still striking in her mackintosh and broad pink hat. In her heyday, she must have been remarkable. Her job now was to wait in Kensington Gardens so the younger women could drop off the goods they'd stolen. She brought them all lunch too.

'What you got?' Delia asked her.

'Ham and boiled egg,' Lulu said. 'And a bottle of Baldwin's.'

Delia took the two remaining sandwiches. They were wrapped in greaseproof paper from the Wonderloaf that had been used to make them. 'Is that all?' she said, passing one to Maureen.

'You're last here,' Lulu said. 'Filled your bloomers for me, have you?'

'Nah. Been showing this apprentice around Barkers. I'll do some proper work with her later. We'll need to look different, though – we were in there hours this morning. Is there anything in those bags we can borrow for the afternoon?'

Lulu assessed Maureen's physique. 'A bit Diana Dors, ain't she? Doubt I've got much for her.'

'We'll manage.' Delia picked up the half-empty bottle of Baldwin's. She took a swig and handed the rest to Maureen, who looked suspiciously at the label.

'What's this?'

'Sarsaparilla,' Lulu told her. 'Ain't you had it before?'

Maureen took a cautious sip. 'Tastes like medicine. Nice medicine, though, not horrible medicine.' She drank down what was left and belched enthusiastically.

In one of the bags, Delia found a silk headscarf and a coat from Harvey Nichols that should fit Maureen well enough. 'Nice. Who nicked these?'

'Rita.' Lulu snipped off the tags with a pair of nail scissors and stowed them carefully in her pocket for later reattachment. 'Don't you damage this stuff, girl,' she told Maureen, handing her the coat and scarf. 'We got customers expecting it perfect. Rita won't thank you if you bring the price down.'

An hour later Delia and Maureen stood on the street outside Barkers, pretending to be interested in the window display. They checked their reflections in the glass. Back in Kensington Gardens, Delia had slipped into a thicket to put on a matronly twinset from Harrods. She'd also taken off her brown wig, revealing her own blonde hair, tied in a bun.

Maureen's Harvey Nichols coat and headscarf had transformed her, and Delia had told her to switch to a paler shade of lipstick. The flash of cherry on the girl's mouth had been the one noticeable thing about her. Otherwise, she was nearly invisible. Delia had spent the whole morning with her, and only had to look away for a moment to forget what she looked like. Maybe Stella was right to have high hopes for Maureen – as long as she had some talent for the work itself.

'Just to be sure,' Delia said, 'we'll go in separate this time. You wait here, and follow me after five minutes. Come up to Lingerie and then Furs, like I told you before. But don't get too near. You aren't with me and you don't know me.'

'I ain't got no watch, Delia. How will I know when it's five minutes?'

'Count—' She paused to do the sum in her head '—three hundred. Slowly. Like this—' Delia took an audible half breath between each number. 'One – two – three – and look in the shop windows. You can walk up and down the street a bit if you like. You got it? Then when you come in, you keep far off, but you watch what I do. Don't try to take anything yourself, not yet. Just pay attention to how I do it.'

Something on the edge of Delia's instinct had started to bother her. It was only the slightest twinge. She made Maureen repeat the full set of instructions twice. Especially the one about her not stealing anything herself.

## Finer Things

As she entered the store, she turned her head for a final check, wondering whether to ditch the whole thing for today. But there was nothing to worry about. Maureen was following orders. The girl shuffled down the road, browsing shop windows, indistinguishable from any shy middle-class newly-wed out looking for homewares. Eyes and memories would slide over her and continue their search for something of interest. Yes, it looked as if the Imps were taking care of her.

While the escalator carried her up to the third floor, Delia enjoyed the freedom of being briefly responsible only for herself. This was how she liked it.

A lot of the girls worked pairs. While one did the hoisting, the other kept a lookout for shopwalkers, nosey customers or zealous assistants. Some went in for play-acting – one of them would accuse a male customer of impropriety, make a big fuss about it while her partner got on with nicking whatever she fancied. All that theatrical crap was, in Delia's view, just asking for trouble. Quiet, alone and unnoticed was what she preferred. And when it went wrong for her, properly wrong, as it inevitably must one day, she'd only have herself to look out for, only herself to blame. No letting someone else down, no being let down herself.

She already knew she was going to steal something from Furs; even so, she went to Lingerie first. The two departments were next door to each other, and you didn't want to spend too long hovering around the thing you aimed to pinch. Lingerie was a useful place to wait for other reasons too. Usually the atmosphere was a little embarrassed, with nobody looking too closely at anyone else. Today, however, a big fat bloke was in there, picking up one pair of silk knickers after another. He wasn't doing anything bad enough to get himself kicked out, but he obviously enjoyed the feel of the fabric between his fingers, and occasionally he'd give one of the garments a discreet sniff. This was a good omen. The Imps must definitely be on Delia's side now. With the assistants' disapproving eyes all fixed on this pervert, she wouldn't draw anyone's attention, and it was easy for her to assess the situation across the aisle in Furs.

Exactly on cue, Maureen appeared. Keeping her distance as instructed, she shuttled through a rack of nightdresses, and avoided any eye contact with Delia. The girl was doing all right. Time to get on with it.

Delia strolled towards the black fox jacket she'd marked down for herself that morning. It was displayed slightly out of sight between a couple of big minks; simple to hoist and very sellable. She moved into its vicinity, her eyes deliberately focused on a hefty-looking red stole in the opposite aisle. She gave her surroundings a final check. Over in Lingerie, the fat pervert was still the centre of interest. Here in Furs there were two assistants on duty. A younger woman sat behind the counter and gazed dreamily off into the distance while the other, a senior saleswoman, dealt with a customer whose English didn't seem very competent. Nobody was even aware of Delia, or of Maureen, who was now pretending to examine an absurd Russian-style fur hat while keeping a careful, and unexpectedly subtle, watch on her teacher.

The moment felt right. Delia leant in and lifted the fox jacket from its display. She would normally have moved completely out of sight for the next part, but she wanted Maureen to see what to do, and circumstances were perfect for that.

She turned her back away from the trio at the counter and, in full view of her pupil, held the jacket upside down. Then, squeezing as tightly as she could, with nimble, practised fingers, she rolled it into a cigar, pulled her skirt forwards at the waist and dropped the fur inside the massive, specially made bloomers beneath. A little shake of her backside and she felt the weight of the coat settle where it belonged, into the space between her legs. Its soft exterior brushed against the insides of her thighs as she stepped out from between the minks and made her confident, innocent way past the younger assistant, who was still gazing distractedly off, and her superior, still trying to explain herself to the foreign customer.

It was always tricky to walk smoothly with something so heavy hidden under your skirt. The tight elastic around her legs meant there was no danger of the jacket falling out of the bloomers, but its swinging needed to be controlled, and she had to adopt an uncomfortably wide gait. Nevertheless, she was confident her movements would seem natural. She felt pleased with herself too, having rolled and hoisted the jacket so brazenly and got away with it.

Then a voice interrupted her. 'Excuse me! I don't think that belongs to you, Miss.'

Someone had been watching her, and she hadn't realised. How could this have happened? She readied herself to run, preparing for the way the fur under her skirt would unbalance her and obstruct her stride.

'Get off me!'

That was Maureen shouting. The pervert from Lingerie had hold of her by both arms, just above the elbows. The girl twisted and squirmed, but the man was strong.

Delia's thoughts tripped over each other, tumbled in confusion. A new shopwalker, obviously. Not a pervert – or not *simply* a pervert. She should have spotted him. How had she not noticed he was watching? Any moment now someone would grab her too. Maureen was only the accomplice after all. Delia had stolen the jacket.

What direction should she go? Maybe if she were to run down the 'up' escalator, she told herself – they wouldn't expect that. But she was frozen. None of the ideas fighting in her head seemed capable of turning into action.

**David Wharton**

Maureen spat full in the shopwalker's face. In return he slapped her hard, knocked her to the floor, wiped off the spit with his sleeve and bent to lift her back to her feet. The two assistants scampered out to help him.

Delia's paralysing incomprehension evaporated. She realised that nobody had grabbed hold of her, and nobody was going to. None of them were even looking at her. They hadn't seen her steal that fox jacket after all. It lay unnoticed between her legs. She was safe, as long as she could keep calm and get out. Maureen was the one in trouble. Only Maureen. The Russian hat the girl had been inspecting was now stuck halfway out of her waistband.

The stupid kid wasn't meant to hoist anything yet. She'd been told that over and over. But when Delia had stolen the fox coat she'd made it look easy, and Maureen must have been so excited she'd forgotten her instructions, hadn't been able to stop herself having a go too.

Now there was no way to save her. Delia started edging towards the escalators.

'Excuse me, Madam.' It was the shopwalker. He'd noticed her moving away. 'Would you mind waiting until the police get here? You might need to make a statement.'

'Oh, I'm so sorry.' Delia gave him her best Knightsbridge posh. 'I'm afraid I was looking elsewhere when all this happened. Nothing I could tell the officers would be of the slightest use.'

'Even so, Madam, I—bloody hell, you little—!' Maureen had stamped hard on his foot.

Delia took the opportunity the girl had given her. When the shopwalker looked for her again, she was gone.

# 2

Elsewhere in the city that same morning, half an hour before Delia arrived in Kensington Square, Tess Green stepped out from the oily heat of the Underground and joined the mass of commuters on Euston Road. To a nineteen-year-old from Dewsbury, the anonymity of the capital was exhilarating. Here nobody meant anything to anyone else. She halted briefly to check her *A-Z*, then pushed forward.

A few turns along the pencil line she'd drawn on the map led her off the main concourse, into streets punctuated by cafes, bookshops and second-hand emporia, mostly still closed at half past nine. In sophisticated cities, she remembered, one did not talk of 'areas' but of 'quarters', and in this quarter the inhabitants obviously preferred to sleep late – or to remain in bed for other reasons. Eventually, she thought, this would be her life too. Though she, being an artist, would never waste the early morning light.

As she walked along, she slipped into a familiar daydream: herself as the sort of painter she'd read about in novels. Birdsong would wake her in the single-room studio where work and sleep and life all blended together. Still groggy from last night's red wine and political argument, she'd make fresh coffee, then turn her attention to the man in her narrow bed, to the painting she was making of him. He'd be unconscious under the tumbled blanket, one arm and one leg uncovered. His spectacles and notebook nearby. Many years later, art historians would build entire lectures around this early work: *The Sleeping Poet*.

She laughed aloud at herself, at the silliness of writing her own epitaph before any of it had begun. Before she had even passed her art school interview. She didn't actually like red wine or coffee, though she had tried both two years ago on a sixth form French trip to Le Touquet. Just acquiring the proper tastes was going to take practice. To begin with, she needed to change into the clothes she was carrying in the duffel bag over her shoulder. Because dressed as she was right now, she'd have little chance of snagging any young poet's interest, and still less of convincing an art school interview board that she was a suitable candidate.

Just ahead of her an elderly woman was unlocking the door of a cafe: *Ginelli's*.

'Are you opening up?'

'Sure, of course.' The woman spoke irritably, with a strong European accent. She was tiny, dressed in a black frock of some rough, heavy material her desiccated body seemed almost too frail to support.

'Do you have a lavatory in there I could possibly use?' Tess asked, remembering Nancy Mitford's rule that it was a sin to say 'toilet' or 'loo'.

'This ain't a public lav, darling. It's a caff.'

'Yes – of course. I'd like a coffee as well, afterwards. But if you could—'

'It's for staff, only. We ain't got no toilet for customers.'

'I'd really appreciate it if you could make an exception. It's just I need somewhere to change my clothes. I've an interview this morning.'

The woman looked her up and down. 'You're dressed pretty smart.'

Smart was not the way Tess wanted to appear. Last night after the evening meal with Mum at their lodgings in Upper Norwood, she had sneaked out and hidden a duffel bag containing her real outfit in a neighbouring garden hedge, to be retrieved in the morning after she'd said goodbye. There was no point upsetting Mum, who had insisted on the clothes she thought would be right: a mid-length skirt, white blouse and patent leather shoes; but Tess was not going to turn up to an art school interview looking like this. Like a provincial secretary with a marital eye on the Area Manager.

'Please? It won't take long, honestly.'

Inside the cafe, the old woman led Tess through a door marked *STAFF ONLY*, down a couple of corridors and into a backyard containing a tiny brick shed only a little larger than a public telephone box.

'It's easiest to go in backwards,' the old woman said, then turned and left her there.

After Tess had followed this advice she swung the door shut against her own face, closing herself into the minuscule interior. She fastened the bolt and began addressing the problem of how to undress with so little room for movement.

First in tiny steps, she rotated to face the toilet bowl. It had a seat, but no lid. Its cistern was right up against the ceiling. This would not be easy. She shucked off the duffel bag, let it fall behind her, and then shuffled around another hundred and eighty degrees so she could sit on the lavatory and remove one of her patent leather shoes. It all seemed quite clean in here, but the idea of putting her unshod foot on the floor didn't appeal. She kept it high whilst she released her garter belt and peeled off her right stocking. Then she put the shoe back on and repeated the process with the other leg. After that it was, if not exactly easy, at least manageable. She replaced the skirt with black canvas trousers, and the patent leather shoes with a pair of red gym pumps. Finally, she swapped the blouse for a fine grey jersey, and stuffed all the clothes she had been wearing into the duffel bag.

Back in the cafe, she took a seat at one of the small circular tables. The old woman stood at a hob behind the counter, heating an aluminium coffee pot and a pan of milk. She had been joined by a dark-haired young man, who might have been her son or her grandson. He sat half-slumped, looking vaguely at the back pages of a newspaper, from which he glanced up in Tess's direction, caught her eye and gave her a bare-toothed grin. She looked away immediately.

A few minutes later the old woman brought over a tall cup and saucer.

'Coffee,' she said. 'Sixpence.'

Tess handed over a shilling. 'I've an art school interview today. Do you think I look like an artist now?'

The old woman stepped back and appraised her customer. 'Ech. You look like a boy. But I see them a lot here, from the art schools. Girls dressed like boys. Where's your interview?'

'Moncourt Institute.'

'Oh yeah. They come in here from Moncourt. Make one cup of coffee last three hours.'

'Dressed like this? Like me?'

'Sure.'

That would do, Tess thought.

The first sip of coffee sent a shudder through her, so she tipped in several doses of sugar. Initially it seemed she'd made it more bearable, but each mouthful tasted sicklier than the last, until finally she reached a brown sludge of half-dissolved crystals at the bottom of her cup. She scooped out a gritty dollop with her finger and ate it. Then another. When it was all gone, feeling slightly nauseous, she left the cafe.

This room must normally be a teaching studio. It was a broad, open interior with raw, paint-spattered floorboards. Abundant light from its many windows illuminated the three people behind the interview table so that they looked, even in their modern dress, like a scene from one of the Dutch masters. *The Merchants of Ghent*, perhaps, by Pieter Codde or some such person.

She knew the man in the middle was the famous Benedict Garvey from all the art programmes on TV and radio, though she couldn't see his face because he was busy muttering and tutting over someone's portfolio. On his right sat a grandmotherly woman, and on his left a piggish man in a pinstriped suit. And the portfolio Garvey seemed to disapprove of so thoroughly, Tess realised with insuppressible horror, was her own, which she had packaged up and posted to Moncourt a fortnight ago.

'Please, take a seat, Miss Green,' the woman said. 'We'll be ready for you in a moment.'

There was only one other piece of furniture in the room: a wooden chair positioned some distance from the interview table. As Tess walked to it, her gym pumps squeaked against the floorboards. The patent leather shoes, she thought, would have made the most appalling racket.

This was a Shaker-style chair, designed for discomfort. She sat on it and became conscious immediately of the twin points of her pelvic bone digging against the wood through their mantle of flesh. Her ischial tuberosity and her gluteus maximus. Tess knew anatomy – she had drawn every important bone and muscle over and over, from every angle, flayed and cross-sectioned, in pencil, in pen, sometimes with a watercolour wash, always with the proper Latin name inscribed beneath. As a result of all this practice, she could sketch the human figure in any position she chose, fluently and energetically, even from memory. Her portfolio was filled with images that proved how well she understood the body's mechanics, its balances, its energy and stasis. Now her very best work lay in front of Benedict Garvey, and she could see it had not impressed him at all.

She waited, listening to him grumble under his breath. The grandmotherly woman smiled uneasily, as if she felt somehow responsible for her colleague's rudeness.

'I'm Jocelyne Weaver. I look after drawing, mainly.'

The piggish man had just fished his pipe out of a jacket pocket. 'Toby Flint,' he said, then made her wait until he had got his tobacco properly lit before adding, 'sculpture.'

It seemed as if Tess should respond. She gave what she hoped was a confident and amiable smile. 'Theresa Green, applicant.'

Flint tilted his head and cupped an ear. 'Beg your pardon?'

She shrivelled inside. It had been the sort of remark that could pass for wit if you dropped it in with sufficient confidence, as long as nobody looked too closely at it. But it was weak. It would not survive being repeated.

'Theresa Green,' she said, louder, minus the 'applicant' part this time.

Flint frowned. 'Yes. We have your form, Miss Green. We know who you are.'

'Of course.' She caught herself about to add 'sorry', but held that back at least. Right at the edge of the table next to Flint was an unstable-looking tower of black portfolios. Thirty or so. All the other hopefuls still to be interviewed today. She wondered how many would pass. How many had failed already.

At last, Garvey raised his face to meet Tess's gaze, revealing to her the patch over his left eye. Though she had seen it several times before in book jacket photographs, and on television, the reality of it disconcerted her. Of course people really did lose eyes, and wear eyepatches. Still, in the modern world of 1962, it seemed strange, like a thing from history or fiction.

'Benedict Garvey,' he said, sliding Tess's portfolio across to Jocelyne Weaver. 'I'm head of the fine art department. You're good at hands, I see.' It didn't sound like a compliment.

Remembering to speak up and be heard, Tess said. 'I enjoy drawing hands. They're expressive, but not obviously expressive in the way a portrait is.' Expecting a question about hands, which everyone said she did well, she had practised this remark endlessly in front of the mirror. It had never sounded as dishonest, as schooled, as it did now.

Jocelyne Weaver held up a charcoal sketch. A young woman, seated, with fingers interlinked in her lap. 'Is this drawn from life?'

'Yes. That's my sister.'

'It's very tender.'

'Thank you.'

Tess wished there was something more she could add, some way to turn the exchange into a conversation. The woman was a kindly sort, and she seemed favourable to Tess's work. Flint would obviously go along with whatever the others decided. But Garvey was the only one who mattered, and perhaps he was right. Perhaps Tess was a fraud after all. The great painters had immersed themselves in the gore of the charnel house; Tess had merely taken the bus to Leeds public library. No wonder Garvey thought her unworthy. All she knew about the human form had come from anatomy books; all she knew about life had come from novels.

He looked down at her application form, and back up. She found herself wondering what was beneath the eyepatch. Images flicked across her mind. Half-skinned faces with one eye socket full, one empty.

'Miss – er – Green, your work is very good from a technical point of view. I daresay you know that already. Tricky business, drawing a hand that doesn't look like a bunch of bananas, isn't it? Took you a lot of practice I should think.'

'Yes,' Tess said. Again Garvey had offered her the words of a compliment, the sound of an insult. Her only hope was to work out what he wanted her to be, and convince him that was who she was.

Flint chipped in now. His voice was as piggy as his face: nasal and stuffed. 'Of course Walt Disney got around the problem by only ever giving his characters three fingers.'

'I believe that's right,' Tess said, trying to guess whether or not Flint approved of Disney's simplistic approach. He'd said he was in charge of sculpture, hadn't he? Back at Leeds School of Art, they said you only took sculpture if you couldn't draw or paint. Well, the drawing and painting students said that, anyway.

Garvey continued, 'Half the young people we take on here haven't a quarter of your skill, I should say. But the thing is, it's all very well being able to turn out pretty representations, and doubtless everyone in – er – sorry, where are you from again?'

'Dewsbury.'

'Lancashire, is that?'

'Yorkshire. I've been doing my foundation at the Leeds School of Art.'

Garvey scowled. She shouldn't have corrected him, she thought. If he said Dewsbury was in Lancashire, perhaps that was where it ought to be. 'Good enough institution, Leeds, in its way. I imagine everyone up there's most impressed by all this verisimilitude.' She was sure she heard him flatten the vowels of 'up there'. Not significantly – not oop thurr – but just enough to let her know he was parodying her accent. 'The fact is, drawing accurately's not such an important qualification for our school as you might think. If a student has real talent, but a deficiency in that side of things, a dozen or so of Mrs Weaver's classes normally sorts it out.'

'They do come on quickly, Ben,' Mrs Weaver said, her tone less emollient than before. 'But hardly in a dozen classes.' It seemed Garvey had annoyed her. Deliberately perhaps.

'There you are. A couple of dozen, and then they can draw hands well enough. With all four fingers, even.'

The pain in Tess's backside was beginning to distract her. As subtly as she could, she shifted herself on the Shaker chair and felt the fabric of her trousers slip against the wooden surface, polished by the ischial tuberosities of all the young men and women who had sat here before her and fallen, one after another, under Benedict Garvey's disdainful right eye.

Mrs Weaver lifted a couple of Tess's pen-and-wash studies. 'These are exceptional, Ben.'

'It's a useful knack,' Garvey continued, ignoring his colleague's remark. 'You'll certainly never starve as long as you can churn out realistic-looking stuff like this. Christmas cards and such. Advertising. If that's how you want to make your living. As you probably know, we have a very strong graphic design department here at Moncourt. Maybe you ought to consider that route.'

'It's not what I'm interested in,' Tess said, too quickly.

'What do you mean? What is it that you're not interested in?'

'Commercial art,' she said, immediately realising how snobbish that must sound. 'I – I don't mean—'

'Commercial art. I see. Well, one wouldn't want to sully one's hands with that, would one? So you prefer to make, what? Uncommercial art, I suppose?'

'I'm not saying there's anything wrong with commercial work. Only it's motivated by money, not by—' What was she saying? Why did she keep talking? None of her sentences could achieve a full stop. If she could only shut up, this would be over with, and she could go from this place where she was not wanted and did not belong – retrace her steps to Ginelli's cafe; change back into who she really was.

Toby Flint sucked on his pipe. Mrs Weaver immersed her attention in Tess's portfolio. Both had evidently decided there was no saving her now.

'Really? Motivated by art?' Garvey said. 'And how about Leonardo da Vinci? Michelangelo? Rubens? You think they worked for nothing, that lot? You think they fed themselves on art?'

'No – of course not. I just mean—'

'Painting the faces of corrupt cardinals onto portraits of the apostles. Turning rich men's mistresses into the Virgin Mary. That's how you made a living as an artist in the Renaissance, Miss Green. Knocking out a few Santa Clauses and robins in the snow hardly compares with that, does it, if we're talking about prostituting your precious talent?'

'Oh – I certainly wouldn't ever compare myself with—' She grabbed for a name that would explain what she really meant. 'What about Van Gogh?'

That wouldn't save her either. Garvey's scorn was unconstrained now. 'Yes. Loyal to his vision, Van Gogh. But do you think he liked going hungry and unappreciated? Do you imagine he didn't want to sell his stuff, didn't dream of being recognised?'

Five days in a row, the whole week *Lust for Life* had shown at the Dewsbury Regal, Tess had joyfully suffered through all the miseries of poor Vincent's life, as portrayed by Kirk Douglas. Yes, Van Gogh was her idea of a proper artist. And now she hadn't the strength to defend him against a man like Benedict Garvey.

She said, 'Well, obviously nobody wants to go hungry. I was only—'

Again, Garvey cut her off. 'Have you read Brecht, Theresa?'

The use of her first name was unexpected. He was talking to her as if she were a child.

'I don't think so,' she said tightly.

'I imagine you'd know for sure if you had.'

'No, then.'

'Well, when you return to Dewsbury in Yorkshire, why don't you take yourself off to the public library. Ask them to order you a copy of *The Threepenny Opera*? Among many fine ideas in that play, you will find the maxim, "Erst kommt das Fressen, dann kommt die Moral." Do you know much German? It means you have to eat. "Erst kommst das Fressen" – first comes grub – "dann kommt die Moral" – then comes morality. What Brecht recognised, you see, was that to imagine you can live on ideas is romantic juvenile nonsense.'

Around each of those last three words, Garvey left a brief, emphatic pause. Then he stopped speaking and settled back in his chair. This, Tess saw, was her cue to collect her portfolio and go, now she had been properly punished for having the temerity to apply here.

The fury that descended on her encompassed everything in the room: Benedict Garvey; the other craven members of the panel letting him say whatever he wanted; the very idea of being interviewed when surely the work in her portfolio ought to stand for itself; the bloody pain in her arse from this bloody, bloody chair.

'Which is it, Mr Garvey?' she said. 'Is my work competent and ordinary or am I a Romantic idealist? I mean, just so I know – for my future efforts to improve. Should I try to be less of a Romantic or less competent? Or both?'

If things were fair, now ought to have been the moment at which Garvey understood. Tess was fierce and true. She might seem small of stature, plain of face, bespectacled and unremarkable, but she had the heart of a real artist. A heart like Van Gogh's.

But things were not fair, and Benedict Garvey was not fair.

'Miss Green,' he said. 'Brecht also tells us that the true sign of intelligence is the ability to hold two opposing ideas in the mind at the same time. I'd say any real artist needs to be able to hold as many as thirty. Thank you for coming in. We'll be in touch with our decision.'

That was all. Garvey was already reaching across Flint to pick up the next candidate's work. Didn't even have the humanity to wait until she'd gone. She had failed her interview for one of the best art schools in London. At least she could lift her aching backside from the Shaker chair.

Mrs Weaver held out her portfolio. Of course, they weren't going to mail it back to Yorkshire. Tess would have to bear the indignity of carrying it home herself. She took it from Mrs Weaver's hands. It felt different from a fortnight ago. Back then, wrapped in brown paper and tied with string, ready to post off to Moncourt, it had been full of brilliance and potential. Now it returned to her containing only rubbish and disappointment. It would be difficult to carry on the Tube too, being so large and awkward.

'Are you travelling to Yorkshire today, or staying in London?' Mrs Weaver asked, through the same sympathetic, hopeless smile she had worn during the entire interview.

'Oh – I'll go back tonight, I suppose.'

How agonising to have to sustain pleasantries, when all Mrs Weaver wanted was to be rid of Tess; and all Tess wanted was to storm out, cursing the lot of them.

'Which station is it for Yorkshire? King's Cross?'

'No – that is, I don't know. I didn't come on the train.'

'Good Lord,' said Flint. 'Did you take the coach, then? That's a hell of a journey just to be— well, just for an interview.'

Just to be rejected, he had been about to say. And he was right, it was humiliating. The lower-middle-classness of it all. Those hours travelling with her mother yesterday; last night in a boarding house; changing her clothes in a cafe lavatory to try and look the part. It came to her that these people didn't deserve her honesty. She could tell them anything she wanted. They'd rejected her anyway, so what did it matter?

'Actually,' she said, lighting on an idea from a television play she had watched with her parents a week previously, 'I hitch-hiked here. I imagine I'll get home the same way.'

Surprise wiped away Mrs Weaver's vapid smile. 'My goodness. Isn't that rather risky?'

Tess wilfully misunderstood the question. 'Oh, I agree it's not the most reliable form of transport,' she said. 'By the time

# Finer Things

I got to Luton, it looked like I was going to miss my appointment. But luckily a nice young man on a motorbike picked me up. He was ever so quick, nipping in and out of all the traffic jams – even went out of his way to drop me right at the door of the college. So I made it in the end.'

This was almost an exact account of a scene from the TV play, which had been called *Girl on the Run*, except the girl in question had not ended up in an art school. In fact, things had gone very badly for her. Tess hoped none of the panel had seen it. She doubted these people watched much television.

'Is it wise for a young woman to accept lifts from strangers? From men?' Mrs Weaver said. 'Surely your parents must be worried?'

They certainly would have been. *Girl on the Run* had terrified them, and her mother now kept referring to 'what happened in that awful play' in support of her argument that Tess should choose a college as near to home as possible.

'Oh, I don't think about that sort of thing,' she said breezily. 'The papers all make such a fuss about it to sell copies. I expect it's very rare really. You just have to be sensible. I mean you'd never experience anything, would you, if you worried all the time about getting murdered? That's what my mum and dad believe too.'

'Do they now?' Garvey said. He had stopped looking at the next candidate's portfolio now, and his manner towards her was different than it had been. Quite by accident, she thought, she might have changed his mind. 'Anyway, as I say, we'll be in touch with our decision. Goodbye, Miss Green.'

As she left, she heard Flint's porcine voice behind her.

'Ben, that thing about intelligence – holding two different ideas and all that. You know, I'm pretty sure it was Scott Fitzgerald who wrote it.'

'No,' Garvey replied. 'It was Brecht. Definitely. In *Der Kaukasische Kreidekreis*.'

'Well, I suppose you must be right,' Flint said.

Jimmy Nichols arrived outside the interview room fifteen minutes before his appointment. There were four chairs in the corridor. Two were occupied by female candidates, quietly keeping their nervousness to themselves. Jimmy took one of the vacant seats. Meanwhile an angular young man in an Aran sweater paced up and down, muttering, 'I will succeed! I will succeed! I will succeed today!'

Handsome, Jimmy thought. But unnecessarily intense. He wondered if the angular young man's idea was to build up his own confidence, to unnerve the competition, or both. In any case he'd soon had enough of it.

'Excuse me,' he said. 'Would you mind not doing that?'

The young man stopped pacing and gave Jimmy a ferocious look.

'Or perhaps you could go somewhere else and do it, if you really feel you need to,' Jimmy added. He wondered if he was about to be punched. 'Only it's quite off-putting for the rest of us.'

Letting out an explosion of a sigh, as if he had just been subjected to the most appalling injustice, the young man stalked off around the corner, where his mantra and pacing continued audibly. It seemed to Jimmy he had stepped up the volume on purpose.

'At least we don't have to *watch* him anymore,' he said to the other two. They smiled but did not reply.

A compact, bohemian-looking young woman came out of the interview room. Through the open door, Jimmy heard someone say something in German. The bohemian dropped her portfolio and sat down heavily in the one vacant chair. With her grey sweater, black canvas trousers and red pumps, she looked exactly like his idea of an art student.

'Bloody hell,' she said, responding to the smile he had automatically given her.

'Tough, was it?'

'Strange.'

'How do you think you did? If you don't mind my asking.'

'I don't mind your asking. But I haven't a clue. Maybe. Probably not.' She shook her head. 'You know it was touch-and-go to start with, but I really think I might have got in.'

If she was trying to convince herself, he thought, it seemed to be working. Anyway, there was no reason to challenge her about it. 'Well done,' he said. 'Benedict Garvey's on the panel, isn't he? He always seems terrifying on those TV programmes. Does the patch put you off?' He'd heard that during the war Garvey was a bomb-aimer in a Lancaster. Apparently a lump of hot shrapnel had hit him in the face and melted the whole eye away. Tragedy for an artist. For anyone, but for an artist particularly.

'I wouldn't say that was the most challenging aspect of the interview,' the bohemian said. Jimmy had lived in Kent all his life, and he liked the unfamiliar music of her northern accent, the air of restrained cleverness that went with it. He was about to ask her where she'd come from when a chubby man in a pinstriped suit leaned out of the door, and scanned the corridor.

'Are you Damian Barratt?'

'No,' Jimmy began, 'I think he's—' but the angular young man was already striding back towards them.

'That's me!' he barked. 'I'm Damian Barratt!'

'Right ho,' the pinstriped man said, retreating into the interview room. 'You're next then.'

'Best of luck,' Jimmy said.

'Get stuffed,' Barratt hissed as he swept by.

The door closed behind him. After a few moments, the bohemian girl said, 'He seems very rude. Do you know him?'

'Just met him for the first time.'

'Well, you obviously make a strong first impression – that should work in your favour in there.'

'So – being as you just passed yours – any tips for my interview?'

She thought for a moment. 'Just be honest. Be yourself. You'll be fine.'

'Was that what you did?'

'Of course.'

Soon after she left, Damian Barratt came out. He leant against the wall and said to nobody in particular, 'Waste of time that was. Fucked it up completely. 'Scuse my French, ladies.' Then to Jimmy, 'Sorry about before, Chap. Got a bit wound up. Not good at interviews.'

'Forget it.'

'Decent of you. That Garvey fellow's an absolute monster. Pulled me to pieces. Christ!' Barratt took the seat the bohemian girl had vacated and lit a cigarette. Having decided there was nothing he could learn from this buffoon, Jimmy let him smoke in silence.

Soon afterwards, the pinstriped man arrived to call in one of the young women. Jimmy didn't hear her name. Barratt shuffled away disconsolately, and two more candidates came along. By then Jimmy had lost interest in talking to anyone. If he didn't get through this interview, he thought, perhaps he should kill himself.

As Tess left Moncourt, her belly snarled at her, and she felt suddenly light-headed. The only sustenance she'd taken all morning, she realised, had been a cup of sugary coffee. She decided to return to Ginelli's. According to the old woman, it was somewhere Moncourt students went, and Tess was more and more certain that she was a Moncourt student now.

The cafe had grown much busier than before: overfull of animated young people chattering self-importantly. A trio happened to be exiting, so she took one of the seats they had just vacated and deposited her portfolio on another, sandwiching it against the melamine table. The old woman had gone, leaving the dark-haired young man to do triple duty as order-taker, coffee-maker and preparer-of-food. He arrived at Tess's table with a tray and began to collect up the detritus left by the previous occupants: jam-smeared plates and knives – and three puzzlingly tiny cups, like toys made of thick white porcelain, their interiors stained umber.

'Morning,' he said. 'What do you want?' She had been expecting a heavy foreign accent like the old woman's, but he spoke like a Londoner. Maybe they weren't related after all.

'Do you have a menu?'

He balanced the now-loaded tray on one hand and with the other used a tea towel to wipe away crumbs from the table. It was a deliberately impressive display of minor competence. 'I can do you toast, eggs, bacon. Cheese on toast. Egg on toast. Mushrooms. We're out of sausages, and I'm not washing out a scrambled egg pan,' he said. 'Fried or poached, that's the choice. And I've got to warn you, if it's poached I'll probably end up breaking the yolk. You'll still have to eat it. Sorry, that's just the way it is.'

'What are those little cups for?'

'Espresso. Ain't you seen that before, then? Really strong coffee it is.' He leaned down and whispered. 'All this lot make out they love it, but I tried it once and it's poison. You never tasted nothing so foul. No fucking wonder they can't get more'n a thimbleful down.'

He straightened up again, looking to see if the casual obscenity had startled her, and grinning in the same ugly way he'd done when she first saw him. This time she held his gaze, refusing to be either unnerved or charmed.

'I'll have an orange juice, please. And a fried egg on toast with mushrooms.'

His intimacy disappeared. 'Good choice, Miss. Be about ten minutes.'

Alone again, Tess wished she could hide behind something to read. She'd left her book at the boarding house, and although she had passed several newsagents on her journey, she hadn't felt confident about buying the right paper. Some of the people she admired on the foundation course at Leeds read a new magazine called *Private Eye*. She guessed that would be an appropriately Moncourt-ish point of reference, though whenever she had tried it she got hardly any of the jokes because she didn't understand current affairs. Try as she might, she couldn't tell what was important and what wasn't, or how she was meant to keep up with it all. Or why she should even take any interest in such distant, unchangeable events.

She looked around her. Everyone here was in a group or a pair, and they were all involved in each other. If she'd brought a pencil and sketchbook she could have set about drawing the clientele. She would have enjoyed capturing these mutually absorbed little groups: the interplay between looks and gestures across tables; the way everyone tried to become whomever it was they wanted others to see; the subtext of every conversation visible in the eyes, the faces; the way they tilted towards or away from each other.

A young woman entered the cafe. Tess thought her perhaps the most arresting-looking person she had ever seen. She was tall, dressed in a vivid pink angora polo neck and workmen's blue denim trousers. Beneath a beret of similar blue, her red hair was stringy and unkempt. Her feet were encased in a strange pair of thick-soled black leather boots with yellow stitching. She had applied her make-up like an eighteenth-century French aristocrat: scarlet lipstick and heavy mascara, sharp against white face powder. All that was missing was a cosmetic beauty spot.

The new arrival stood in the open doorway for a moment, perhaps looking around for some friend she had arranged to meet. Then she caught Tess's eye and headed in her direction.

'You on your own?' she said, her accent exactly as upper class as Tess had expected, but her voice surprisingly high-pitched. 'Mind if I join you?'

'Not at all,' Tess began, though her new companion was already pulling out the remaining empty chair.

'I'm Penelope Hoxworth. Penny.'

'Theresa Green. Tess.'

Penny Hoxworth waved to the man behind the counter. 'Espresso, Luca, when you've a minute,' she called. He looked up from frying Tess's egg and nodded. Penny indicated Tess's portfolio. 'Interview?'

'Yes. This morning at Moncourt Institute.'

'Oh God. Ben Garvey?'

'That's right. Do you know him?'

'I'm a second year at the Slade. Garvey was there before he got the job at Moncourt. Taught me painting for a term. Did your interview go well?'

'I'm not sure.'

'Really? I wouldn't have said Ben's the sort to keep his feelings to himself. Do you know, one time, he described me as "that talentless bulldyker". Charming, yes?'

'Gosh.'

'I know!' She leaned back in her chair and framed her face with her hands. 'Not directly, you understand, not actually to me, but in my hearing. And the thing is, I'm not – a lesbianist, that is. As for talentless – from Ben Garvey. I mean! Did you see his last exhibition?'

Tess had been wondering whether *lesbianist* was an actual word, and it took her a moment to realise that Penny had asked her a question.

'His exhibition? Erm. No,' she said.

'You wouldn't have. It was a decade ago. In fifty-two. That's what teaching art does to you. Kills the muse!' She mimed a pistol shot to her own head. 'Never try and teach anyone anything, Tessie. It'll be the end of you as an artist.'

Luca arrived with the food, Tess's orange juice and Penny's espresso. As he handed over the miniature cup, he said, 'You shouldn't listen to this woman, Miss. She's not right in the head.'

'Ignore Luca,' Penny said. 'He's a man-child. Typical Italian male, notwithstanding his second-generation Lundunner persona. His only interests in life are spaghetti and titty milk.'

First *lesbianist*, now *notwithstanding*: a word Tess had never heard anyone say before in actual conversation. And people in this city were so routinely vicious to each other. Penny's rudeness, however, did not seem to bother Luca at all.

'One and thruppence for the orange juice, toast and egg,' he said with affected weariness. 'And half a bob for the espresso.'

Tess handed over a ten-shilling note.

'Oh, very kind,' Penny said. 'Thank you.'

Luca looked at Tess quizzically. 'That right, Miss? One and nine?'

'I suppose so, yes.'

He gave Tess the change and left them. Penny tossed the espresso into her mouth, swallowed and pulled a face. 'I don't know if Luca makes these badly or whether the stuff really is just foul,' she said. 'Where are you from? I hear an accent. Yorkshire, is it?'

'Dewsbury. Yes.'

'So you'll be needing somewhere to live, won't you, when you move down here?'

'If I've passed the interview, I suppose I might. But I'm waiting on some other offers too. Lancaster and Canterbury. And Leeds have already told me they'd like to keep me on the diploma course after I finish my foundation.'

39

'Obviously you've passed the interview. You're clearly very talented. And you can't possibly choose Canterbury or Leeds – or that other place you said. Of course you'll go to Moncourt and live in London.'

Penny produced a notebook from a trouser pocket, tore out a page and gave it to her. There was a number on it. 'I always keep a few prepared,' she explained, 'for emergencies. Look, I'm sharing a house in Camden with three other girls, and one's moving out at the end of the summer. The rent's not too bad, and there's a telephone – incoming calls only, of course. Honestly, none of us are sapphists, despite my lovely boots. Give me a ring when you get your offer.'

After she exited the cafe, Tess wondered what she would do next. It was almost twelve. On the other side of the city, her mother was going to check out of their boarding house, drop their cases off in the left luggage at Victoria Coach Station, and then go shopping in Oxford Street. To avoid having to join her, Tess had invented an afternoon programme of tours and talks for all the Moncourt hopefuls. Under that pretext, she had intended visiting a gallery on her own, but she found she had gone off the idea now.

When no better alternative occurred to her, she went to the Tube to ride around the lines. Every year since she'd been eight, she had received a diary for Christmas, always with a schematic map of the London Underground on the back pages.

'Why not put in the Bradford bus timetable instead?' Dad would invariably complain. 'That'd be just as much use to most folk.'

Tess had enjoyed her Tube maps. She loved their thick, brightly coloured lines and, like the teams in the football results on the radio, the names of the London stations had a soothing, mysterious poetry, especially when she said them aloud. Chalk Farm, Maida Vale, Chiswick Park, Clapham Common, Barons Court, Elephant and Castle.

By now it was the middle of the afternoon, and the Underground was stuffed with tourists. Her bulky portfolio was even more of a nuisance down here, getting in people's way and making it difficult to negotiate the narrow tunnels between platforms. She decided to get out at Blackfriars, a name that for her had always conjured a gothic cathedral out of Poe, attended by sinister, silent monks.

Of course the place was not at all as she had pictured it. Just a jumble of mouldy Victorian red brick, ancient stone and bare new concrete, and the thick, sluggish river, stinking of sewage. She sat on a bench by its banks and decided that if Moncourt offered her a place she would accept. And Moncourt would offer her a place, she was sure of that.

Penny's number, which Tess had slipped into the top of her portfolio after their encounter, was her one proper connection with the city that would be her home in a few months' time. She untied the boards and looked for the scrap of paper. Here it was, tucked among all her old pictures.

Seeing her work unexpectedly like this, in the context of thinking about something else, she was struck by how impressive so much of it was. How beautifully done. She had been correct to feel proud of these pieces, and Garvey had no right to dismiss them. She lifted up the first three in the stack and stood them against the bench, then stepped back for a proper look.

The one of her sister that Mrs Weaver had admired really was very good, she thought. You could see Sally's petulance and vulnerability in it. The other two satisfied her less – but they were only quick studies, sketches of people she'd seen on the bus from Dewsbury to Leeds, refined a little in the studio at college. An old man and a schoolboy. Looking at them now, she wasn't sure why she had even included them in the portfolio.

A female voice behind her said, 'How much?'

She turned. A couple stood on the riverside path, arm in arm. A man and a woman, middle-aged. The woman who had spoken to her wore a red headscarf and polka dot dress, the man a trilby and blazer with sharply pressed trousers and tieless shirt.

'I beg your pardon?' Tess said.

'How much are the pictures?' the woman repeated.

'Oh,' Tess began, 'these aren't— that is, which one?'

'How about the old fellow in the flat cap? I rather like the look in his eye.'

'That one's fifteen pounds.' The number hadn't entirely come out of the air. A few months previously, a young man on the foundation course had received fifteen quid for his painting of a cow – the only piece anyone in her class had sold all year. A butcher had bought it to hang in the shop.

'How about we give you a fiver for it?' said the man, reaching into his inside pocket.

Tess understood. This was haggling. She could probably get herself ten pounds – for a picture that only a few moments ago she had dismissed as substandard. She should say 'twelve' next, she supposed, and he would say 'seven', then they would split the difference. But, though she knew that would have been correct form, the words she found coming out of her mouth were, 'No, sorry, it's fifteen pounds. That's what it's worth.'

'I see,' the man said, stuffing away the pair of five-pound notes he had taken out of his wallet. Tess cursed herself. Chance had just offered her the possibility of more money than she had ever held in her hand at one time, and she had refused it out of capriciousness. He replaced the wallet in his inside pocket and made as if to continue walking. 'Well, best of luck.'

His companion stopped him with the lightest of touches on the arm. 'Good for you, young lady. Stick to your guns. Fifteen pounds it is.' With that, she took the picture and began rolling it up. 'Give her the money, Graham.'

He laughed and reopened his wallet. 'You've sold yourself short there my dear. The mood my wife's in today, you could probably have got thirty out of her.'

'It's only worth fifteen,' Tess replied.

'Quite,' the woman said. 'Don't be such an ass, Graham. The girl knows her own value. What are you, dear, an art student?'

'That's right,' answered Tess. 'At Moncourt Institute.' The more she said it, the truer it would be.

'Good school. You should make the most of it.'

After they had moved along, Tess thought the woman had been right, she did know her own value. But it seemed others might estimate it more highly, and she would have to remember that.


At Victoria Coach Station, she found her mother sitting on one suitcase and holding onto another, looking warily about her as if at any moment some passer-by might push her to the ground and make off with all their possessions.

'Whatever happened to your clothes, Theresa?' Mum said.

She realised she'd forgotten to change back, but she was becoming used to lying now. The falsehood came smoothly and easily. 'I went and bought these after my interview,' she said, 'so I'd be more comfortable on the journey home.'

Her mother looked unconvinced. 'With what money? I only gave you enough for your lunch.'

'Ah. I sold a picture.'

'Sold a—? Which one?'

'Mum, aren't you going to ask how my interview went? I think I passed it.'

'Well, I hope you haven't. This is a terrible place. I'm glad to be on my way home, and I'll be happy if I never have to see it again.'

Tess realised, with a wave of guilt, how her mother had spent the day. 'Did you not go shopping, Mum?' she said.

'I was going to. But I had such an awful time on those undergrounds getting here. And when I went to the left luggage place, the woman in charge didn't look too trustworthy.' She had already dropped to a whisper. The last word she mouthed silently. 'Anyway, I thought I'd best keep an eye on our things myself.'

So she had waited since ten that morning at the coach station, too much on edge even to go and buy herself a cup of tea. Thinking about it now, Tess saw that had been inevitable. She ought to have known; ought not to have deserted her.

'There isn't anything worth stealing in those cases. It's only our dirty clothes.'

'A thief wouldn't know that until he opened them up, would he? And you're forgetting the cases themselves, Theresa. Good quality cases can fetch quite a bit, even second-hand.'

'Well, it's still ages until the coach comes. I'll buy you a cup of tea and a slice of cake. Like I said, I sold one of my drawings today.'

'Oh yes. Which one? Not that nice picture of our Sally, I hope?' Mum had been trying to convince Tess that the portrait of her sister would look lovely framed in the front room, but the idea had met stolid resistance from both of her daughters. Sally was so shy, it had been almost impossible to persuade her to sit for Tess in the first place – putting the image on display in the house would be agony for her. And Tess felt no desire to subject her work to the ill-informed praise her mother's friends were bound to shower over it.

'Just a drawing I did on the bus of some old man.'

'But, who bought it?'

Obviously, she couldn't tell Mum about her encounter on the riverside; that she had gone wandering around this dangerous city on her own. 'Someone at the college,' she improvised. 'Jocelyne Weaver. She's one of the teachers there.'

'Well, they would know good stuff from bad, wouldn't they? How much did she pay you?'

Tess really should have thought her story through before bringing this up. The three five-pound notes currently sandwiched between a couple of pen-and-washes in her portfolio would be incomprehensible to Mum, who knew art could be expensive, but would surely not countenance any picture costing more than—

'A fiver.'

'Five pounds! Oh, Theresa! Was it one of the big ones? I suppose it must have been.'

'No Mum, it was just a little sketch.'

'A little one! Well! How long did it take you to do?'

'I don't know. Twenty minutes.'

Mum went quiet, probably thinking of the hourly rate. Finally, she said 'You should put what's left of that into your savings at the Post Office.'

'I'll need to buy art supplies,' Tess said. 'Paint, paper. Brushes are really expensive.'

'But five pounds!'

After a couple of hours, the coach arrived and they boarded for the long journey back to Yorkshire.

Relieved and exhausted, Mum fell asleep soon after they departed, her head against the window and her daughter reading silently beside her. Every once in a while, however, she would stir in her seat and repeat some variant on the same theme.

'Five pounds, Theresa. For a little drawing. Wait till Dad hears!'

# 3

Panic was the enemy. No matter what happened, you stuck to the routine.

Delia headed out of Barkers' revolving doors, her pace brisk like she had an appointment to keep. She became someone other than herself: a housewife late meeting her husband. In rapid strokes she built a mental picture of the life such a woman might lead. The details she'd invented formed a picture. Kids away at private school. Long, silent evenings. The menace beneath the comfortable superficialities. Her waiting husband was five years her senior, balding, with an office in the city. A stockbroker, drumming his leather-gloved fingers on his Daimler's steering wheel. Bruises under her clothes. One time, when he was hitting her, she'd pissed herself in terror that this might be the time he finally, inevitably, lost all control. Both of them gracious at dinner parties with his colleagues: everyone guessing; nobody saying.

Delia had used this trick before. Humiliation and pain, if you imagined them properly, could become part of who you were, would turn anyone's eyes away from you. That was why nobody saw her as she made her way out of the store and up the Kensington Road.

Sticking to routine. Not panicking. The long hike across Kensington Gardens with the fox coat swinging between her legs all the way back to Peter Pan, to Lulu, now surrounded by more shopping bags. The others had done well today, it seemed. Delia took a seat next to the old girl and explained what had happened.

Lulu peered around her. There was nobody to be seen in either direction. 'You're sure you weren't followed?'

'Certain.'

'Sounds like it was just one of them things. Give me the fur.'

Delia dragged the fox jacket out of the top of her bloomers and dropped it into one of the bags.

'Good,' Lulu said. 'Itchy Pete'll be along in a bit to help me carry all this lot to the taxi. You'd better get off before he turns up. Don't worry, I'll explain to Stella when I see her. You can talk to her later on.'

At seven that evening, when Delia arrived at the Lamplighters, she found the pub door obstructed by a huddle of pavement kids, some playing jacks, some eating fish and chips out of newspaper. She recognised one of them, an unkempt ten-year-old girl with coarse yellow hair and gypsy features.

'Your mum and dad in there, Maggie?' Delia asked.

The girl was sucking a lolly. She pushed it into her cheek with her tongue. The thin white stick hung from the corner of her mouth like a cowboy's cigarette. 'Dad is. 'E 'ad a win this afternoon. Give us all sweets an' fish an' chips.'

'Spending the rest on drink, is he?'

'Fink so.'

Little Maggie Chisholm's mum, also called Maggie, had previously been a sort of brass. She was a remarkable-looking woman, and her husband, Albie, whose many vices did not include jealousy, had quickly seen the potential. During the early, romantic days of the marriage he'd only pimp her out once in a while, when he couldn't get work for himself and cash was short – but by six months in, Albie never got work anymore and cash was short all the time. One night at the bar in the Lamplighters, he had offered his wife to a Soho businessman, out East to do some deal or other with Stella. This businessman, who was called Finlay (first or second name, Delia wasn't sure) wasn't interested for himself, but he saw Maggie's potential and took her on, maybe just in time to save her from hardening off, from losing the sweetness that had made her profitable for Albie.

No more amateur pimping for him. That was done with now. Instead, Maggie worked as a hostess in one of Finlay's Soho clubs, making blokes feel welcome and encouraging them to buy drinks. Men there came in two sorts, she said: big mouths who pretended they had full wallets and others, not always big mouths, who really did. Her job was to sniff out the latter sort and introduce them to people who'd help shake off their burdens.

Albie had mixed feelings about his wife's new position. He wasn't going to stand in her way, especially since the money was so much better, but he'd preferred it when he was boss. There was a bit more dignity in that, as he saw it. The current situation left him, the man of the house, to look after the kids, a task to which he was not well-suited. Mostly he'd spend his afternoons in the bookies and his evenings in the pub, leaving his eldest daughter in charge of the others. He wasn't a bad bloke, as blokes went, Delia thought; just a selfish drunk, none of whose children looked much like him.

'Where's your brothers?' she asked Little Maggie.

'Sleepin',' the girl replied. Then she added proudly, 'I made 'em Ovaltine.'

Out of nowhere, Delia had a hideous presentiment of Albie staggering home and deciding to fry himself an egg for supper – the house burning down with all the children inside. The Imps whispered the story in her ear. She wanted to ignore it. It was probably nothing. The Imps' messages didn't always mean what they seemed to on the surface. Except, what if it were to come true? The guilt would be unbearable.

'You ought to go and sleep 'round your aunt Jemima's tonight, Maggie,' she said. 'Take your brothers too. Go and get them now.'

The girl pouted, spotting an opportunity. 'Dad says he'll give us another two bob when he comes out.'

'Oh yeah?' Delia said. 'And you think he'll have two bob left, do you? When he's finished drinking?'

'Prob'ly.' Maggie had chosen her story and would stick to it. Delia admired that, in a melancholy way.

'Here, I'll give you thruppence.'

'Ain't you got six, Delia?'

'Sixpence, then. Now promise you'll take yourself and them boys to Jemima's house?'

Maggie pocketed the coin, removed the lolly for extra solemnity. 'I promise,' she said, and turned and ran.

It was busy tonight in the Lamplighters, and passing through the pub door took Delia right back to her own childhood, the years before the war. There was an old familiarity in this transition from cool, quiet night into hot, noisy fug; from dark isolation into bright society, into a horde of miserable people pretending they were happy. Maybe it was because of the encounter with Little Maggie that it reminded Delia so unpleasantly of every time her own mother had sent her out to retrieve her father.

Off to her left, a drunken cluster sang around the out-of-tune piano. Little Maggie's dad, Albie, was among them, his hand on the arse of some old bird twice his wife's age and without a quarter of her looks. He seemed happy enough, though.

Delia pushed through the crowd of men, through the muddle of jokes and arguments and boasts, through all the competing stinks of beer and bodies, until she found Stella at work behind the bar, flustered and aggravated. The boss was

49

forty-eight years old, peroxide blonde and so thin you might imagine she was breakable. That would be a mistake.

'Short-handed,' she said to Delia, scrunching her face to keep her nostrils closed as she pulled a pint of Watney's. 'All I got tonight's Scotch Tam. Christ! How can anyone stomach this stuff?' Though she was the landlady of an East End pub, Stella disapproved of alcohol worse than any Methodist. Hated the smell of it too. She lifted the glass to the bar, and a little liquid slopped over her hand. She shuddered in disgust. The fact that the boozer's profitability trumped all her objections to drink told you things about Stella you'd be wise to pay attention to.

At the other end of the bar, Scotch Tam winked at Delia and handed a couple of whiskies to a customer.

'Ginny and Alf both off with the flu,' Stella continued. 'I'd put Teddy on it, but—'

She let out a sigh of dispirited realism. Teddy was too prone to giving free drinks to his pals and couldn't be bothered working out anyone's change. If he thought nobody was looking, he'd fill his wallet from the cash register. Little brother or not, Delia thought, Stella knew how useless Teddy was. Delia, on the other hand, had always been reliable, always a good earner. This thing with Maureen wouldn't change any of that.

'You need any help, Stell? I can take over if you like.'

'God love you, Dee. Can you do an hour for us?'

'Course I can.'

'I'll pay you for it. Double rate.'

'No need for that,' Delia said. 'You go round the back. I'll come and see you when it quietens down out here.'

Stella smiled, maybe out of relief to be getting away from the bar, maybe to acknowledge this act of atonement for transgressions as yet unspoken of. She handed Delia an apron.

❧

Barmaid: another career she could have chosen for herself. She had a knack for this work – remembering all the orders, keeping the crowd moving, not letting anyone wait too long. Delia could be charming too, flirtatious but not slutty, pitching her tone just right to make the men laugh and still keep them from pitying her or thinking they had any chance. All the tips she made, she dropped into a pint glass behind the bar for Scotch Tam. You never knew who you might need on your side. Always worth sacrificing a few bob to keep someone friendly.

She noticed Teddy wasn't in the pub. Nor were Itchy Pete or Tommy the Spade. That was something to take into consideration. If Delia was to find all three of them waiting for her in the back room with Stella, she could be certain her punishment had already been decided. Most likely, in that case, she wouldn't see the end of the night.

After an hour and a half, the pub was still full, but everyone was running out of money, and business had subsided enough for her to leave Tam on his own at the bar. In the landlady's kitchen she found Stella sitting at the table, pouring tea from a big brown pot. Teddy was there too, lounging against the back door like he was guarding it. From his self-satisfied look, she could tell he'd been putting the knife in; but he was on his own, no Pete or Tommy. They might be waiting in the garden. It was dark out, and she could see little through the window.

'Sit down, Dee,' Stella said.

They waited a moment in silence. Stella pouring a cup of tea for Delia, Teddy smirking behind his sister's back.

'It's calmed down out there now,' Delia said.

'What happened with Maureen today, Dee?' Stella said. No messing around.

Delia had her strategy ready. Don't apologise. Explanations not excuses. Careful to keep her voice level, her tone factual, she said, 'Girl got herself caught. I'd told her and told her, don't try nicking anything till I say otherwise. She was only supposed to watch me hoist the fox coat, see how it's done, like—'

'Nice bit of stuff, that coat,' Stella said. 'You done well there.'

Teddy's expression soured. So Stella had seen what Delia had brought her, knew the day hadn't been a total loss. That would be thanks to Lulu. Delia pressed the advantage. 'Went down beautiful, that fox, Stella. And the girl was watching to see how I did it.'

'Then I suppose she got carried away, did she?'

'Must've done. She tried to shove a great big fur hat down her skirt.'

Stella exploded with laughter, halfway through a mouthful of tea. 'Fucking fur hat? Jesus Christ!'

Delia felt droplets land on her face. Knowing better than to wipe them away, she laughed too. 'One of them enormous Russian ones it was. Girl didn't even have proper bloomers on – I don't know how she expected to keep it down there.' It felt mean, making fun of Maureen like this, but there was the compensation of Teddy's obvious displeasure at how well Delia was getting on with Stella. Out in the darkness of the garden, only just visible through the kitchen window, something or someone moved.

As abruptly as Stella's hilarity had overtaken her, it vanished again. 'I've seen it before with these young 'uns,' she said, regretfully. 'Think they can't be caught, don't they?'

Who was out there? Was it Tommy? Pete? Getting ready to come in and hold Delia's arms while Teddy popped a bag over her head and—

'That Maureen didn't strike me as too bright,' Delia said. 'Poor thing's a danger to herself.' Teddy looked at the floor, as if he was actually capable of shame. She knew it was only fear of getting caught. If she kept away from the subject of what Teddy had done with Maureen that morning, resisted the temptation to drop him in it, he'd owe her. She kept her expression neutral, hiding her pleasure at that thought, as Teddy left his place by the kitchen door to join them at the table.

'You think the kid might grass us up?' he said to her.

'Doubt it. She isn't too clever, but she knows what's right. Brave too. Gave that shopwalker a good hard kick so I could get away.' She turned back to Stella. 'Did you send for Grayson?'

Maybe the shape in the garden was just something moving in the wind. No use worrying about it.

Stella reached for the teapot. 'Nah. They caught the girl in the act. There weren't no doubt about what she was up to, was there?'

Delia remembered Maureen wriggling in the shopwalker's grip, the hat sticking absurdly out of her waistband. 'Not as I could see, Stell.'

'Well then. The way it stands, far as they know she's on her own. A lawyer like Grayson turning up'll only make 'em suspicious. Get 'em thinking there's more to it than meets the eye. Then they'll look deeper, maybe. We don't want that.'

Teddy blurted, 'Surely we got to do something, Stell? Make sure she don't grass.'

A misjudgement. His sister's face hardened. 'You telling me how to run my own gang, Teddy?'

'I only thought—'

'You didn't think nothing,' Stella snapped. 'But, bein' as everyone's so interested in how I handle things around here, I'll explain what I've done, shall I? I've sent Lulu. She can pretend to be the girl's grannie. Tell her how to go on with the coppers. First offence, ain't it? Can't see it going too hard, 'specially if she tells 'em it was only one of them moments of madness. Respectable young woman, not even eighteen yet, desperate after she lost her job at the hairdressers and that.

Shame she ain't prettier. If she could bat her eyes at the judge, she might have got off with probation.' Stella drained her teacup. 'I reckon six months reform school. Nine at most. So I says to Lulu, "Let the girl know we'll be grateful, and we'll look after her properly when she gets out again." Grayson'd do more harm than good, in the circumstances.'

'Course,' Delia said. She knew Lulu would also make sure Maureen understood the alternatives – would leave her in no doubt about what happened to grasses. Well, it served everyone's interest to keep the kid right.

'The only other thing is the stuff Lulu gave the girl to wear. Coat and a headscarf, weren't it?'

Delia nodded. 'Rita's. Whatever that was worth, just take it out of my pay.'

'No, no, no,' Stella said. 'None of this is your fault, Delia. I landed you with the girl, didn't I? So I'll look after Rita. It's only fair. And I'll pay you for the shift you just did in the bar too. No arguing.'

The figure in the garden, which Delia was sure now was a man, was too small to be either Pete or Tommy. Stella spotted her looking, and said, 'Well then. That's that. I got other business now. If you don't mind.'

Delia stood and turned to go. Teddy caught her arm. 'Don't make no arrangements for next Wednesday night, Dee, all right?'

'Why's that, Teddy?'

'Ignore him,' Stella said.

Delia didn't know whether she meant Teddy or the man in the garden. She said, 'I'm going to take a few days off, if you don't mind Stella. All this with Maureen, it's upset me.'

'You do that, Dee,' Stella replied. 'Long as you want.'

She went out into the hall. Before she reached the entrance to the bar, someone inside closed the kitchen door. Though she was tempted to sneak back again and listen outside, she didn't.

Whoever was about to come in from the garden, Stella wanted him keeping a secret. Safest to go along with that, because sometimes knowledge gave you power, but it usually brought danger too. And Delia still didn't know for sure how close she'd come today to being in serious trouble – or, for that matter, whether she really was out of it yet.

On their days off, most of the girls wouldn't get up until the afternoon. It wasn't just laziness – hoisting wore you out in ways you didn't realise: being always in danger, and constantly on your guard like that. They needed to take the rest when they could get it. Many had a regular bloke too, someone to persuade them to stay in bed. Delia had been without that distraction for over a year now, and sleep was no remedy for her exhaustion. Mostly, her dreams left her more drained, not less. She found the waking world a far more soothing environment to inhabit.

At five in the morning she looked out from the window of her flat, over the rooftops of all the sleeping houses. It came back to her then how she'd been afraid last night of the Chisholm kids burning to death – how she had given Little Maggie sixpence to take her brothers to her aunt Jemima's. There was nothing in it, she thought. She'd just been feeling upset because of Maureen. Nevertheless, she decided to go to Jemima's paper shop, and take a detour down the Chisolms' street on the way.

It was still dark when she set off. Already, men in flat caps were out with their horses and carts, going who knew where, to pick up who knew what. Scrap metal, coal, beer. In other parts of London you felt like you were in the city, in the modern world. In the 1960s. Out here in the East End, it was still half-rural. Horseshit on the streets. The only cars you ever saw in Fenfield belonged to visitors from elsewhere, or more recently to local criminals doing well for themselves. Stella was thinking of getting herself a nice sedan. Teddy had passed his test in the army and could drive her around. Maybe she'd make him wear a chauffeur's uniform. Delia hoped so.

Finding no sign of any fire at the Chisholm house, she stood outside for a few minutes, looking and listening for anything unusual. Doubtless, Albie had wandered home drunk, but it seemed he'd found his way into bed without causing a catastrophe. Delia wasn't exactly disappointed – she wasn't a monster. It was just that if the place had burned down her instincts would have been proved right; she'd know the Imps were on her side again, might feel able to trust them once more. She'd made a bad judgement and Maureen was going to be locked up because of it. And the fact that the girl had helped Delia get away left her feeling even worse.

Inside the newsagent's shop, Delia watched while a paper boy waited for Jemima to fill his delivery bag. He was stunted, underfed. You might have taken him for eight or nine, but he was probably thirteen at least. When Jemima's back was turned, he nicked a handful of boiled sweets from an open jar and stuffed them in his pocket. Delia looked him right in the eye. He didn't flinch. As far as this kid was concerned, Delia was free to grass him up. He'd take the consequences if he had to.

Jemima handed over the laden bag of newspapers. The boy hefted them across his shoulder, and wobbled out of the shop, unbalanced by his burden.

'You shouldn't leave jars open like that,' Delia said.

Jemima screwed the lid back on and returned the jar to its shelf. Its label read *Lemon Suckers*. 'You saw the size of him,' she said. 'Do you think he'd manage the whole round without a few sweets in his pocket?' She took Delia's money for a *Daily Mirror* and a packet of Rothman's. 'Anyway, you didn't half put the wind up Little Margaret last night. Kid turned up at our house with her brothers at half ten. Terrified, she was. What did you tell her?'

'Nothing. Albie was getting pissed in the Lamplighters, that's all. I thought they'd be better off with you and Ern.'

'Well,' she said. 'They woke us up. He weren't happy, I can tell you.'

Her husband, Ernie, was a postman, and Jemima always took the early shift at the newsagent's. Early to bed, early to rise, both of them. Still, Jemima looked pleased to have had her niece and nephews for the night, and Delia would bet Ernie was too. They had no children of their own. Something not right with one of them.

'Sorry about that,' Delia said. Nevertheless, she was glad to hear Little Maggie had done as she'd told her – had not just taken the sixpence and gone home. Even though the Chisholm house had not burned down after all, something was wrong, she was sure.

As it turned out, Delia's premonition had been right in a general sort of way. Albie hadn't set his house on fire, hadn't even gone home, but he had died that night after all. It took a few days before anyone knew about it, and then there were varying accounts of exactly what had happened. The one Delia trusted most came from Jemima, who had been with Maggie when the police came around to break it to her.

Evidently the husband of that woman he'd been groping that night was in the Lamplighters too. Knowing better than to start a brawl in Stella Bilborough's pub, this husband waited until closing time, then he suggested Albie might want to come back to his house to play cards, pretending he wasn't much bothered one way or the other about how Albie had been going on with his wife.

Having won unexpectedly large that afternoon, and despite buying rounds for the last four hours, Albie had been unable to run through more than half of his spoils. This must have sat badly with him. He was the sort who preferred to go to bed with his pockets light. His luck had already been stretched thin that day; a few games of three-card brag would surely break it. So they all set off together: the husband, the husband's two friends and the wife, who continued to drape herself over Albie's shoulder as they strolled along, the same way she'd been doing all night. He had no idea what was really going on. He found loyalty and jealousy equally incomprehensible, and thought other men were just like himself.

'We'll take a shortcut here,' the husband said, pointing to a gap in the barbed wire fence where someone, a looter or a truanting kid, had once broken through. Beyond lay a stretch of half a dozen bombed-out streets, flattened in the Blitz and still not rebuilt over twenty years later. The place was all open land now, scattered with debris and punctuated by unfallen half-houses – bedroom and parlour wallpaper exposed to public view, like the open interiors of doll's houses.

Albie wasn't sure. He could see how, crossing this abandoned territory at night, you would soon be out of the street lights' glow and stumbling around in total blackness.

'Looks dangerous.'

'Nah, I know my way across,' the husband said. 'Stick by me, mate. It'll save us half an hour's walk.'

The wife realised what was up. Drunk as she was, she knew her husband. She leaned closer to Albie.

'I shouldn't go that way if I was you.' It was meant to be a whisper, but it was loud enough for them all to hear.

Her husband grabbed her by the shoulder to shove her away from Albie. She lost her footing and fell to the ground. He gave her a kick in the back.

'You keep your mouth shut, slag!' he hissed.

The husband's friends had happily joined the scheme to lure Albie to a bombsite and put him in the hospital. That plan had seemed both entertaining and morally righteous. Now things had taken a different turn. Beating a woman was unacceptable, at least in public, and they couldn't be party to it. So they wandered away and left the other three to sort out their disagreements among themselves.

The wife lay sobbing on the ground. Her husband stood over her, his determination to be revenged draining away rapidly. Albie balled his fists. He wasn't the sort to go looking for a fight, but he always enjoyed one when it arose in the natural way of things.

'That weren't nice,' he said.

At that, the husband turned and fled through the gap in the barbed wire. Albie ran after him into the moonless dark of the bombsite, drunk and reckless, pursuing the sound of his quarry's retreating feet, barely able to see where he was going.

This was the husband's regular shortcut; even with no light he could navigate it with ease. He was soon out the other side and weaving through the backstreets beyond. Meanwhile, the wife had picked herself up from the ground, stopped crying and set off for home. Each had resolved to apologise to the other, forgive the other. Never to do such things again.

So far, the story was more or less reliable, built on testimony. The wife and the husband had told their tales to the police, and later, with other details, to anyone in the Lamplighters who might be interested. The rest of it, how Albie Chisholm actually died, was all guesswork, probabilities. He'd been alone in the dark. Nobody could know quite what had happened. The police said it was probably like this: that after ten minutes of stumbling over debris, over bricks, lumps of concrete, broken furniture, over bits and pieces of lives destroyed by the Luftwaffe, Albie lost his enthusiasm for the chase and decided to find his way out of the bombsite. He climbed to the top of a high mound of earth, hoping to see enough from there to map his route back to the lighted streets. Then he turned too sharply, tripped over some half-buried object, and tumbled down the side of the hill. Unluckily for him, his fall was broken by a rusted iron pole. It pierced his chest on the right side, smashed two ribs, slid through his lung and exited his back.

Afterwards he lay there for a couple of days, until a beat constable spotted a couple of stray dogs chewing at the body and chased them off. The copper who broke the news to Maggie Chisholm told her Albie couldn't have taken long to die. Who knew really, though? No point upsetting a grieving widow with the horrible truth, the hours and hours of suffering.

According to Jemima, there was something else. 'He told me someone must have found Albie before the police,' she said. 'Because the money in his pockets, everything he had left from his winnings that afternoon – it was all gone!'

For the last forty-eight hours, Delia had been feeling dopey. She'd slept some of it, but not much. Mainly, she'd prowled around her flat. Listened to the wireless. Read. For long stretches in a state of shut-down wakefulness she had stared out of the window or at the wall. It made no difference: she saw nothing.

Itchy Pete came to her door with a summons from Stella, and the news about Albie. 'Funeral's next week,' he said. 'Monday.'

'What's happening with Little Maggie and the boys?'

He stood in the doorway, scratching. It made you itch yourself – like when you heard some kid had nits and you'd get to feeling as if you had them crawling about your own hair too. 'Their ma can't look after 'em, can she? Not with all her hostessing down Soho. They'll stay with Ern and Jemima, I reckon.'

So that had worked out all right. The whispering Imps hadn't misled her. Albie had been destined to get himself in bad trouble that night.

'Stella need me hoisting again, does she? That what she wants to see me about?'

'She don't tell me what she's thinking,' Pete said shiftily. 'All I know's she sent me to fetch you.'

Delia remembered the person lurking in Stella's back garden. What was it Teddy had said? Stella had shut him up about it pretty quick.

'This about next Wednesday night?'

'Like I said, I dunno.' Pete scraped his fingernails rapidly up and down his neck just under the left ear, a dog chasing its fleas. The itching always got worse when he was on edge. He did know something. Probably not much, though, and he was loyal; if Stella had instructed him to say nothing, he'd say nothing.

'I'll get dressed and be round in twenty minutes.'

She recognised the Jaguar parked outside the Lamplighters, which belonged to Maggie Chisholm's boss, Finlay. The pub door was locked, so she knocked on the frosted window and Tommy the Spade let her in.

At a table in the bar-room Stella and Finlay were sitting with five of the other girls: Rita Lovage, Jenny Wicks, Mary Baker, Alice Boone and a newish one called Kathy something. With Delia, that made half of Stella's hoisters.

Finlay was sharp: tall, well-dressed, with Brylcreemed hair, and he wasn't quite thirty yet. Ten years ago, he'd been a Teddy boy, dancing to Bill Haley and picking fist fights on the street. Even now he kept knuckledusters and a flick knife in his pockets, spoiling the line of his Saville Row suit.

'Brought it on himself,' Stella was saying. Obviously they were discussing Albie Chisholm.

'Was always going to happen, the way he went on,' added Rita, a hoister of long standing. Second-best thief in the gang, after Delia.

'How's Maggie taking it?' Delia asked Finlay. She knew he'd be pleased to see Albie out of the way. It must have been an irritation to him, his most useful hostess worrying all the time about her husband and kids – her work suffering because of it. It wasn't the sort of thing you could solve with a threat or a payoff. Maybe he'd been toying with the idea of having someone tidy Albie away. Maybe he'd been thinking about doing the job himself.

But Finlay was on the cusp of maturity, Delia thought. These days, every time it became necessary to show some of his own muscle, he'd find it a little more distasteful, a little further beneath him. That sort of thing, waving blades around, giving out beatings, was for kids on the way up.

'Maggie's upset of course,' he said.

'Of course.'

'She'll get over it.'

He was probably right. And now that Little Maggie and the boys were with their aunt and uncle, they'd be looked after properly. Albie had done everyone a favour.

Stella took control. There was business to discuss, and it had nothing to do with Albie Chisholm. 'Now, girls. Finlay here's got some work for you.'

Rita said, 'What sort of work's that? You got a commission in mind, Finlay? You want us to pinch you a load of cocktail dresses?'

Some of the other girls cackled at the implication. Finlay was rumoured to have a private interest in female clothing.

'No. It's not quite your usual line,' Finlay replied, ignoring the subtext. 'I'd like you to meet some people, be entertaining, that's all.'

'Oy! We ain't brasses, Finlay,' Alice Boone said. A couple of the other girls expressed their outrage at the very idea. This was somewhat dishonest, Delia thought. They all thought themselves better than prostitutes, but most of them would lead a drunk on with a promise if the chance arose, then roll him for his wallet.

Finlay held up both hands in supplication. 'You misunderstand me, ladies. No offence, but if I was looking for girls to do that sort of work, I wouldn't come round here.'

Jenny Wicks pouted with mock affront. 'What's that mean, "no offence"? Are you telling me I ain't good enough to open my legs for your punters?'

'Quiet,' Stella said.

Under Finlay's pose of boredom, Delia could see he was aggravated at the way these women refused to respect him. He knew they were making fun of him, saw how they'd shut up for Stella, not for him, and he didn't like any of it. He said, 'All I want you to do is come to a club I own, two or three of you each night. Drink a few drinks. Talk to the customers.'

'Talk to men?' Delia asked.

'Men, women. People at the club.'

'What about?'

'About whatever you want. Just be yourselves. Within reason.'

Stella said, 'You can tell these people you're hoisters if you want. They won't care. They'll like it. But no details. And nothing about me at all. You understand?'

'I'll pay you each a fiver a night,' Finlay said. 'Bonuses if you do 'specially good work. Plus all your drinks for free, as long as you're sensible.'

Kathy, the new girl, asked, 'Is this the same club where Maggie works?'

Delia had been to that club, the Ferrara, twice. In a back room there she had helped sell stolen furs and dresses to a procession of debs and their boyfriends, any of whom could easily have afforded to buy the same goods legitimately.

Finlay said, 'This is the Gaudi. Completely different sort of clientele. More bohemian.'

'What's that mean?' Kathy asked.

'Artistic.'

'Like a strip club?'

Finlay gave her a weary look. 'If I mean strip club, I'll say strip club. The Gaudi's my artistic establishment. It's a boozer for your creative types. Painters, writers, musicians. You get a lot of that sort in Soho these days. They like to think they're on the outside of what you might call conventional society.'

Rita's voice was full of contempt. 'You mean they like hanging about with criminals?'

'That's right, sweetheart. They love hanging about with criminals. Criminals are their favourite sort of company. They'll be interested in you, and all you got to do is look as if you're interested in them. Listen to what they talk about.'

'Don't forget,' Stella said emphatically, 'keep it vague. No details about our business. So, do you lot fancy helping Finlay out?'

It wasn't a question. Not really. Stella wasn't democratic, but this looked like a good deal.

'Can't argue with a fiver plus drinks just for a night's socialising,' Delia said. 'And that's all there is to it, right?'

Finlay paused, then said, rather too casually, 'Maybe from time to time, me or Stella here might ask you about what one or other of 'em has to say on a particular subject.'

'That's that,' Stella said. 'We'll let you know which nights we need each of you. Delia, wait back a minute, love.'

After the others were gone, Stella told Delia the news about Maureen. In the normal way of things, if one of her hoisters was brought to trial, the boss would send Teddy or Lulu or one of the others to sit in the courtroom, partly to keep an eye on events, partly as a visual reminder of the consequences of grassing. But being only seventeen, Maureen was tried at juvenile court, where there was no public gallery. The cases weren't even reported in the paper. Luckily, Finlay knew some kind of bribable official, through whom Stella was reassured that during all her testimony Maureen had kept faith and done as she should: stuck to the story, maintained she'd acted alone and on impulse.

Grayson, Stella's lawyer, had agreed he shouldn't be involved directly. Being of previously good character, the girl would likely get away with probation, especially when the time she'd already served on remand was taken into account.

What none of them knew, however, was that a year ago, Maureen had been involved in a car theft. The three young men with whom she'd been found travelling in a stolen Ford Zodiac were all convicted of taking and driving away, but the judge believed her story that she'd innocently accepted a lift. He gave her the benefit of the doubt and let her off with a warning to be more careful in future.

'Bad luck she's still underage,' Grayson had said. 'If she'd been a legal adult, they'd have suppressed her juvenile record.'

Maureen was only seventeen, and now she had pleaded guilty to stuffing a fur hat into her knickers at Barkers of Kensington. This time, there was no doubt for which she could be given the benefit. The judge concluded that she was a young woman of mendacious and criminal character who had failed to respond to his predecessor's generosity. He sent her down for six months to Bullwood, the girls' borstal in Essex.

# 4

The mail dropped noisily into the cage behind the letterbox. Mum was at the grocer's and Dad was at work. Tess's younger sister was still asleep. There were three letters for her parents, two for her. She opened the one with a London postmark, leaving the other, from Lancaster, amongst the rest. Then she walked three streets to the nearest telephone box and called the number Penny had given her a fortnight previously.

Through the sound of the pips a female voice, not Penny's, said, 'Hullo?' Tess pushed a coin into the slot.

'Could I speak to Penny Hoxworth, please?'

'Just a moment.'

The silence that followed continued so long that the pips went again and she needed to put in more money. Eventually she heard a familiar drawl.

'Penny Hoxworth speaking.'

'Penny? It's Tess Green. I don't know if you'll remember. We met just after my interview for Moncourt, and you said—'

'Oh yes. At Ginelli's. I told you you'd get in! I was right, wasn't I?'

'You were, yes. I heard a few days ago.'

'Well! Congratulations.'

The lie about when she had received her offer had slipped from Tess's lips without thought, out of a subconscious decision to avoid looking too keen, she supposed. 'Thanks. Anyway – as I said, I was wondering about the room in your house.'

'Ah. That one's gone, I'm afraid.'

Suddenly, the fantasy of London had become unreal again. If she couldn't live in Penny's house, how could any of it be possible?

'I see. Well, thanks for—'

'Hold on though, Tess. That girl who answered the phone – Emma's her name. Not that it matters – she's moving out next month. It's not such a nice room as the one you missed out on, but—'

'I'll take it,' Tess said.

Back at home she found her mother in the hall, sorting through the mail.

'Where have you been?'

'Getting some fresh air. Anything for me?'

'Here. It's from Lancaster.'

Tess tore open the envelope. 'They've said yes too.'

'Who's left?' Mum asked, though she knew perfectly well.

'Only Moncourt. The one in London.'

'I must say, I don't know why you don't just stay on at Leeds.'

She had made the same remark on the arrival of each of her daughter's previous acceptances: from Canterbury, Newcastle and Stoke-on-Trent. She made it again a few days later when Tess finally showed her the letter from Moncourt. And again, tearfully, when Tess told her she was definitely going to London; and one last time, most tearfully of all, at Dewsbury Bus Station in September, as she watched the driver load Tess's cases into the belly of the coach.

Tess could think of no reply to 'I don't know why you don't just stay on at Leeds' that would not be either hurtful or incomprehensible. She certainly could not have told her mother the truth: that the question she kept asking contained its own answer.

❧

## Finer Things

Maureen served only four weeks of her sentence in the end. After that, they released her to a hospital in Braintree, and from there into the supervision of her 'grandmother' Lulu, who brought her to London on the train. There was a little Welcome Home gathering for her in the kitchen at the Lamplighters when she got back: just Stella and Delia.

According to records, the girl had injured herself in an accident whilst on work detail in the turnip fields, but her smashed-in face and broken leg suggested a different history.

'Christ! You've been in the wars, ain't you?' Stella said. 'You fall into one of them combine harvesters or what?'

'It was the screws,' Maureen was hard to understand. Her mouth hadn't healed properly yet. Her face would never look right again. 'Couple of them took against me, said I wasn't working quick enough. I told them I couldn't go no faster, and—'

Maureen choked back a sob at the memory. Stella took the girl's hand between her bony palms and said, 'That's why you got your sentence shortened. They're covering up what they done. Disgusting. But it's an ill wind blows nobody any good – at least you're out, eh? And remember we promised if you did right by your friends, we'd take care of you?'

Maureen nodded, conscious perhaps that 'take care of' had many possible meanings. She sipped gingerly at the hot tea.

'We'll put you in a nice little flat I've got next door to Delia here,' Stella told her. 'She feels ever so bad about all this, you know.'

Maureen turned to Delia. 'It wasn't your fault I got myself caught, Dee.'

Oh, but it was, Delia thought. She should have spotted that shopwalker. The Imps had expected that of her. When she failed, they'd sacrificed Maureen. 'You did well helping me get away,' she said.

68

Stella let go of Maureen's hands. 'She's got a big heart, Delia does. Even asked if she could go out to Bullwood to see you on visiting days.'

'I'd have liked that,' Maureen said.

'Well, I couldn't let her do that of course.'

'Of course,' echoed Maureen.

Her parents had cut her off after the incident with the stolen car. During what had evidently been a hellish month at the girls' borstal, her only visitor had been Lulu in the role of grandmother, there to remind her of the importance of keeping her mouth shut.

'Anyway,' continued Stella, 'Delia wants to make sure you're all right now you're out. So it'll be good for you to be living right by her.'

A look of concern crossed Maureen's face. 'What about the rent?'

'Don't worry about no rent. When you're properly better we'll find you a bit of work to do. But like I said, you done right by us, and we owe you.'

Stella gave Delia a glance that meant *we understand each other*. It was obvious Maureen would never be able to work as a hoister now but she had done her duty and kept silent, so Stella would let her have a flat for free, with a paid job on top. And these rewards would redeem Delia's portion of the debt too. It was an arrangement that would neither be spoken of nor recorded in the ledger where Stella kept her secret accounts.

Delia knew it was more complicated than Stella understood. She was glad the girl was being looked after, but it wasn't enough. She could feel wrongness in the balance of things, heard it in the whispering of the Imps. What she had done to Maureen could not be remedied with money alone.

る

69

'Lucky this place was empty,' Maureen said, opening the door.

'Yeah,' Delia replied. 'Lucky.'

As they entered the flat, she glanced at the doorframe where a week ago, Teddy had repaired it, grumbling about Pete and Tommy as he did so. 'Fucking idiots,' he'd said. 'There was no need for this. Stella gave them a key.'

The flat's previous occupant had been a brass by the name of Suzy. According to Stella, she had been late with her rent too often and, in contravention of the rules, brought customers back to the flat. Suzy had refuted both complaints, perhaps with justification. Delia didn't know whether she had always been on time with her money, but she had certainly never seen or heard any men in there.

On Monday morning Itchy Pete and Tommy the Spade had resolved the dispute by kicking in her door and putting Suzy out on the pavement with all her stuff. Delia had no idea where she went afterwards. Maybe her pimp found her somewhere else.

Knowing nothing of this, Maureen explored her new flat gleefully. Like Delia's, it had a separate kitchen and bathroom, but it was smaller, with only one bedroom. The place was near-enough unfurnished. All Suzy seemed to have needed was a bed, a kitchen table and a portable gas hob.

'It's nice here. I've been in bedsits ever since I moved out of Mum and Dad's. I'm so pleased you and me're going to be neighbours.' Maureen flinched at an unexpected twinge of pain. Her excitement had made her careless of her injuries.

'That thing Stella said about me having a big heart. It ain't true, Maureen.' This point seemed important to Delia. It might help the girl recognise the reality of her situation.

'But you've been really good to me, Dee.'

'I haven't done anything for you.'

'You were going to come and visit me at Bullwood.'

'I was. But I didn't.'

'Only 'cause Stella said you weren't to. I understand why. And you're going to keep an eye on me now, aren't you? Help me get settled in?'

'I ain't got a big heart, Maureen. I've barely got any heart at all, and what I do have is hard. But I believe in doing right.' Delia hesitated. How much could she tell Maureen about the Imps, their demands for sacrifice and balance? 'It's my opinion that the more you do right, the less goes wrong for you.'

Maureen looked out of the window, down at the street. 'You know my mum and dad don't have nothing to do with me no more?'

'I heard that, yes.'

'It was the first time I'd ever been in any trouble, and I hadn't even done anything wrong. I was really frightened, locked up in a cell at the police station, and they just turned their backs on me. My dad never spoke to me again, not properly. Mum said it wasn't my being in a stolen car so much as— they thought I'd done *things* with those boys.'

'Had you?'

'No,' Maureen said. Then she laughed. 'Well, not much, and only with Derek. He was the nearest I ever had to a proper boyfriend. If he hadn't been driving the car I'd never have got in it. I tried explaining to my mum, and I asked her if she couldn't at least try to get Dad to understand, but she just kept saying, "You broke his heart" over and over. "He's got a big heart, your dad, an' you've broke it, Maureen." Like it was all my fault. I believed that.'

She turned her injured face back to the room. Delia saw there were changes in her beyond the physical damage. Maureen was no longer exactly the girl who had followed her into Barkers of Kensington.

'Your parents should have looked after you, whatever you'd done.'

'I know that now. Back then I was just so sorry for hurting my dad, even though I'd never meant to and it was only a mistake – and I hadn't even done half of what he thought I had. Seemed like it was my fault he was so upset.' She looked around this flat she had been given. 'Things have worked out all right, haven't they, with me here and you looking after me?'

'It's all Stella, really,' Delia said. 'This is her place. I couldn't have done this for you. I'll help you get some nice furniture, though.'

It was hard to read Maureen's expression, because of the damage, but a couple of fat tears rolled down her cheeks.

'You know what I realised in hospital?' she said. 'I realised I wouldn't have been there if it wasn't for Dad's big broken heart. If him and my mum would've looked after me better, I wouldn't never have tried working for Stella, wouldn't never have tried nicking that stupid hat, wouldn't never have gone to borstal and wouldn't never have got beat up.' She took a breath, grasping at this stream of hypotheticals and finding a conclusion among them. 'So all in all I'd rather have someone with a small heart, trying to do the right thing. Someone like you.'

# 5

As the closest pub to Moncourt, the Lord Nelson was almost an outbuilding of the college, filled with students and staff every night. Jimmy had gone along there with this or that new acquaintance several times since beginning his studies a fortnight ago, and usually regretted it. Tonight he was already half-cut by eight o'clock. Best stop now, he thought, before I lose control. Then he kept drinking. At nine he was entirely drunk, and talking to Tess and Penny.

He wasn't impressed with Penny, but Tess, he had decided, was the first person he had met here who might become an actual friend. She wasn't, it turned out, nearly as sophisticated or as bohemian as he had imagined when he'd met her before his interview.

The noise from an excitable cluster of students and staff at the next table, together with the alcoholic fuzz in his head, made concentration difficult. It was a struggle to follow the story Tess was telling him. Something about her fooling Benedict Garvey with a lie about hitch-hiking. When she reached the end, Jimmy had made enough sense of it to know he should find what she had done both hilarious and admirable. He told her so.

'I'm not sure,' she answered. 'It sort of feels like I'm here on false pretences.'

'Everyone's here on false pretences,' Penny announced.

'Well, I certainly am,' Jimmy said, and immediately felt annoyed at himself for being drawn into her game of stupid proclamations. 'Anyway, speaking of false pretences, have you read *Art Matters* yet?'

Garvey's book on criticism and theory was required reading for the course. After four pages of the introduction Jimmy had hurled his copy at the wall of his room. It was still lying where it had landed.

'I have,' Tess replied. 'It's all right. Not well written, though, and quite self-regarding. Reminded me of bad poetry sometimes. I don't think he always has any idea himself what he means. It gets better in the second half.'

Penny said, 'I wouldn't read anything by that man. You know he once called me—' She took a drink, and waited for Tess, who had obviously heard this story before, to complete the sentence for her.

'—that talentless bulldyker!'

'Quite. Men like Garvey need to learn: a woman in trousers isn't necessarily a lesbianist. Not that I have any objection to homosexuals of either persuasion, you understand.'

She threw Jimmy a sly glance, and he wondered how it was that so many people could see so easily? He wasn't camp or obvious, as far as he could tell, but there was at least some usefulness to being identifiably queer. Since coming to London, he had already discovered what it could facilitate for him in a swimming-pool changing room or public toilet. But when the likes of Penny Hoxworth made it known she'd spotted what he was, he felt his privacy invaded.

'So,' he said, looking for revenge. 'What about the "talentless" part?'

Penny blew him a kiss across the table. 'Touché. Not for me to judge that one. Don't much care, either.'

For that remark, he thought, she was due some respect at least.

A chunky young man at the noisy next-door table turned to speak to them. He wasn't bad looking in a dull-faced way,

Jimmy decided, despite a prematurely receding hairline that added ten years to his age.

'You lot are first years at Moncourt, aren't you?'

'They are,' Penny told him. 'I'm not.'

'Not a first year?'

'Not at Moncourt either.'

He regarded her with interest. 'That explains why I've not seen you in here before. I'm doing Business and Accounts at the Laughton Institute. My name's Marius Shearsby by the way.'

He was still addressing himself entirely to Penny. Jimmy did his trick of raising a single eyebrow and was pleased when Tess had to cover her mouth to suppress her laughter.

Shearsby glanced distrustfully between Jimmy and Tess, then returned his attention to Penny. 'Anyway, there's going to be an impromptu later, in Primrose Hill, if you and your chums want to come.'

'We'll think about it,' Penny said, in the manner of some-one who had no intention of doing so. Nevertheless, it was with a look of accomplishment that Marius Shearsby turned back to his companions, one of whom immediately leant across to whisper something in his ear.

'Mission complete, Marius,' Jimmy said to Tess and Penny. 'I don't know about you two, but I'm not going anywhere with a bloke who talks about *impromptus* and *chums*.'

Despite which, when the pub closed, Jimmy found himself carried along with the tide of students and staff all heading for the Primrose Hill party. Hours later here he still was, in a house that could have swallowed his father's terraced cottage three times over. Apparently it belonged to a couple of post-graduate students, or rather to one of their parents. Right now, Marius Shearsby was droning away to him about this 'invest-ment', glancing around himself all the time, looking for Penny, Jimmy supposed. No point in that.

Half an hour previously, Toby Flint, the piggy-faced head of sculpture had started dancing drunkenly to someone's American jazz records. That was when Tess had suggested it was time to go, and Penny had agreed. Marius, hooting with laughter as Toby fell on his pinstriped backside, hadn't noticed their exit. Jimmy knew now he should have joined them in their taxi. Apparently they lived near the house in Camden where he rented a room. But at the time he'd been engaged in conversation with an interesting-looking second year from graphic design. Now the graphic designer was elsewhere, Flint was snoring on a Chesterfield sofa, and Jimmy was trapped with Marius Shearsby.

'What do your people do?' Marius asked him.

'My people? You mean my mum and dad? He's a coal miner. She used to work in a shoe factory, but she died last year.'

Soon after that, Marius invented an excuse to wander off, and Jimmy decided to try and find the graphic designer again. Passing by the unconscious Toby Flint, he saw that a trail of drool had leaked out of the corner of the tutor's mouth and almost filled one of the sofa's buttons to the top. It seemed bizarre to him that any of the Moncourt staff would come to a thing like this. Awkwardly conscious as they all obviously were of their off-duty status, it couldn't be much fun for them. What on earth did they get out of it? Then again, it wasn't much fun for Jimmy either, and yet here *he* was, prowling around the house in search of a probably heterosexual young man.

In the kitchen, he discovered a cluster of marijuana smokers. Finding the aroma of the drug pleasant, he stayed, leaning against the cooker. The lights were low, and it took his eyes a while to adjust after the brightness of the hallway, but he made out a couple of familiar faces. The joint, he saw, was currently with Roger Dunbar. Roger was the tutor in charge of first-year painting, a well-maintained fifty-year-old, sloppily but nattily dressed, with a mop of greying hair and an untidy, matching beard. He was the kind of man who'd been unremarkable when younger, grown briefly more attractive with age, and was now on the cusp of a decline. Jimmy wondered if he found that sort of thing attractive – an idle question, since the tutor was married with several kids and notorious for his pursuit of female students.

Next to Roger, to Jimmy's unsurprised disappointment, the attractive graphic designer was busy kissing some young woman and trying to thwart her half-hearted efforts to keep his hands off her breasts.

Roger offered the joint to Jimmy.

'No thanks,' he said. 'I don't have the constitution for it. Tried it once when I was fifteen and I nearly passed out.'

'Oh, that happens to everyone first time, Nichols. Give it a try. It frees the imagination.'

Roger stood up to give Jimmy the joint. He took it and drew deeply, burning his throat and lungs. His brain shrank inside his skull. A vignette closed in around the edges of his vision. His mouth filled with saliva and the contents of his stomach began to rise. In a panic, he shoved the joint back into Roger's hand and raced for the sink, reaching it just in time for his body to release a ferocious jet of vomit. It was mostly beer. Afterwards he ran the tap to wash it away, and poured himself a glass of water.

Several of the marijuana smokers, including the graphic designer, were giggling.

'Sorry about that.' Roger passed the joint to one of the others, then opened the door onto the rear garden. 'Let's get you some fresh air.' Then there was a hand against the small of Jimmy's back, guiding him almost without pressure into the welcome cool of the night.

# FEBRUARY – MARCH 1963

# 6

Penny lay on Tess's bed, reading her tattered *Lady Chatterley's Lover*, a pirate copy from before the end of the ban. She'd been out in the snow to the greengrocer's and was working her way through a bag of satsumas. Meanwhile, a few squiggles of muddy ice had fallen from the treads of her German boots onto the bedcovers.

Tess sat at the desk, trying to type up an essay about Allan Kaprow for an optional course she was taking in contemporary artists. The dirt on her bed and the satsuma peelings on her floor were among several Penny-related irritations about which she was currently keeping her feelings to herself. The Imperial Model B typewriter was another. A month ago, browsing a local second-hand shop, Tess had been drawn to a little green plastic Olivetti, marked *barely used*, but Penny had managed to persuade her that the peculiar and ancient Imperial represented the more stylish investment.

Aesthetically, she was right. The Model B was a skeletal, black and sepia construction in wood and iron. Made before the First World War, it seemed to Tess more like some half-cannibalised device from a destroyed future. As an artwork, it fascinated her. As a typewriter, its main drawback was that it didn't work. The carriage return would triple-space of its own accord, the caps lock liked to disengage itself, and the 'm' key stuck. None of these quirks occurred consistently. Tess sometimes wondered if she might find a way to avoid the machine's idiosyncrasies by choosing her words cautiously to avoid particular sequences of letters, but there seemed no discernible pattern to the Model B's misbehaviour.

'Do you want to go somewhere interesting this Thursday night?' Penny said, just as the word 'immediately' jammed eight type-hammers into a clump against the ribbon. Wearily, Tess set about untangling them.

'Where?'

Penny dropped her *Lady Chatterley* among the satsuma peelings on the floor and sat up, depositing a few more of her boots' frozen runes on Tess's bed. 'Soho. There's a club. Marius can get a few of us in, he thinks.'

'I've got to finish my essay for Monday.'

The hammers all dropped back into their home positions. Tess cleaned the ink from her fingers with the damp cloth she kept on her desk. She typed another sentence, two-fingered, looking at the keyboard, but fast and accurate. If she could keep writing, she thought, the ideas behind Kaprow's work might begin to make sense to her.

Many commentators find it difficult to accept the notion that an artwork can be a scripted event, an idea rather than an artefact. It could be argued, moreover, that Kaprow's soi-disant 'happenings'

Too pretentious, she decided.

~~It could be argued, moreover, that Kaprow's soi-disant 'happenings'~~ It could be argued that Kaprow's so-called happenings have more in common with theatrical performances than they do with a painting or a sculpture. However, there are some interes

'Francis Bacon goes sometimes, I've heard. Allen Jones too.' Clearly Penny wasn't going to let Tess concentrate until she agreed.

'How can Mr Business and Accounts get *us* into a club with Francis Bacon and Allen Jones? Hardly sounds like his sort of thing, does it?'

'Well, I'm not promising they'll *both* be there.'

'Why do you encourage that awful bloke anyway?'

She knew the answer. Penny selected and maintained her friends entirely on the grounds of usefulness and convenience. Marius's social connections, along with his romantic obsession with Penny, made him useful. Tess on the other hand did not flatter herself she was anything more than convenient; someone reasonably interesting to talk to. The other tenants in the house were both secretaries in the same typing pool. They worked long hours and their sole interest was in swapping mundane anecdotes about their colleagues and bosses.

'Marius's father's some kind of novelist, or playwright, or poet. Used to be an Angry Young Man. Now he's an irritable middle-aged man. That's what Marius says. Anyway, whatever he does, he's well-known for it and that gets *him* in. He'll recommend us, and that'll get *us* in.'

'Why would he do that? He has no idea who we are.'

'Paternal indulgence, darling. We're Marius's friends. That's enough for Daddy. You can bring the passionate young Mellors too, if you like.'

Penny delighted in every opportunity she could find to promote the absurd notion that Tess's and Jimmy's friendship barely concealed their seething lust. There was something else in the way she talked about him too, some not-too-subtle subtext Tess could hear, but couldn't get at.

'All right,' she said. 'If Jimmy wants to go, I will too. But that means I really do need to finish my essay now.'

'Don't mind me. I shall return to my study of literature.' Penny grimaced as she retrieved her *Lady Chatterley*. 'Though I have to say, I wouldn't have believed it possible to write this unsexily about fucking.'

Jimmy had a contact at the medical school through whom he had acquired thirteen human skulls.

'They're real ones,' he'd announced the first time he'd opened the sack to show them to Tess. 'Not plaster or anything. These are actual skulls out of actual people's heads. Thirteen people. Imagine that.'

At first, seeing the skulls all jumbled in a sack like murderers' trophies, she had found them hideous. Their jawbones reattached with wire. The hollow craniums with their hairline cracks. All the chips and scars – damage that might have happened before death or after. Now that Jimmy had assembled them into a pyramid, they were easier to look at. Five skulls formed the base, four the next layer, three the next, and one sat on top. He had arranged them so that their faces all pointed away from him.

As usual on Monday morning, their tutor Roger Dunbar had not yet arrived. Two dozen first-year fine art students were scattered around the studio: some in groups of three or four, many in pairs, and one or two in isolation. Each was equipped with an easel and a small table. Unlike every other class at Moncourt, Tess's year were not allowed their own permanent working spaces.

'If you stay in one place, your imagination and your eye stagnate,' Roger had explained. 'Far better to start everything fresh each morning. Your mistakes won't hinder you, and your successes won't turn into mannerisms. So every night we'll clear the room, and every morning you'll choose a new spot.'

He never seemed to notice, however, that each morning they all returned their equipment to more or less exactly the same positions. You couldn't fight human nature, Tess supposed. She and Jimmy liked it here, towards the back of the room. Jimmy had even cut his initials into a table and easel, to ensure he could always retrieve the same ones: *his* kit.

Their current task was to 'find and paint an object of symbolic value, so as to explore the idea of *meaning* in visual art'. In response, about a quarter of the class had brought in musical instruments, which they were approaching in various conventional ways – here a straightforward still life, there a Picasso-esque collage – all of which struck Tess as avoiding the challenge. Others had found crassly meaningful subjects: political books, bits of army uniform, religious insignia.

Tess was painting a scruffy old toy bear. Jimmy was depicting his pile of skulls in oils, with crude strokes of harsh colour.

'I've seen one a bit like this by Cezanne,' Tess said.

'I know it. Fewer skulls, facing the painter.' Jimmy sounded like a bad ventriloquist. He had a paintbrush gripped between his teeth, the way a dog in a cartoon might carry a bone.

'So why are you painting the backs of their heads?'

'More interesting.'

He put down the brush he'd been painting with, removed the other from his mouth and used it as a pointer to emphasise his explanation. 'When the eyeholes are staring at you, they're all the same. But this way round – look at the variation – texture, shape, colour. The back of the head, that's where the real individuality is.'

'But you aren't painting the subtleties, are you?'

'Aren't I?' Jimmy shut his left eye to suggest a patch, and mimicked Benedict Garvey's punctilious, oddly emphasised delivery, familiar from their weekly art history and theory lectures. 'Yes, by *painting* the backs of these skulls, I seek to *reveal* a delicate individuality, which would *otherwise* be overwhelmed by the obvious and clichéd *memento mori* symbolism of the *forward*-facing death's head. Do you *mean* to suggest, *Miss* Green, therefore, that this somewhat naive *rendition* I'm making here might be at odds with those *lofty* intentions?'

It was an old game between them by now. His perfect impersonation only required a standard response from her.

'Yes,' she said. 'And no.'

'Yes indeed. And, of course, no.' He stepped back and admired his own painting. Dropped back into himself again. 'I'm pleased with it. It looks good, doesn't it?'

'Yes – but I can't say why.'

It was odd. Neither Jimmy's patience nor his technique was up to much, really, and this picture was typical, with its apparently shoddy draughtsmanship and a composition that ought by conventional standards to be weak. Yet it succeeded because of qualities so indefinable that you had to fall back on vague ideas like 'painterly' to explain them.

'Yours is great, Tess,' he said. 'I wish I could just *get* things like you do. The fur . . . it's so believable. And there's a mood about it too.'

He was just being kind. She knew her technical perfection served only to emphasise what the painting lacked, and Jimmy's had, which was *Art*. It was fun to sneer at Garvey, but ever since starting the course, she had become increasingly convinced that the man had been right about her, that what he had seen within a second of opening her portfolio was true. Unless she could find a way to become a different kind of artist, she might as well give up: leave Moncourt and get herself a job drawing surgical enhancements for newspaper ads.

The class had been working on their paintings for an hour and a half when Roger Dunbar finally entered the studio. Poor punctuality was one of many liberties the tutor denied his students but allowed himself.

'You know he's been to bed with three of these girls since the Christmas holiday,' Jimmy murmured.

On the far side of the room, Dunbar leaned in close to a female student and guided her brush hand to indicate where work needed to be done.

'No – who?'

'Jill, Olivia, Zoe.' When Tess did not reply immediately, Jimmy added, 'Not all at once – obviously.'

After a moment's reflection, she said, 'At least an orgy would be dramatic. Working his way through the first-year girls one by one is just unambitious.'

'You shouldn't try so hard to sound like Penny, you know. She's not worth half of you.'

After that they both focused on their paintings for a couple of minutes. Tess was cross at him because he was right. Penny's style of showy glibness would only impress the sort of people whose good opinion was worthless. Still, he didn't need to be so nasty about it.

He had been adding highlights in yellow. Now he dipped his brush in the jar of turpentine, dried it on a rag and loaded it with burnt umber mixed with a little purple. This he began applying carefully to the spaces between the skulls. Tess saw how the deep shadows would transform the picture. They would define and separate each skull from the others, reveal its individuality.

'Do you want to know something else about Roger Dunbar?' Jimmy murmured. 'A proper secret?'

'What's that?' she said, because in own his way he was apologising, and to reject the offer would be petulant, though really she'd have preferred to abandon the subject entirely.

'Later.' He gave a tilt of his head to indicate that the tutor had made his way to their part of the room and was within earshot.

Roger strolled from canvas to canvas, finding some remark to make about each student's work. When he reached Jimmy's painting, he just paused long enough to say, 'Rough, but strong,' before he moved on to Tess's canvas. 'Beautifully done, as always. And you've avoided the risk of tweeness. Is the bear your own?'

'From when I was little,' she replied, though actually she had found this bear only a week ago, rain-soaked, on the street, taken it home and dried it out on a windowsill. She glanced at Jimmy, looking for support, but he was determinedly focused on his own work.

'What does it *mean*?' Roger asked.

'My grandmother gave it to me,' she said. 'I forgot I had it. Then when I was eight, my little sister found it and started playing with it. Of course, I immediately wanted it back, and we ended up in a massive argument. So my mum said she'd throw it on the fire if we couldn't agree who it belonged to.'

'Like King Solomon and the baby,' Roger said.

'That's what I thought. And knowing that story, I knew what to do. I said I couldn't stand to see the bear burned, and Sally could have it. But then it turned out Mum didn't know the story of Solomon at all. She just gave the bear to my sister. After a couple of days Sally lost interest, so I went in her room and took it back. She didn't even notice.'

'I see.' He hovered around the inevitable question before landing on it. 'And how does this picture communicate that meaning?'

'It doesn't,' Tess said immediately. 'I'm not all that happy with it, if you want to know.'

He moved nearer. She did her best not to flinch or stiffen at the dry warmth of his palm around the back of her brush hand.

'Here,' he said softly, as he made her draw hieroglyphs in the air. 'The problem is, you've only painted what you see. It looks like a toy bear.'

Close up, she saw signs that Roger was beginning to unravel. His skin was drab. There was tobacco on his breath, and the sour odour of last night's drinking. She slipped her hand free of his.

'What *should* it look like, then, Mr Dunbar?'

'Think about a real bear,' he said. 'A real bear wouldn't comfort a little girl, it would kill and eat her. So why do we feel the need to transform this savage creature into something so *safe*? And how does all that fit with you and your sister? You can't answer those questions, so you mustn't try. But if you get the picture to ask them, maybe it'll mean something.'

'I don't know how to do that,' Tess said.

Roger looked back at her evenly. 'Give it a try.'

He moved on. Tess stepped back from her painting, and wondered what to do. She was in her second term at one of the so-called best schools in the country, and so far all she had learnt was that art wasn't fair. You spent hours and hours trying to paint what things *were*, only to find yourself falling short of painting what they *meant*. Dunbar was no help. It sounded meaningful when he talked, but underneath his pose of wisdom her tutor could barely express what he was looking for. As far as she could see, that made him typical around here.

Once Roger had worked his way all around the room, he called for everyone's attention.

'There's good stuff here,' he told them all. 'Some better than others, of course, but generally, yes, rather impressive. Well done.' He paused, created a sense that what he was about to say next would be momentous. 'Now, as you all know, once you've all done your final pieces in a few months, there's the first-year show for the examiners. Normally that's a quiet affair, not open to the public like the third-year show. But you'll be aware that I recently took over as head of the first-year course, and I've seen some real potential in this group. So I'm pleased to announce that for the first time ever, your examining panel this summer will include an important art dealer.'

Olivia Rackham put up her hand, and without waiting for acknowledgement asked, 'Which dealer is this, Roger?'

Remembering that Jimmy had named Olivia as one of the girls Roger had been to bed with, Tess caught her friend's eye. He grinned back at her and nodded.

'I can't tell you that right now,' Roger said, 'but I can say she's influential.' He hesitated, realising the pronoun had narrowed the field. 'It's not likely this dealer will *buy* anything, of course, but it's an excellent opportunity for each of you to make an impression. I hope you'll all take best advantage of it.'

There was a murmur of excitement around the room. Tess didn't care. She had already concluded that passing the first-year exam and surviving into the second year would be enough for her. Looking around at her peers, she thought most of them really ought to be feeling the same way.

Roger put a finger to his lips. 'Listen, I can't tell you anything about how the viewings will be arranged – it's all behind closed doors. However, what I *can* say is that my recommendations are respected. And good work is good work. It's not a matter of opinion.'

Tess returned to her painting, and realised the story she had just told Roger was not after all a complete lie. Now she thought of it, she was fairly sure there *had* been a real child-hood dispute rather like the one she had described, though it was over a doll rather than a bear.

Her mother really had threatened to resolve the argument by chucking the thing in the fire, but there the similarity to the Solomon story ended. As Tess recalled, neither she nor Sally would give in, leaving Mum no choice. Once the toy began crackling irretrievably in the flames, Sally did at last turn despondent, and begged, too late, for its salvation. Tess, however, rather enjoyed seeing it melt and burn. In the circum-stances, destruction had felt like the only possible victory.

Had all that really happened, though? The recollection flickered irritatingly in her mind. It might have been a dream, or something she had invented.

She resolved to ask about it when her mother telephoned at the weekend.

'Can't face all that suet,' Jimmy said as they left the studio at lunchtime. On Mondays, the refectory always served meat pudding followed by spotted dick. 'Want to walk to Ginelli's for lunch? I could do with some fresh air.'

Tess had hoped to enjoy an hour in the refectory's comfortable fug, but instead found herself trudging alongside Jimmy through the harsh February cold. For almost two months, snow had fallen over the city. Its obviating whiteness seemed strange and symbolic at first, a marker of all the newness in her life, until time turned it into an uncomfortable bore to be endured as long as it lasted. Even kids had stopped bothering with snowballs after a couple of weeks.

Last Saturday, while taking a walk along the banks of the Thames, she'd witnessed a car pulling a skier along the river's frozen surface. The surrealism of the scene had barely occurred to her.

She struggled to keep her footing on the compacted ice and tried her best not to be bad tempered about it.

'What do you think about this dealer looking at our work?' she asked Jimmy. 'I don't see much point in it myself.'

'Ah, but you're forgetting Roger's behind-the-scenes influence.'

Tess laughed. 'Poor Roger. He really wants to be important, doesn't he?'

'He's a shit,' Jimmy said. 'Have you noticed he never uses anyone's name? Students, I mean. I don't think he knows what any of us are called. Not even the girls he's *fucked*. That's pretty unforgivable, don't you think?'

It had not taken Tess long to grow accustomed to the well-spoken vulgarity affected by most of her middle-class contemporaries at Moncourt, but she knew Jimmy preferred to keep his swearing for the times he really felt he needed it.

'What were you going to tell me before?' she asked him. 'You mentioned you knew a proper secret.'

'Oh. That. I probably shouldn't say.' He picked up pace. 'We'd better get a move on, hadn't we? We've been dawdling. At this rate we'll barely have time for a snack.'

Tess decided she'd already let him push her around enough for one day. She stopped walking. He took a couple of steps further and then halted too.

'Just tell me,' she said.

He sighed. 'All right. But we have to keep going. Come on.'

They set off again.

'So?'

He stuck his hands in his coat pockets. 'The thing is, when it comes to sex, Roger isn't *only* interested in females.'

At first, she thought she understood what Jimmy meant. But so what if Roger Dunbar was bisexual. Surely, after all the art history she'd studied, Jimmy hadn't expected her to be shocked by *that*?

'I have to say, that's hardly—' she began. Then she realised. 'Oh Christ, Jimmy.'

They walked a few more steps in silence. She was going to have to hear all about this, she supposed, however uncomfortable she felt about it. He needed a confidante, was waiting for her to take that role. There was no way out.

'So how—I mean—when—?'

He kept his eyes focused on the road ahead and continued in a determined monotone. 'Right at the start. Do you remember that awful party Marius Shearsby dragged us to in Primrose Hill? It was after you went home. I got in a bit of a state, I'm afraid. Roger was sympathetic. We went out into the garden where it was dark and there were trees we could hide behind. Anyway, everyone else was in the house. Once we were finished, he told me to wait out there for twenty minutes after he'd gone in, so nobody would guess what shenanigans we'd been up to. That really was what he called it – *shenanigans*. I should have known then how he'd be afterwards. By the time I went back into the house, he'd left.'

'He could go to jail,' Tess said.

'We both could.'

'You'd be his victim,' she said. 'You're under twenty-one.' She wasn't entirely sure of the law, but she'd read reports about this type of thing in her father's *News of the World*.

'Except it wasn't my first time, Tess.'

'Oh.'

'Hadn't you guessed?' Jimmy said. 'I mean, you've never thought of me as a possible boyfriend, have you?'

That was true. He was just her friend. But then, Tess seldom thought romantically about any actual person. Her fantasy objects always lay somewhere in the future, were more abstractions than people: just stories she told herself.

'You don't look like one,' she said. 'Or sound like one.'

He grunted in response. Perhaps she'd offended him, she thought. All she had meant was that he didn't speak in one of those voices she sometimes heard in radio comedies, full of archness and italics. Everyone knew that way of talking was code for 'queer', though nobody ever said so. She'd met young men whose manner was like that – not so exaggerated, perhaps, but definitely in the same category. It occurred to her now that maybe it wasn't exactly natural to them; maybe they chose to speak that way on purpose, to tell the world what they were. If so, she thought, that was a tremendously brave thing to do.

'I'm just saying you just don't seem like an obvious homosexual to me. Nor does Roger.'

'Plenty of poofs don't flounce around yammering in Polari,' he said. 'But a lot of people do spot it in me, you know. Penny saw it right off, for example.'

Of course. *That* was the real joke, the now-totally obvious subtext, underlying all Penny's ribbing about 'Tess's little beau'. Thinking of that, she blushed at her own stupidity.

'As for Roger,' Jimmy continued, 'he isn't really a homo. He just dabbles once in a while. I suppose all those compliant nineteen-year-old girls must get dull for him. Still, after he's been with a boy – I mean, immediately after – he does find it necessary to provide a list of all the women he's had sex with. That's how I know about those three in our year. Because Roger's not a *degenerate*, you see.'

'Is that why you're angry at him? Because he's—' she scrambled about for the right word '—uncommitted?'

'It annoys me that he won't talk properly to me about my work anymore, that's all. He's being such a child about it. But I suppose that's my own stupid fault for getting in the situation in the first place. And you could be right – about him being frightened of jail.'

'Or of losing his position at least.'

'As far as that goes, I think they're allowed as much fun as they want with the students, Tess. It's not just a perk – most of them think it's part of the job. Sentimental education, they call it. You know about Joe Reid, don't you?'

Reid taught in the sculpture department. According to gossip, he'd got a student pregnant last year, or possibly the year before, and the girl had died during a botched backstreet abortion. Or anyway she had got so ill she hadn't been able to stay on the course. Despite this travesty, the story went, there had been no sanctions whatsoever for Reid. There might have been some truth in part of it, Tess thought, but surely there was a lot of hyperbole too.

'That's just rumours,' she said, perhaps a bit too primly.

'No smoke without fire,' Jimmy replied, as if that settled the matter. She let it go.

They arrived at Ginelli's, and found themselves alone there, apart from Luca and his mother, bickering in Italian behind the counter.

'Looks like this place got unfashionable without our noticing,' Jimmy remarked as they took their seats.

'Good,' Tess said.

# 7

As long as she kept herself reasonably sober, Delia was allowed whatever she wanted from the bar. It turned out she didn't really want anything. She sat alone, not touching her tonic water, taking a break for now. In half an hour or so, she'd have to be sociable again, earn her keep for the evening. She'd need alcohol then.

It was nine forty-five, and the Gaudi was half-full – which was as full as it ever got. At scattered tables around the tiny club, self-involved customers chattered over the equally self-involved musical accompaniment provided by the Les Jensen Jazz Trio, playing on the tiny stage at the side. When she'd first come here, Delia had found the clientele strange and glamorous: men in black sweaters or checked shirts; women in blue jeans and dramatic spectacle frames. But she had soon realised that the appearance of being interesting was about as much as most of these people could manage.

At a table near the stage, Rita and Kathy, the other two of Stella's girls here tonight, were noisily entertaining a group of actors. From time to time, Les Jensen scowled down from his piano in disapproval at this disrespectful racket.

Delia liked rock and roll best, and she didn't mind some jazz – Kenny Ball or Acker Bilk – the stompy, old-fashioned sort you heard on the wireless sometimes. But the Les Jensen Trio sounded nothing like that. Their music was flashy, abstract and syncopated. Delia's untrained ear could find nothing in it resembling a melody or a rhythm. There were no songs, no breaks in the performance, just a long, vague

95

improvisation in which no note lasted long enough to sound completely wrong. Occasionally, the group would slip, probably by accident, into something recognisable as music, but after a bar or two, they would spot their mistake and return to tuneless virtuosity. Every fifteen minutes one member took a solo (always following the same strict cycle: piano–drums–bass) during which the other two could leave the stage for a break. Thus they were able to play on relentlessly all night.

Bill Shearsby arrived at her table during the night's fourth bass solo. By way of greeting, he mimed along on an imaginary instrument.

'*Dum-dum-du-dum-du-dumdum-dum-du-dum.* Can I join you?'

She could have told him she wanted to be on her own. He'd have understood, wouldn't have taken it personally. But she liked Shearsby. He was also one of the half-dozen customers Finlay especially wanted the hoisters to talk with. What for, she wasn't sure. He didn't seem well-off enough to be a candidate for blackmail, and there was nothing obviously crooked about him. She smiled and nodded, and he took the seat opposite her.

'Ah well, at least there's no bloody *poet* this time,' he said.

One night a couple of weeks previously, the Les Jensen Trio's performance had been augmented by a bearded Australian ranting semi-comprehensibly about sex and politics. Some of it had been hilarious, but Delia had not known if she was allowed to laugh.

'You writing anything at the minute, Bill?' she asked. 'It's plays you do, isn't it?'

'Oh, let's not talk about that, Delia.'

She knew he didn't mean it. 'What are they about, then? Your plays.'

'All sorts. It depends.'

'Ain't you got a main subject, though? Something you keep coming back to, no matter what the story is?'

'You mean my *theme*? For a shoplifter, you make a fair literary critic, Delia.'

Shearsby was a heavily built bloke, in his middle forties she'd guess, with some kind of country accent. He said *sharpliffur* for shoplifter and *lurtery* for literary.

'I ain't a shoplifter, Bill. I don't know where you got that idea.'

'Course not. Just my imagination running away with me, I expect.'

'Well, I like reading. Always have,' she told him. 'Charles Dickens. He's got a theme, ain't he? Always writing about lost kids.'

'Like *Oliver Twist*? You read that one, Delia?'

'Started once or twice. Never got away with it.'

He grinned. 'Bit too close to home, maybe?'

'I seen the musical. New Theatre about three year ago. Gent I was walking out with at the time took me. Proper cultural, he was. We went to quite a few plays together. Not just musicals, neither. Harold Pinter, John Osborne, Rattigan. Any of your plays been on up the West End, Bill?' She realised she had slipped into playing up her accent – as if she was some character out of *Oliver* herself. Or Eliza bloody Doolittle.

'Once upon a time they used to be,' he said. 'These days my sort of play doesn't appear to be required in that part of town. Seems I'm a little too 1950s for a contemporary theatrical audience. Funny, really. 1950s was exactly what they wanted five years ago.'

Delia laughed. Not that it was especially funny, but she recognised the cadence of a joke. Bill looked pleased.

'Anyway,' he continued, 'I mainly write for the telly now. Had a play on the BBC about six months back. Maybe you saw it? *Girl on the Run*. It got some good reviews. Caused a bit of a stir for a few days. Was even mentioned in parliament.'

'Haven't got a television,' Delia said, reining in the cockney.

'Teenager leaves her parents and hitches to London to find her fortune. It all ends up badly for her.'

'Sounds cheery.'

'I've done what they call light entertainment too. Couple of episodes of *Dixon of Dock Green*. One about a librarian who accidentally kills her mum, and one about a retired soldier who tries to rob a bookie's.'

'Oh yeah?' The last time she'd watched anything on the TV had been in Stella's back room – Spurs winning the 1962 Cup final 3-1 against some northern side. Teddy and that lot alternating between abuse and yells of encouragement. Tiny men on the black and white screen. Not very interesting.

'Telly's the future,' Shearsby said. 'In ten years there probably won't *be* any big theatres in London. They'll all be converted into bingo halls or cinemas. Good thing too. Put the plays back where they belong, among the ordinary people – rooms in pubs, town halls – not in the bloody Shaftsbury, with the Lord Chamberlain telling you what what's right and wrong, what you can and can't say. A man can do serious work on television and reach the whole country. Have you seen that thing on ITV? Just a street in Manchester. Ordinary people, ordinary lives. It's wonderful stuff. Bleak, funny, truthful—'

All you needed to do, once you'd started him off, was make noises every now and again, so he'd think you were still listening. Delia didn't mind. Shearsby was *angry* all right, but anger came in different varieties. Teddy Bilborough's, for example, was selfish – entirely directed at the past: all the promises he thought life had made him and not kept. Shearsby, on the other hand, was full of hope; he lived in the belief that things could be better, would one day be better, and he was annoyed at them for not changing anything like fast enough.

They spotted Marius Shearsby waiting on the other side of Leicester Square. He was standing near the doors of the

Odeon cinema, huddling himself in his overcoat, and sheltering from a mercifully light snowfall. Even from this distance his disappointment at the sight of the three of them was obvious.

'Oh God,' Jimmy said. 'He was expecting you to be on your own, Penny. That idiot thought this was a bloody *date*, didn't he?'

'You can't back out now,' Penny muttered. 'You two are my bodyguards.'

'You knew?' Tess had always envied her housemate's capacity to say and do whatever she felt like saying or doing, without embarrassment or fear of being judged. But perhaps it wasn't exactly that Penny didn't mind *what* anyone else *thought*, more that she didn't care *how* anyone else *felt* – and that seemed much less admirable.

'I brought these two along,' Penny said to Marius as soon as they arrived. 'Your pa won't mind, will he?'

'I don't know.' Then, evidently deciding to make the best of things, he said, 'It'll probably be all right. That is – the other chaps who were meant to be here had to drop out, so—'

Jimmy regarded his efforts with obvious amusement. 'Last minute problem, was it, Marius? Something come up?'

'Shall we go?' Marius said, offering an elbow to Penny. She didn't take it.

They passed through the chaotic beauty of Chinatown, drenched everywhere in red, yellow and black, and on to the grubbiness of Soho, where suddenly there were far more men on the streets than women. Oily little characters outside shop fronts marked *Peep Show*, *Gentleman's Club* or *Private Cinema* accosted passers-by and tried to encourage them in.

'Want to see some titties, fellers?' one of them called to Jimmy and Marius. 'You can bring the ladies in too, if you like. Free of charge.'

'How much to let you see ours?' Penny replied, giving the man a wink.

Recognising Marius's discomfort at the way the situation had let him down, Tess felt unexpectedly sorry for him. 'I gather your father's a well-known writer,' she said. 'One of the Angry Young Men?'

'Used to be,' Marius replied, seizing the opportunity to deliver his joke. 'These days he's more of an irritable old man, though. And he doesn't write for the stage anymore, thank God.'

'Why "thank God"?' Jimmy asked. Tess had never heard of the man, but it was the chance of meeting William Shearsby that had persuaded Jimmy to join them this evening. Apparently one of Shearsby's plays had affected him quite deeply.

'Know who he is, do you?' Marius said. 'Not too many people remember him these days.' Clearly his dislike for Jimmy was deepening by the moment.

'William Shearsby? Of course I do, and I'd say he's still very well known as a dramatist.'

'Bloody hell, he's not William *Shakespeare!*' Marius replied. 'And you wouldn't ask why I'm glad he's stopped writing plays if you'd had to sit through every one of the miserable damn things, like I did. Night after night, sometimes. Three hours of some washerwoman complaining about her life. Honestly, you've no idea.'

'You're talking about *Consider This Your Notice*?'

'So you know it?'

Tess had seldom seen Jimmy so unguarded. 'I went to a touring production when I was in sixth form. It was brilliant.'

'Really?' Marius drawled, killing off the sympathy she had felt for him a moment ago. 'As I say, I didn't get much out of it myself, other than his being on time with my school fees for once, I suppose. But I'm sure he'll enjoy you telling him what a wonderful writer he is. He's generally pretty keen on that.'

Marius led them into a back alley between a Greek restaurant and a dangerous-looking pub. A chef from the restaurant was busy emptying a vat of hot water down a drain. Fishy-smelling steam enveloped them as they passed. About halfway along the alley, they found a portable billboard set out on the pavement.

'Here we are,' Marius said. 'Don't forget, if anyone asks, you two are both twenty-one, all right?'

Next to the billboard, marked *Gaudi Club – Licensed for Alcohol and Entertainment – Members Only*, was an unpromising blue door, which Penny pushed open to reveal a staircase, barred at the bottom by a table. A heavily scarred man sat behind it. He looked up from the Western novelette he was reading.

'Members only,' he said, far more mildly than Tess had expected. 'Didn't you see the sign?' The cover of his book bore the lurid image of a man in a sombrero firing revolvers from both hands. It was called *Bandito Pedro*.

'We're guests of a member,' Marius said. 'Well, *I'm* a guest of a member, and these are *my* guests.'

'Which member would you be talking about, Sir?'

'Mr William Shearsby. The playwright,' interjected Jimmy, attracting a sour glance from Marius.

The scarred man put his book down on the table. 'Wait here,' he told them, and headed up the stairs.

'Hello Lenny,' Delia said.

Caught up in his own rhetoric, Shearsby hadn't noticed the compact little man waiting for his attention.

'Evening, Miss,' Lenny said. 'Excuse me, Mr Shearsby. Sorry to bother you. Young feller at the door, says he's your son.'

Lenny Boden was crop-haired, his leathery face scarred from twenty years as a flyweight boxer who couldn't dodge or dance. His particular skill was the taking of punishment. Thump after thump and he'd still come back fighting. That was how he'd won his matches – endured the barrage until his opponent wore himself out. Finally it wore him out too. Now he worked the door at the Gaudi.

'Oh, yes, that's right,' Shearsby said. 'I spoke to Finlay about it earlier. The boy's twenty-two. He's here at my invitation. If that's what you're asking. Let him in by all means.'

'And his friends, Sir?'

'Friends?'

'There's another young gentleman with him, Sir. And two ladies. Can you vouch for all four of them?'

Shearsby was obviously annoyed at himself for having, in some moment of paternal indulgence, invited his son into this arcane segment of his world – an invitation the boy had apparently seen fit to extend to his friends too.

'Sod it,' he said. 'Better go and check, I suppose, before I give the OK and let 'em all in here. Who knows what kind of troublemakers Marius could have fallen in with—'

He followed Lenny out to the lobby.

While Shearsby was gone, Delia looked around the club. The group of actors at the table with Rita and Kathy included several barely famous faces – the sort you recognised from one-line roles in *Carry On* movies and suchlike but couldn't put a name to. From the expressions Rita was pulling, Delia surmised she must be telling her story about the wide-mouthed frog. It was the only joke Rita knew, but it was a good one. Everything was in the performance.

*There's this wide-mouthed frog. He lives in a pond and spends all his days eating bugs and flies. Until one day he thinks, I wonder what there is in the world outside here? Perhaps there's other animals to see. And maybe they eat things other than bugs and flies. So this wide-mouthed frog sets off wandering about the forest. And after a while, he comes across a long-eared, furry creature, so he says—*

This was the moment for Rita to put a finger to each corner of her mouth, stretch her lips out sideways as far as she could, and put on the frog's honking voice:

'*Good afternoon, friend. Who are you and what do you like to eat?*' *says the wide-mouthed frog.*

Then an impersonation of the frog's interlocutor:

'*I'm a rabbit,*' *answers the rabbit –* '*cause that's who it is, a rabbit.* '*I'm a rabbit,*' *he says,* '*and I like to eat carrots and greens.*'

'*How delicious that sounds,*' *says the frog.* '*Carrots and greens, eh? Well, I'm the wide-mouthed frog, and I like to eat bugs and grubs.*'

*And off he hops through the woods to see if there's other animals he can find out about. After a while, he meets a . . .*

Rita could spin this out for twenty minutes or longer: each iteration of the wide-mouthed frog funnier than the last; every animal with a different voice.

'*Good afternoon, friend. Who are you and what do you like to eat?*'

*[high-pitched squeak]* '*I'm a mouse. I like to eat the cheese that's left out in the night.*'

*[dopily]* '*I'm a worm. I like to eat soil.*'

*[seedily]* '*I'm a dung-beetle. You've probably guessed what I like to eat.*'

*[grunting]* '*I'm a pig. I like to eat whatever the farmer gives me.*'

So important was the wide-mouthed frog joke in Rita's social repertoire that she had gone to the trouble of stealing a book from the public library, *Wildlife of the World*, so she could research a wider variety of animals and learn about their dietary habits.

'*Good afternoon, friend. Who are you and what do you like to eat?*'

*[slightly drunken slur]* '*I'm a pangolin. I like to eat ants and termites.*'

'*How delicious that sounds,*' *says the wide-mouthed frog.* '*Well, I'm the wide-mouthed frog. I like to eat bugs and grubs.*' *And he hops off through the woods to see if there's other animals he can find out about.*

Delia saw Finlay at the bar. He must have arrived while she'd been talking to Shearsby. Most nights the club boss tried to get around all four of his establishments, to make sure everyone remembered who was in charge. Maggie Chisholm sat with him, sipping at a Martini. The little dress she had on, Delia herself had nicked from Selfridges a week ago. Anything black counted as mourning, she supposed. It seemed, anyway, that Albie Chisholm's death had cleared the way for more than just hostessing work. In fact, Maggie hadn't done any hostessing now for over two months.

Here's to you, Maggie, thought Delia, and she raised her tonic water in a toast. On the far side of the club, the young widow acknowledged the gesture with a smile, and a four-finger wave over the rim of her glass.

*[dreamy and vague, sing-song] 'I'm a blue-throated moun-taingem hummingbird. People think us hummingbirds don't live on nothing but nectar. Well, it's true I do like nectar best of all, but I'll gobble up any insects and little spiders I can find too.'*

Shearsby returned, with his bohemian son and his bohemian son's bohemian friends. Two skinny boys in polo necks, two girls in checked shirts.

'This is Marius,' Shearsby said. 'Marius, this is Delia.'

'Pleased to meet you, Delia,' Marius said. He was handsomer than his father, but had inherited none of Bill's natural charm. He held out his hand like a businessman closing a deal. She took hold of it. It was dry and warm. After a single decisive shake, he let her go, and she realised with a bolt of nostalgia that this was the first time in over a year she had touched another person's skin.

'This is my friend, Penny,' Marius said. 'And this is her housemate, Tess, and Tess's friend from art school—ah—'

'Jimmy,' the other boy said.

*[buzzes] 'I'm a honey bee. In the summer I fly about and eat nectar, like the hummingbirds do. In the winter I huddle together with the other bees, and we live on the honey we made when the days were long and warm.'*

They all sat. After a few moments of awkward settling, the girl called Penny said, 'So, Delia, how do you know Marius's pa?'

'From here,' Delia said. 'From the Gaudi.'

'We chat from time to time,' Shearsby added.

Delia knew Shearsby was divorced from Marius's mother, that he had a girlfriend, quite a lot younger than himself, who had been in one of his plays once. Having messed up his family enough already, he'd be keen to make sure Marius knew his relationship with Delia was, what was the word? Platonic.

'Are you a writer too, Delia?' Jimmy asked. If she had to bet on it, she'd say the boy was most likely queer. Not that he was making it at all obvious. Sometimes you could just tell. Conversely, Penny seemed to be trying hard to look like a dyke, but it was all pose. Delia knew a few lesbians. They were authentic. Penny just wanted to make people think she was something interesting.

'I work in a shop,' Delia said. 'Are you all going to be artists, once you finish studying?'

'The three of us are,' the one called Jimmy said. 'But Marius isn't an art student. He's doing Exploitation of the Working Classes at Moneygrab College.'

'Learning to make a living, you mean,' Marius snapped. 'I'm studying Business and Accounts. That's nothing to be ashamed of.'

People only said that when they *were* ashamed, Delia thought. She wondered what these young men were fighting over.

'Anyway, one doesn't *become* an artist,' Penny asserted. 'One either *is* an artist, or isn't. We don't go to art school to learn how to be artists, but to find out whether or not that's what we are.'

Her pronouncement had the ring of something that had been said more successfully on some previous occasion. This time, however, it hung in the air for a few seconds, with nobody really knowing what to do with it. Then Bill, not bothering to keep the irony out of his voice, said, 'And have you found out yet, Penny? Whether you're an artist or not?'

Penny smiled benignly. 'Certainly I have.'

'And—?'

'I'm not.'

'Oh, come on, Pen,' Marius said. 'Don't be so modest. Your stuff's brilliant.' Whatever he thought about Penny's sexual leanings, it was obvious her good opinion was important to him.

His, however, seemed of no interest whatsoever to her. She sighed. 'It's really not, Marius.' Having dismissed him, she directed her explanation to Delia. 'I'm good enough to pass. After that, I shall most likely get a job in some second-rate private school, teaching young ladies to draw and paint. They'll all have terrible crushes on me, of course, and that'll be fun. But I'll never be a real artist. Who would want to, anyway? It's an awful life.'

From what Delia could see, Penny looked as if she would make a perfect schoolmistress, with her bossiness, her trick of seeming to like people she couldn't really care less about. As to the little queer and his so-far-silent girlfriend – maybe they were real artists, whatever that meant. Now Delia could see Bill Shearsby getting twitchy. If she wasn't quick, he'd be off first.

Over on Rita's table, the joke was reaching its climax.

*'How delicious that sounds,' says the wide-mouthed frog. 'Well, I'm the wide-mouthed frog. I eat bugs and grubs.' And he hops off through the woods to see if there's other animals he can find out about.*

*After a while, he comes across a long, low creature with skin like one of Stel— like one of my boss's handbags, and a great big mouth full of the sharpest teeth he's ever seen. And what do you think Mr wide-mouthed frog says to this funny-looking animal?*

By now, her whole audience was joining in. All the third-rate actors around her table pulled their lips as wide as they could and honked out the chorus, *'Good afternoon, friend. Who are you and what do you like to eat?'*

Rita raised her left eyebrow. *[voice of a public-school bully]* *'I'm a crocodile,' this new animal says, 'cause that's what he is, he's a big old crocodile. 'I'm a crocodile,' he says – pause – and I like to eat – pause again – wide-mouthed frogs!'*

The key was not to rush the final moments of the joke. Rita took it slowly, pantomimed all the frog's reactions – terror, confusion, decision – building laughter around the table. Finally, she puckered her lips into the tiniest possible *o*, and squeaked the payoff:

*'Well, you don't see many of those fuckers round here, do you?'*

Uproar from the actors. Much imitation of the punchline – the face and the words – by the third-rate actors.

'Scuse me,' Delia said, getting to her feet. 'I just need a word with Finlay over there.'

Shearsby's rueful smile acknowledged she'd beaten him to it. A look of surprised disappointment crossed the face of the so-far silent Tess.

'Oh—I—'

'What is it, darling?'

'Nothing. I was going to ask you something. It doesn't matter, though.' There was a pleasing music in Tess's northern accent. Delia found herself wanting to be kind to her.

'You sure?'

'Honestly. Some other time,' the girl said.

Once the woman, Delia, had left them, Tess knew it was just a matter of *when* Shearsby would feel he had done enough of his duty and could break off the encounter too.

Jimmy said, 'She doesn't really work in a shop, does she?'

Shearsby ignored the question and turned to Tess – his back closing off further discussion of Delia, or any other topic, with Jimmy.

To smooth over this rudeness, Penny said something uncomplimentary about the jazz trio – a springboard from which the other two leapt gratefully into a conversation about music, leaving Tess to deal with Shearsby.

'What sort of an artist are you?' he asked her.

'Not one at all, yet,' she said. 'I hope I'll be good enough to be a painter one day.'

'Not like your friend, then?'

He meant Penny's idea of becoming a schoolteacher at a boarding school. That ought to have come as a surprise to Tess, since Penny had never mentioned it before. But it was a lazy, pragmatic decision, and there was nothing unexpected about it.

'No. When did you decide you wanted to be a writer?'

'Never did. Still don't. It's not a calling. It's – I don't know – unavoidable, don't you think? I mean, what would *you* do if you couldn't paint or draw?'

She had no answer. Despite all her recent uncertainty this was not a question she had ever considered.

'Well,' Shearsby said. 'That's my point.' He kept glancing away from her towards the bar, where Delia was now talking to the club boss and his pretty companion. A look of hostility briefly crossed his face.

'What's your view on things in South Africa?' he said.

'South Africa?' What did he mean? A moment ago he'd been talking about art. Being an artist. What did South Africa have to do with that? Marius must have been listening out for this turn in their conversation. He dropped the exchange he was having with Penny and Jimmy.

'Dad,' he said. 'We're just out to have some fun. There's no need—'

'—to talk about anything that actually matters?' Shearsby interrupted. 'Aren't your *friends* serious people, at least?'

Marius looked down at his drink. Tess flinched at the idea this unforgiving man might think her as frivolous as his son.

## David Wharton

'I'm a serious person,' Jimmy said, quietly.

Shearsby seemed not to hear him. 'It's terrible, how things are over there, and hardly anyone in this country knows about it. There's a march in a couple of weeks' time, if you're interested.' He put some kind of leaflet on the table, then addressed his son. 'I'm sorry I was sharp, Marius.' When Marius did not look up or speak, he said, 'Well, I'd better be going. I've writing to do. I'll just say goodbye to Delia.'

Jimmy picked up the leaflet. 'I'd like to find out more about all this.'

Seeing Shearsby about to ignore him a third time, and Marius preparing to say something unpleasant, Tess added, 'Me too.'

'Well then,' Shearsby said with something approaching a smile. 'Maybe I'll see you both at the march.'

Up close, Delia could see Maggie wasn't right. Despair lay immediately beneath the make-up. Her eyes kept trying to focus and then letting go. Mother's little helpers, most likely, prescribed by the crooked doctor her new boyfriend paid to look after his girls. More than once, Delia had heard Finlay refer to this man as 'the vet'.

'Who's that lot with Shearsby?' Finlay asked her, as if he was only making conversation.

She told him, 'The one in the middle's his son. The other three are his son's friends.'

'Yeah, Lenny told me.'

Why bother asking, then? Delia thought. 'They're all students,' she said.

Finlay pretended not to be very interested in the answers to the questions he kept asking. 'What were they talking about?'

'Nothing. Themselves.'

'Oh yeah? Like what?'

'That girl on Shearsby's left, the taller one. She's going to be a teacher in a private school. The son, Marius, is doing

109

some sort of business certificate. The other two are just art students.'

For the moment he seemed to have all the information he wanted. He fell silent and watched what was happening over on Shearsby's table.

Maggie said, 'You seen my kids recently, Dee?'

'Few days back, I did, yeah. Jemima was walking them to school. Making sure they didn't get lost on the way in.'

Maggie laughed. 'When Albie was looking after them, the truant officer used to be round our house all the time. Jem won't have none of that. How'd they look?'

'Healthy.' Delia wasn't sure how much to say, how Maggie would feel about her children not needing her. It might be a relief, she supposed, but it might hurt her too. 'They were happy, far as I could tell.'

Still with an eye on Shearsby's table, Finlay said, 'Not too sorry about their old man, then?'

'Kids are tough,' Delia replied.

Without looking at Maggie, Finlay laid his hand on her arm. It might have looked like a sympathetic gesture. Maybe that was how it was meant. But Delia doubted it. She remembered one time when she was a kid, evacuated to Somerset. A farmer had brought his dog to heel with a tiny click of his tongue, barely audible, and then winked at the child. Men like Finlay were that way with their women, always showing off their control, never guessing what they were really demonstrating was their weakness.

Maggie finished her drink and called to the barman for another. Finlay signalled his permission with an exasperated sweep of his hand, like he was batting away a moth. He probably didn't want Maggie drinking so much, but he had other things to worry about. He returned his attention to Delia.

'What about before?' he asked her.

'Before?'

'When you were talking to Shearsby on your own. What'd he have to say for himself?'

'Oh—' she'd already started forgetting that conversation. 'His plays. Things he writes for the telly.'

'He writes for the telly?' Maggie said.

'Yeah. *Dixon of Dock Green*, apparently. And he did a play about a young woman who runs away from home.'

'Ooh. *Girl on the Run*?' Maggie said.

'That's the one, I think.'

'I saw that. It was ever so good. He *wrote* it?' Full of admiration, she gazed across at Shearsby, who was talking animatedly to the girl called Tess.

'That all?' Finlay said. 'No politics?'

Delia decided to improvise. Give the man something he might want to hear. 'He's writing a thing for the telly about the blacks,' she said.

'Oh yes? Which blacks is that?' Finlay was always keen to hear about any talk to do with the blacks.

'The usual ones. Them that go on all the marches in the States.'

At that he lost interest again, for real this time. Wrong sort of blacks, obviously.

'You don't think about someone *writing* it,' Maggie said. 'When you're watching a story, you just imagine it's real people.'

Shearsby was standing up now, saying goodbye to Marius and his friends. He came over to the bar.

'I'm off home,' he said to Delia. 'Writing to do.'

Finlay ground out his cigar. 'We're going too, Bill. Whereabouts do you live?'

'Clapham.'

'That's well out of our way. But still, we ain't got nothing better to do. Why don't we give you a lift?'

'You're all right, Finlay. I'll take the night bus. Public transport's good for writers. Sitting in expensive cars, you lose touch. But thanks anyway.'

Finlay caught Delia's eye and inclined his head slightly towards the table Shearsby had just vacated, where the four students were still sitting. She gave him a tiny nod of understanding.

'All right,' he said to Bill Shearsby. 'We'll walk downstairs with you, anyway. C'mon Mags.'

'See you Dee,' Maggie said. She stood and put on a fur coat, which looked very like that fox jacket from the day in Barkers when Maureen had got herself caught. Quite possibly it was the same one. Delia pushed aside an echo of sadness, of guilt, and made her heart small and cold.

Some kind of disagreement had broken out between the art students. The two boys had stood up and were facing each other off. Neither of them looked much like a fighter, but if she had to guess, her money would be on the queer rather than the bore. Anyway, nothing would happen. Lenny the doorman was on his way over to deal with it.

'Typical,' Marius said, right after his father had left them. 'He can't bear to be around me for more than quarter of an hour.' He was drunk, Tess saw. Drunker than the rest of them. Otherwise he'd have kept that thought to himself.

'Maybe he's—' Jimmy began, then decided not to finish the thought.

'What?' Marius asked. 'Maybe he's *what*?'

'Sorry, it's none of my business, is it?'

'Go on,' Marius insisted.

Jimmy smiled artlessly. 'Really. Let's talk about something else.'

He won't leave it alone, Tess thought. This conflict was in motion now, and if Jimmy was forced into a fight, he'd do anything necessary to win it. Marius imagined he had the upper hand, was too drunk to understand that he really ought to stop. Leaning in, he fixed his eyes on Jimmy's. 'You obviously understand my father better than I do. So let's hear it, Mr "I'll come on your march, Mr Shearsby, Sir".'

'Listen,' Jimmy said, his voice level, meticulous. 'I'm not the one who abandoned you when you were a kid, and I'm not the one who doesn't like you now.' He stopped speaking, as if he was finished, but Tess knew he was waiting deliberately for Marius to open his mouth. She was right: as soon as he did so, Jimmy interrupted him. 'Well, no, that's not true exactly. I *don't* like you, but that's neither here nor there, is it? We're nothing to each other. Why not show some guts? Go and take it out on your dad, rather than me.'

Marius slumped in his chair. 'I'd like you to leave,' he said.

Before she could think about it, Tess found herself saying, 'Oh, don't be so absurd!'

Furiously, he turned on her. 'You can get out too, you little slut. I saw what you were up to. Flirting with a man twice your age. It's disgusting.'

Was that really how it had looked? It was a horrible, insulting lie. Tess wanted very much to punish Marius for it, but Penny did the job for her.

'Speaking of your father, we're all *his* guests, aren't we, rather than yours? He's on his way out now with that owner chap. I'll nip over and ask him if we can stay, shall I?'

Marius was suddenly all supplication. 'I didn't say *you* were to leave, Penny. Just these two.'

'Well, of course I can't stay if you throw out my friends,' she said.

Tess felt grateful for this defence, though she knew it was mostly an excuse for Penny to exercise power over Marius. She looked over to the bar, where she saw William Shearsby glance back across at his son's table, realise what was going on, and turn to leave the club. Marius saw it too. And he saw her see it. He rose to his feet, accidentally knocking his glass over in the process. Spilled beer crawled across the table towards the flyer Shearsby had left there.

Jimmy grabbed the piece of paper. 'Careful chum.'

Marius narrowed his eyes. 'Fuck off, you fucking degenerate!'

Jimmy stood too, a smooth, controlled motion. 'Do you want me to punch you, Marius? You could try and hit me back then. Would that make you feel better, do you think?'

Then there was a third person standing by their table. The scar-faced little doorman, with a bar towel in his hand. 'Everything all right here?' he said.

'S'fine,' Marius replied. There was, Tess thought, relief in his voice.

'You've had a little accident, I see.' The doorman righted the glass and spread the towel on the table. Then he took hold of Marius's upper arm. 'All right, Sir. I'll help you find your way out, shall I?'

'I know the way,' Marius murmured, allowing himself to be led to the door.

'You might catch up with your old man, if you're quick,' Jimmy said. Marius affected not to hear. Before he sat back down, Jimmy folded the soaked bar towel into four and dumped it on Marius's empty chair. 'Well that was awful,' he said.

Penny chuckled unkindly. 'You terrified the poor thing! What would you have done if that bouncer hadn't arrived?'

'Oh, there was never any danger of that. I'd seen him heading for us before I stood up.'

'Still, if it *had* turned into a proper fight, would you have won, do you think?'

'No idea.'

Tess said, 'Anyway, I'm glad he's gone. I can't believe he accused me of flirting with his father.'

'Well, of course you weren't,' Penny said, and for some reason that unthinking dismissal annoyed Tess more than the original accusation had.

Jimmy opened the leaflet. It was a single sheet of white paper, covered on both sides with heavy black type.

### David Wharton

**ANTI-APARTHEID MARCH & RALLY**

*March from Portland Place (just north of
Broadcasting House) to Trafalgar Square
2.15 p.m. (nearest tube: Oxford Circus)*

# NO BRITISH ARMS
# FOR SOUTH AFRICA

**Sharpeville Memorial Rally**

**at TRAFALGAR SQUARE
on SUNDAY, MARCH 17th at 3 p.m.**

He turned it over and read the other side. 'It says the United Nations have called for a weapons boycott, but Macmillan's refusing to honour it.'

'Commie rot,' Penny said. 'These people want to hand Africa over to a lot of savages. My uncle and aunt had to move out of Kenya during all that Mau Mau business. Even in Rhodesia, where she is now, you can't trust the servants not to murder you in your sleep.'

Hearing them talk like that, Tess felt shamed by her ignorance. Apartheid, Mau Mau, Rhodesia, United Nations – she knew these were the kind of things on which she ought to have a view. Everyone else – Jimmy and Penny and Bill Shearsby – seemed to understand all about them, while she herself had only the vaguest idea. Macmillan was Prime Minister, of course, leader of the Conservative Party; and there had been other names on the leaflet – people scheduled to speak at the rally – whom she half recognised as politicians of some sort. Barbara Castle and Harold Wilson. They were from the Labour Party, she was pretty sure.

In a year's time, she'd be twenty-one, old enough to vote, and it was likely there would be a general election soon after.

She was going to have to make an informed decision. Her parents had always voted Conservative in a ward that invariably returned a Labour MP. What was the point of that? Or any of it? One person's political argument always sounded as convincing to her as another's, and whenever such matters came up, she struggled to prevent her thoughts from drifting away. Realising they had done so now, she refocused her attention, and found that for some reason Jimmy was talking about George Orwell having shot an elephant. She wondered if he'd noticed her not listening.

'Mind if I join you again?' said a voice behind Tess. It was that woman from before. Bill Shearsby's friend.

'Certainly,' Penny said. 'Did you perhaps notice the recent display of manly ferocity?'

'I saw your friend got a bit upset. What was that all about?'

'Nothing much,' Jimmy said. 'Marius thinks I've got designs on his sister. He was trying to defend her honour.'

Delia took a seat between Penny and Jimmy. 'Well,' she said. 'I suppose that's understandable.' Tess didn't think she sounded convinced.

'I came over,' continued Delia, 'because I was wondering what it was you wanted to ask me before?'

'Oh, that,' Tess said. With everything that had happened since, the thought had quite gone out of her head. Now Delia had reminded her, it seemed an even more essential idea. 'It's just – would you let me paint your picture?'

Delia raised her eyebrows. Smiled. Tess had the feeling the request had surprised her, that she was trying to look as if it hadn't, was taking a moment to formulate an answer. 'I'd have to come to your studio, I suppose?'

'I don't have a studio of my own. Anyway, I'd rather come to your place, if that's all right – for the sketches anyway. I'll do the painting itself back at college.' The switch from conditional to definite was deliberate. Tess hoped it would somehow confirm the idea in Delia's mind, give her the impression she had already agreed to something.

'How long would these sketches of yours take?'

'I don't know. A couple of hours perhaps.'

'I got work to go to in the day. It'd have to be a weekend.'

'How about Sunday? And you can have some of the sketches to keep, once I'm done. If you like them.'

Jimmy said, 'Might be worth a bit, those, if she gets to be a famous artist one day.'

Delia gave him an appraising look. 'Everything isn't about money, young man.'

He looked ashamed, but Delia agreed to the offer, so perhaps it wasn't such a bad move after all. She drew a little map for Tess, directions on foot from Fenfield Underground Station to her flat on Doddington Road, under which, in the graceful, schooled handwriting of a previous generation, she added instructions, turn-by-turn.

'Sunday afternoon, then. After church,' Delia said and Tess couldn't tell if she was joking or not.

Later, Penny told her, 'You probably shouldn't go there. It's not safe.' When Tess said she was going, safe or not, Jimmy offered to accompany her. She refused.

# 8

She had imagined she was getting to know this city. The truth, she realised as she walked alone through Fenfield the following Sunday afternoon, was that she had been confined only to the narrow track between her house in Camden and the Moncourt Institute. For half a year, under the impression she was experiencing London, she had been holidaying in a Butlin's Bohemia: a world created from *ideas* – and ideas that were not even indigenous. Its artistic passion and sexual carelessness had been borrowed from Paris, its jazz music and beatnik clothes from New York, its espresso coffee from Rome. All this time, there had been an entirely different London just a few Tube stops away from her house, beyond the walls of the camp.

At least the weather had changed. Almost all the snow was gone: melted away over a couple of days and washed into the drains by a night's rainfall, so she could see Fenfield uncovered.

The reclaimed marshes that had bequeathed this part of the East End its name were long gone, but there were still horses on the streets. One clopped by her now. The old man leading it wore trousers held up with rope, and beneath his flat cap, rheumy eyes squinted out from a labyrinth of black-grained lines. He might have been ninety. His great grandparents could have seen the eighteenth century; lived during the French Revolution. His grandfathers might have fought in Nelson's navy. Perhaps his parents had sat in the cheap seats of a theatre and sobbed to hear the deaths of Nancy and Little Nell read by Dickens himself. This old man was a reminder of a city now unimaginable: one that pre-dated these dirty Victorian brick tenements, these rows of doors and stacks of windows.

But here too, more recent history was erasing the deeper past. She walked by a Blitzed-out street where kids played hide and seek in the rubble, undeterred by barbed wire fences and *UNEXPLODED BOMB* signs. After that, she came across a bank of peculiar, semicircular iron buildings, like giant tin cans half-buried in the ground. She recognised them as Nissen huts, the sort you would find on any army camp. These ones must have been thrown up in the post-war years to provide short-term housing for families displaced by the bombing. Their temporariness forgotten, they had evolved into homes, prettily painted, with tidy gardens. All very nice, Tess thought, but you'd surely freeze in winter; in summer you'd boil; and finding furniture to fit against those curved walls must be impossible.

As she walked past one of these Nissens, a threadbare ginger cat jumped up onto a picket fence and picked its way clumsily beside her, mewing and imploring. It slipped on a white-painted paling and had to scrabble frantically to regain its foothold, so Tess stopped to comfort it. At once, the creature's character transformed. It hissed and swiped at her. Tiny beads of blood bubbled out of the four long scratches its claws left on the back of her hand.

'Little shit!' She jabbed it in the head with her elbow, and knocked it to the lawn. Down on the grass, the dazed animal looked back up at her in confusion and bafflement. As if it had no idea what could have brought such violence upon it, the cat recommenced its plaintive miaows, playing pitiable once more. A woman inside the Nissen hut raised a window. Stout, in her forties with a raw, ignorant face, a headscarf and an apron, she looked like something left over from the war herself.

'What you do that for?' she shouted.

'It scratched me.'

'Oh boo hoo. You must've been doing something to aggravate her.'

Tess walked away. Behind her the cat's owner kept yelling. 'You ain't from round here. No wonder Tuppence didn't trust you. You don't belong. You better not come this way again, girl, if you know what's good for you.'

When she reached the corner, Tess looked behind her. The woman had come out to her gate

'You hear me, girl? You show your face on this street again and we'll soon see what's what.'

'Sod off, you stupid cow!' Tess yelled back. Then, surprised by her own forthrightness, and afraid the woman might come after her, she hurried off around the corner.

Doddington Road was a couple of streets further on. A long, broad thoroughfare. According to her directions, Tess was looking for the first floor of number 158.

*Just shout up at the window,* Delia had written. *I will hear you. It is always open.* So Tess looked up and saw that sure enough there was an open casement.

'Delia!' she called, keeping her voice low, not wanting to disturb the neighbourhood. Her nerves were still jangling from the encounter with the woman in the Nissen hut. She felt bourgeois, ill-fitting. When nobody answered, she called a second time, raising her voice to an unexpectedly satisfying bellow.

Delia's face appeared at a different window, further along the wall. 'Oh, hello there. I didn't know if you'd come.'

'Sorry. I've been shouting up at the wrong place.'

'No, that's mine all right. I'm in my friend's flat. She's doing my make-up. Hold on, I'll come and let you in.' Delia vanished inside again. A moment later, someone else stuck her head out of the same window. This must be the friend Delia was visiting: a young woman, blonde, around Tess's age. Her features were terribly damaged, the bottom jaw misaligned, the left eye almost closed, the nose broken.

'You the one 'oo's painting Dee?' she said, revealing that several of her front teeth were missing.

'That's me.'

'Nice. Make a better picture than I would, won't she? Face like mine!' There was no bitterness in the young woman's voice, only gloomy acceptance.

'Actually—' Tess began. She was about to explain that suffering and loss were the most interesting things to paint, and this ravaged creature would make an excellent subject. But she realised how unkind this sort of truth was, and she stopped herself.

'Yeah?' the young woman said.

'I'm here for Delia today. But I could come back another time.'

The door to 158 opened. The face at the window vanished indoors.

Delia was barefoot, in tight high-waisted grey trousers and a white cotton blouse, like a man's business shirt cut for a woman's body. Precise, well-made clothes, incongruous in this rough doorway on this run-down street. Her broken friend had done an excellent job with the make-up too, just enough to sharpen and underline her features. Tess had guessed Delia must make her living from men somehow. Clearly she was doing well out of it.

In the living room, Delia sat self-consciously on a battered leather settee. Tess paused from drawing.

'You don't need to keep so still, you know.' She tried to sound like it wasn't a criticism. 'It's not that sort of portrait.'

'Sorry.' Delia changed her unnatural pose for another just as bad, then she froze again.

The room was furnished in a jumble of styles – from, Tess assumed, whatever had been around when necessity arose. A ponderous 1930s sideboard stood next to new melamine shelves. The coffee table's pointed legs and rounded corners had been fashionable ten years previously.

There was one of those spring-loaded ashtrays on an art deco pillar. The sort that looked like a flying saucer. Before now, Tess had only seen them in coffee bars, never in anybody's house. The green of the linoleum on the floor had faded here and there where the light fell most strongly, and in what appeared to have been the only consciously aesthetic decision anyone had made, the walls had been painted cream, not quite obscuring the wallpaper's pattern of tiny pink flowers beneath. Shabby as it was, everything looked clean. Delia owned no dust-collecting ornaments, had hung no pictures on the walls. The only remotely personal items Tess could see were a few books on a shelf. As well as the entrance to the flat, there were three other doors: two closed and an open one, through which the kitchen was visible.

'How long have you been here – in this flat?' Tess asked.

Delia counted out the time on her fingers. 'Twelve years.'

'Is it rented? I rent a room myself. It's hard to make it personal, I find,' she said, in a feeble attempt to make some kind of connection. Really, Tess's study-bedroom was filled everywhere with markers of herself. There were novels she loved; a promotional poster for *Lust for Life* she'd persuaded the cinema manager in Dewsbury to let her have; picture postcards she had received; bits of her own artwork. The crazy, ancient typewriter.

Delia wasn't taken in. She remained cagey. 'This building belongs to my boss – Stella. The rent comes out of my earnings.'

'I see. I suppose she doesn't allow you to change too much of it?'

'She don't care, long as you don't burn the place down. A lot of the girls in here've made their flats really nice. Me, I don't like a lot of clutter.'

'No. I can see that.'

'You never know when you might have to move on, do you?'

Twelve years of that attitude must feel like a long time, Tess thought. But she'd broken through to something more honest, more personal, so she pursued it. 'So, Stella owns the shop?' she said.

Delia looked puzzled, 'The shop?'

'Where you work? You mentioned at the Gaudi that you work in a shop.'

'Yeah, that's right. Stella owns the shop. It's a little couturier's in Chelsea.'

Tess had become something of a liar herself recently. It had given her an ear for it. She put down her pencil and said, 'Thanks for letting me do this.'

Delia reached down the side of the settee for her handbag and took out a silver cigarette case. Something about the way her manner had changed reminded Tess of the cat that had scratched her earlier.

'Why are you here, Tess?'

'You know why. To do some sketches of you for a portrait.'

'But why a portrait of me? What makes me so special, to bring you all the way out here to the East End?'

'I thought you were interesting, that's all. That is—' There was a liberating, thrilling quality about telling the truth. Careful, she thought, once you start, you might not be able to stop. 'You struck me as the sort of person who has secrets.'

Delia tapped her cigarette against the flying saucer ashtray. 'Secrets?'

'Well, I don't know what you do, but I don't believe you work in a shop.'

'Good,' Delia said. 'That's better than trying to wheedle things out of me all roundabout. If you want to know anything, just ask. Here, let me show you something.' She crossed to one of the closed doors and opened it. 'Come and take a look.'

# Finer Things

When the house had been carved up into flats, this must have been intended as a bedroom. Delia had turned it into a wardrobe. There were several rows of metal rails, the kind you saw in shops, on which hung uncountable coat hangers bearing dresses, blouses, skirts, jackets and coats. A long theatrical dressing table stood against the far wall with lights around the mirror. On it, Tess saw half a dozen wigs of different colours, four jewellery boxes and a vast array of make-up.

'It's only me in the flat,' Delia said. 'So I sleep in the box room and I keep all my things in here.'

Tess stepped inside. She didn't know much about fashion, but she could see how expensive this hoard must be. Time to risk some genuine truth telling, she thought.

'So you're a thief, then?'

'A hoister,' Delia said.


The girl, Tess, left her two of the sketches she'd drawn. They were very good, very realistic, Delia thought. Had it been a mistake, though, to let her come to the flat? To tell her so much about the business? The Imps had steered her that way. And Tess was connected to Bill Shearsby's son – if Stella asked, that would be the story: that she was building up a connection with Bill. Even so, better to put the drawings somewhere out of sight. She quite liked the idea of hanging them on a wall, on display, but that would be unwise. No need for the girl to come back, either. Except there were the Imps, whispering.


On the Wednesday after Tess's visit to Fenfield, Roger Dunbar told the first years they were starting a new project.

'I'm giving you complete freedom from now on,' he said. 'You should start developing ideas for the final exam.' It sounded like a gift, but there was a shiftiness about Roger's manner, a grudging quality that suggested none of this was his own initiative.

'Someone's been putting him in his place, looks like,' Jimmy said.

Roger had been uncharacteristically punctual for over a week now, present in the studio every morning before any of his students. However, his teaching had worsened. To compensate for the loss of his usual lie-in, he'd invariably settle into a chair in a gloomy spot at the side of the room and by mid-morning slip into near – or actual – unconsciousness, from which he would not be raised for the remainder of the day.

While Tess and most of the other first years moved on immediately to something new, Jimmy continued doggedly with his pile-of-skulls paintings. He declared it was all he was going to paint ever again. Tess doubted that.

For her part, she was delighted to abandon the bear. When asked over the phone about the doll-burning incident, her mother had been unable to recall it. Of course that proved nothing: it was the kind of parental behaviour she might have suppressed out of shame. Possibly Tess would return to it in the future, but right now she had a more exciting subject.

After throwing her three paintings, all her preliminary drawings and the bear itself into the waste bin at the back of the studio, she returned to her easel to consider the material she had brought back from her weekend excursion. Several sketches she'd made of Delia at the first sitting looked like they had potential, but she left those to one side for now. Instead she decided she would try to paint the broken-faced girl she had spoken to at the first-floor window. Strangely, she could not get it right. Usually, if something made an impression on her, Tess could recreate it from memory, even many days afterwards; yet for some reason every attempt she made at this picture took a different form, and the girl's true image remained elusive.

Over the next couple of hours, she produced four versions, rapidly and simply, in acrylics on hardboard. Each time, she'd start convinced she had something accurate – the eyes, the nose, the jawline – and then there would seem to be no way of fitting all the other parts correctly around it. The rest of the face wouldn't work. Once, that would have felt like a frustration. Now the failure excited her. For the first time in many months, she was confronted by a challenge. She took her latest effort and laid it on the floor, next to the previous three.

'That's not your usual style,' Jimmy said.

'I'm sick of my usual style.' She was glad to have caught his interest. Recently, for some reason, a little of their easiness had gone. They needed a way back to each other.

'What is it?' Jimmy said, 'Post-cubism?' He tilted his head and squinted at the pictures on the floor. 'I like them. They make a good group, don't they? I don't think they're finished, though.'

'No, they're only sketches. I'm trying to paint her from memory.'

'Her? Oh, are they all the same person? I didn't see that. It's not that Delilah woman, is it? That prostitute from the Gaudi?'

'Her name's Delia. No, it isn't her. And she isn't a prostitute. That is, Delia isn't. This is her friend, Maureen.'

'And is Maureen a prostitute?'

'I doubt she'd make much of a living that way. Her face is all smashed-in.'

Jimmy returned to working on his own picture. 'You'd be surprised. Some men have very particular interests.'

'Some men are disgusting,' Tess said reflexively, aggravated by the way everything always seemed to come back to sex. To sexual intercourse. Like the way Penny encouraged everyone to think she was a lesbian, so that when they discovered she wasn't, they'd find that even more interesting. Like the way Roger Dunbar couldn't say anything to Jimmy about his paintings now because of sex. Like the way Marius Shearsby had accused her of flirting with his father. Like the way, six months into her life as an art student, Tess was still a virgin, and was being made to feel more and more that this was a problem she needed to remedy. That maybe if she could clear the blockage of *fucking*, other people might finally start taking her seriously.

Sooner or later, she supposed, she was going to have to get it out of the way. It oughtn't to be too difficult if she just put her mind to it. Of course, she'd had opportunities already, once or twice when she was on the foundation course in Leeds, and several times since she'd arrived in London. Somehow circumstances had always seemed against her seeing it through.

But perhaps she had not ever wanted to submit to those circumstances. It wasn't that Tess believed herself incapable of falling in love. She had her old fantasy of the sleeping poet, for example; but that had never been about passion, only its aftermath. It was like the point in a film after the camera veered discreetly away. The difference was that in a film the sex had to be implied because it was the most important factor, whereas for Tess it was the least. Not frightening, not disgusting, merely a necessity on whose existence far more interesting things seemed always to be predicated. To paint a picture of the young poet *afterwards*, she needed something for an *afterwards* to come after.

'She's a hoister,' she whispered.

Jimmy stopped painting. 'I beg your pardon?'

Moving nearer to him as if to appraise his picture, she spoke rapidly and quietly. 'Delia's not a prostitute, she's a hoister.'

'What's that?'

It was exciting to have this new and arcane language at her disposal. It felt as if she were drawing Jimmy into a secret world, even if it was a second-hand one. 'She works in a shop-lifting gang. They steal expensive women's clothes from the big department stores – I mean *really* expensive – and sell them for half the price. It's like a proper business. Organised. People actually order particular items. And that bloke Finlay, that gangster she and Mr Shearsby were talking to at the Gaudi, he lets Delia's boss run her fashion shows in his clubs once a month to sell the rest of the stuff off. Invitation only.'

'Bloody hell. Who buys it? Who goes to these things?'

'All sorts. Bank robbers and their girlfriends, debutantes and their boyfriends, rock and roll singers. Drag acts.' This was the list Delia had reeled off to Tess when she had asked the same question the previous Sunday. 'It's quite glamorous, actually.'

A rattling noise interrupted their conversation. Someone was trying to open the studio door. Its handle didn't work properly and usually took a few tries before it caught properly.

Startled into sudden alertness, Roger jumped to his feet, and headed for the easel of the first student in range, a young man working on a dull piece of abstract impressionism. By the time the door opened, Roger was wide awake and apparently engrossed in the process of advising this baffled student.

'Bloody hell. What's Garvey doing here?' Jimmy muttered.

The head of department paused in the doorway and surveyed the room. Because of the eyepatch, she noticed, he had to turn his head to take everything in. The student Roger was advising kept flicking nervous glances towards the front of the studio, where Benedict Garvey waited to be acknowledged. Roger, however, pretended to be unaware of any of it.

Garvey was probably not fooled by this charade; nevertheless, he gave in to it, and coughed artificially a couple of times. Raising his head innocently above the student's canvas, Roger said, 'Oh, hello Benedict. Can I help you?'

'Don't let me get in the way Roger.' Garvey opened a little black notebook and wrote something down. 'It occurred to me this morning that I hadn't been around the classes this year. Thought I'd have a look at what everyone's up to. Please – continue with your teaching. I'll do my best not to get in the way.'

'Good to see you taking an interest, Ben,' Roger said. 'I think you'll be impressed. There's some precocious work going on in here.'

'Precocious, eh?' Garvey said, as if to signal that Roger had made some unspecified error in his choice of language.

The head of department made his way around the room, looking at students' work, making occasional comments and writing notes in his little book. So far, Tess had only ever encountered him behind a desk or in a chair, static. Now she saw it wasn't just his eye that was damaged: his left arm and leg seemed stiff and restricted; he moved as if on constant guard against the threat of pain. She'd heard a lot of stories about Garvey's injuries: a car accident; a street fight; a kettle of boiling water hurled by an angry lover. Various wartime escapades involving all three of the services. Whatever it was, Tess thought, he had surely suffered other wounds too. Maybe there were old burns under his clothes – shiny red skin, tight as boiled bacon; fire-shrivelled nerve endings ready at any moment to be set howling by the memory of a terrible heat.

He stopped to ask Jimmy where he'd got his skulls and why he wasn't painting the eye holes. Jimmy answered respectfully. Whatever he thought of Garvey, he was evidently pleased to have a chance to talk seriously about his work. Meanwhile, Tess hoped furiously that the head of department wouldn't come and look at what *she* was doing. But of course he did.

'Ah. The hitch-hiker,' he said, leaning uncomfortably to scrutinise the paintings on the floor, then turning to the one on her easel. 'What are these?'

'Paintings,' she said. A few moments passed before she realised that wasn't an appropriate answer. 'Of a woman I saw in Fenfield last weekend.'

'Really? You're quite the adventurer, Miss Green, aren't you?' He'd remembered her name, she thought. That must mean she had made some kind of impression on him. 'I've not been in Fenfield for years. What were you doing in the East End?'

'Visiting a friend.'

He seemed to approve. 'A friend in Fenfield? Well this looks like a change of approach for you.'

'They're only rough ideas.' Was he telling her he preferred these daubs to the work he'd seen previously? That she was finally developing into his idea of an artist? She really shouldn't be hoping so.

'Do you know Veronica Wilding?' he asked.

She guessed he must mean some painter with a similar style to this. 'I don't think so.'

'Veronica runs a little gallery in Hampstead. Coincidentally, I was at her house the other week. Curious thing – she had a picture hanging in her hallway. Pleasant little drawing, quite competent. I thought I recognised it. Then I remembered I'd seen it in your portfolio. From what she told me, it sounded like you must have sold it to her yourself on the same day as your interview.'

She felt suddenly that she was in a trap. The drawing of the old man that couple had bought by the Thames. Of course it was.

'That's right,' she said, trying to sound like the sort of person who sold pictures all the time.

'How much did she get Graham to give you for it, if you don't mind my asking?'

She wanted to say she *did* mind. 'Fifteen pounds.'

'Decent price. Very business-minded of you, very practical. Easier than lugging it all the way home too, I suppose.'

'I suppose,' she echoed.

'Then again, you did have all the rest of your portfolio to carry. Unless you sold those too?'

'Only that one. It was more luck than anything. I wasn't trying to—'

'It must have been terribly difficult, hitch-hiking all the way back to Yorkshire with that thing under your arm.'

'It would have been,' she said, impressed by her own adroitness. 'Except I used some of the money from that drawing to buy myself a train ticket.'

'Ah. Of course. How clever you are.' Garvey glanced over at Roger, who was still advising the same student on his abstract. Panic seemed to have locked him where he was. 'Mr Dunbar's found an awful lot to say about that rather boring painting, hasn't he? From here it looks duller than Mondrian and sloppier than Pollock – which is some kind of achievement, I suppose. I'll go and give it a closer look, I think. Nice to have met you again, Miss Green.'

'Fifteen quid,' Jimmy said excitedly, once Garvey was out of earshot. 'You never told me you'd *sold* one. Don't you see? I bet this Wilding woman's the mysterious art dealer on the exam panel. I wonder if all that's got anything to do with her having bought your painting.'

Tess was barely listening. 'He knows I didn't hitch-hike,' she said. 'He knew all the time. But he offered me a place here anyway.'

# 9

At the Gaudi, Bill Shearsby sought Delia out.

'That was embarrassing last week,' he said. 'I don't know why Marius wanted to come here in the first place. And then he was such a fool. Sorry you got drawn in.'

'I'd forgotten all about it,' she told him, seeing no reason to mention anything about her having gone back to talk to those art students, or about the girl Tess's visit to Fenfield. Anyway, Bill didn't really want to talk about what had happened with Marius; his apology, it transpired, was just a way of leading up to other questions. He wanted to know if she was interested in coming on a march with him the following Sunday, in support of the blacks in South Africa. Delia didn't know much about South Africa, but she was against ill-treatment of anyone, and as Shearsby explained, those South African blacks were being treated especially badly. She also realised these must be the blacks Finlay was so interested in hearing about, and that was information she might find useful in future.

When Bill saw she wasn't saying no to joining the march, he moved on to his main purpose, which was to ask her to meet him an hour before it started.

'What for?' she asked.

'So we can talk. Find out about each other. Maybe become friends.'

'Aren't we friends already? And we're talking now.'

'You're at work here, Delia. It's your job to entertain. To be friendly. To add atmosphere. We both know that. So why not meet me when it's your day off, and you don't have to pretend to be anyone other than yourself.'

Fat chance, she thought. But when he put a hand over hers she felt no inclination to pull away, though that was bound to get back to Finlay and to Stella. Anyway, it seemed to her that meeting Bill Shearsby on her day off, away from the Gaudi Club, might be something she wanted to do.

'Will your girlfriend be there for the march?'

'Girlfriend? Oh, Philippa you mean? That's been over for weeks.'

'Then I'll come,' she said. It was an instinctive agreement, uncomplicated by all the questions that would arise after she'd had time to think.

On Friday evening all the hoisters waited their turn to be paid. They sat in pairs and threes around the Lamplighters, watching for the signal from Itchy Pete, who was standing guard outside the snug.

It had been a good week. At the start of March the shops had launched their new lines: 'Spring into Summer' and so on. This was always a profitable season. There were plenty of thin fabrics, easy to roll up and drop into your bloomers, and plenty of troublesome customers to keep the staff distracted. Yesterday, at John Lewis on Oxford Street, Delia had picked up a half-dozen frocks and four pairs of capri trousers; at Harrods, a couple of thin cardigans; and from Dickins and Jones, some sun hats and an evening jacket.

Kathy had been called into the snug five minutes before. She should be out soon. Meanwhile, Delia listened to Rita boast about lifting baby clothing in Barkers of Kensington.

'You can get a load of them in your knickers. Ten or fifteen easy, twenty, if you push it. And you wouldn't believe the prices. I reckon anyone who'll pay that kind of money for a bleeding Babygro must be off their head – but there's plenty as will. You should take a look, Dee. Barkers is the easiest.'

It was bait. Everyone knew Delia wouldn't go into Barkers now. What had happened with Maureen had jinxed the place for her. She changed the subject.

'What's this job Tommy's got lined up?' she asked.

'Butcher shop in Ealing. He's after a load of meat and whatever's in the till. He's promised me some pork chops.'

'Romantic.'

'I'll take a bit of pork over a bunch of flowers any day. Don't mention it to Stell, though. You know how she feels about the blokes working for themselves.'

'Like she doesn't already know everything he's up to,' Delia said.

Rita gave a sage nod. 'Knowing and being told is two different things, though, ain't they? There's plenty Stella don't mind, as long as nobody actually tells her.'

At last, Kathy reappeared, snapping her handbag shut and looking pleased with herself. As she walked out of the snug and headed for the bar, she whispered a name to Itchy Pete – not that you saw it happen: she neither looked in his direction nor paused, but he heard her all right. Enjoying the power at his disposal, he yawned ostentatiously. The way he rubbed the back of his head with the heel of a hand reminded Delia of a chimpanzee she'd once seen at Regent's Park Zoo. He caught her eye, held it just for a moment.

'My turn,' she said.


She was smart, Stella. Hoisters got caught, muscle got caught. Stella was never caught. She had learnt her trade between the wars with Alice Diamond's Forty Elephants gang, and she knew how to keep herself safe, to ensure that she, who always profited the most, was never the one the police put their hands on.

On pay day, she was especially cautious. Her particular concern was that some stick-up gang would get a sniff of the cash box and try robbing her. With a thing like that, the money was secondary, compared with the disruption it could cause; the attention it might bring her way. So Stella had a system. Every Friday between six and seven she sat in the snug at the Lamplighters and had the hoisters sent in one at a time, in what seemed a random order. Pete on the inside door, Teddy out the back, Tommy on the front.

She flapped a hand at Delia, telling her to sit. The Book was already open at the right page. Tracking down the left-hand column with a long red fingernail, Stella read each aloud, and decoded it.

'*Item 100 x 6* – that's those dresses. *Item 1003 x 4* – the capri trousers. *Item 650 x 2* – them cardigans.'

It would be a while before Stella actually sold this stuff. None of it had been stolen to order, and there wouldn't be another open sale at the Ferrara Club until the end of the month, but Stella paid her workers upfront, and she paid fair: a third of what she expected she'd get for each item, plus the hourly rate for any nights worked at the Gaudi. There was a minus column in The Book too, recorded in red ink. For Delia that was only the rent on her flat, which she made sure she cleared every week, whether she'd earned or not. Stella's interest rates weren't unreasonable, but they were compound, and half of the women in her debt only ever paid off the interest, never cleared the capital. They didn't anticipate the future – that was their problem. Not anticipating the future usually meant you ended up trapped, assuming you survived into it.

'*Hrs We x1* – that's Wednesday night at the Gaudi,' Stella continued. 'How'd it go there?'

This could be an innocent question. Neither Stella nor Finlay had been at the Gaudi on Wednesday. Even so, Delia knew word about Bill's hands on hers would have been passed back to them, and she was going to have to say something about her arrangements for Sunday, much as she might prefer for now to keep that information to herself.

'Bill Shearsby asked me out on a march against South Africa.'

Maybe Stella knew that already, maybe not. Anyway, she acted as if she didn't, asked a lot of questions and, once Delia had explained everything, went off to the back of the pub to telephone Finlay.

'Thought so,' she said when she returned. 'If you go to this thing with Shearsby, Finlay says he'll pay you double – what with it being a Sunday.'

'What do I have to do?' Delia asked.

'Keep your eyes and ears open. Remember the names of people you meet and the things they say. Tell Finlay about it afterwards. Or, actually, you tell me, and I'll tell Finlay.'

'I don't understand why Finlay needs to know all this,' Delia said. 'I mean, what use is it to *him*?' She was sure now that he was especially interested in the South African blacks rather than the American ones, but there had to be some specific reason.

'Nothing for you to worry about,' Stella said, closing The Book to mark the end of the conversation. 'Less you know, the less trouble you can get yourself in. Or anyone else.'

*She'll tell you more* the Imps whispered. *Push her a bit.* So Delia persisted. 'It's hard to know what I have to listen for, Stell, if I've got no idea why I'm listening.'

Stella bought that, or seemed to. 'All right. You might have a point, I suppose. You've heard about the Richardsons, haven't you?'

Delia had. They were a gang operating out of some scrapyard in the south of the city who ran protection rackets on Finlay's Soho clubs. 'Why would the Richardsons be interested in Bill Shearsby?'

'I don't know the details. Finlay says it's because they've got business friends out in Johannesburg. Shearsby wrote a letter that might hurt some of them.'

'What sort of letter?'

'No idea. And I don't want to know. The Richardsons want an eye kept on Shearsby. They pay Finlay. He pays me. I pay you. As far as I'm concerned that's all there is to it.' Partial as this information was, Stella had given Delia something, and she wanted something in return. 'You know,' she continued delicately, 'if this Shearsby bloke turns out to be interested in more than talking—'

So she *had* heard about his hand on Delia's. It had been a mistake to allow it, she thought. She should have pulled away.

'I ain't going to sleep with him, Stell.'

'No,' Stella said, pretending to be hurt by the suggestion she would even consider such an idea. 'Course not. That wasn't what I was going to say. But just mind, Dee – if he *does* try anything like that on, you be sure and let me know about that too.'

There were some things Delia wouldn't do for Stella, even under orders, and Stella knew that. But she might do them for herself. And if she did, that was none of Stella's business.

The following Sunday Delia made her way up Regent Street, through a part of the city she'd never needed to visit before, along by the high hotels and embassies of Marylebone, past a burnt-out theatre and the BBC building, and towards the tower of All Souls Church, where Bill had said he'd wait for her. It was a peculiar building, not what she'd expected at all: two circular white stone tiers, the upper one half the size of the lower, and a tall, piercing spire above, like someone had shoved a spike up from underneath a wedding cake, right through and out the top.

Bill sat waiting for her on the bottom step. Though he was almost in silhouette, she could tell it was him from the way his head leant, as if it was slightly too heavy for him to carry. He saw her approach and waved. She increased her pace, because she didn't like to think of him noticing such things about *her*.

He raised himself to his feet, stiffly and with a grunt of discomfort. 'I wonder when I got too old for sitting on the ground. Good job we said one forty-five. It was seething here when I arrived. Congregation for the midday service. I'd forgotten about it being Sunday. They all went in quarter of an hour ago.'

As if on cue, a hymn started up inside the church. 'When I Survey the Wondrous Cross'

'I nearly didn't come,' Delia said.

He looked away, just over her shoulder. 'I'm pleased you changed your mind. Shall we take a walk, before all the duffel coats arrive?' As they turned, he slid his arm briefly around her waist, squeezed her to his side then let go again before she had time to respond. 'Sorry,' he muttered.

She kissed him on the cheek. His clumsiness had intensified her softness towards him. It was the same feeling that had almost overwhelmed her a few hours ago, when sunlight through her window had warmed her out of sleep, and her first thought had been that she shouldn't go.

It was too confusing. Fear and loyalty and obligation meant she couldn't refuse Stella, and at the same time, for reasons she was more cautious about naming, she didn't want to spy on Bill. So far, she hadn't formed any kind of plan. She had simply reacted to each of these irreconcilable pressures as they occurred, one at a time. The trick was not to think about more than one thing at once. As for what the Imps thought about all this, she had no idea yet.

Walking with Bill away from All Souls, she found herself taking a side. Whatever the Richardsons wanted to know, she was going to try to keep it from them. If she could, she would protect this man from the harm they intended to do him. And she supposed that was bound, sooner or later, to work out badly for someone. Herself, most likely.

❧

They had been walking for a while, apparently without direction. She'd intended to ask Bill more about the reasons for the march, to get him to explain the situation in South Africa and his part in the Anti-Apartheid Movement, but they'd spoken only about personal things. She had discovered that the farm she'd been evacuated to when she was ten had only been a few miles from his home town of Bridgwater, though by the time she arrived there he had already left, having turned eighteen three days after conscription started.

'I was home a few times on leave,' he said. 'Then, as the war carried on, I saw less and less point in the place. Once it all finished I went to university on an ex-soldier's scholarship, and I'd barely visit home even in the holidays. I feel bad about that now – I was married, with a baby son by then, so I thought I had a life of my own. But it upset my parents terribly I'm sure.'

'My ma and pa were glad to get rid of me for a bit, I reckon,' she told him. 'By the time I saw them again in forty-five, they'd nearly forgotten me, and I'd nearly forgotten them.'

'What were they like?'

'Horrible. My pa died in 'forty-seven. Ma's still going. Still horrible. I don't have anything to do with her.'

They walked on quietly for a while. Delia saw that Bill understood she didn't want him to push her for details about her parents, just as she had known not to ask him about his experiences in the war. And she felt more intimacy in these cautious avoidances than she would have in any opening of the heart. She realised he had brought her round in a circle, and they were heading back up Portland Place towards All Souls, where the other protestors were now congregating.

Feeling an urgent need to tell him something personal and real in these last few minutes before they were swallowed up in the march, she said, 'Reg and Janet, the people I was sent out to, they were kind to me. Not that I made it easy for them. It weren't what I was used to, decency, so at the start I took it for weakness, and I took advantage, as I thought. There were other kids there too, three of them – some better than me, some worse, and all of us miserable when we arrived. But Reg and Janet kept being lovely, no matter how shitty any of us brats were, until they won us around. That was lucky, I know. There were plenty of evacuees got treated badly where they were sent, came back broken from it. I came back fixed. Partly fixed, anyway. I could read and I could swim, and I knew what it felt like to be happy.'

'Are you still in touch with them?' Bill asked.

'I never went back. Never even wrote.'

'Why?'

'Soon as I got back to London, I started working for this woman who's still my boss now.'

'Shoplifting?'

'Mainly. In those days we'd do other stuff too. Short cons. Factory break-ins. All sorts. Then after a few months we started to specialise, as it were.'

'And that was why you didn't contact Reg and Janet?'

'I suppose I was ashamed of myself. I'd let them down, slipped back into what I'd been before. They saved me in a way, and I never even thanked them for it.'

They had reached the fringes of the crowd. A force of mostly young men and women, cheerfully serious. As Bill had predicted, at least half were wearing duffel coats. Some of the protesters carried placards bearing messages. *No Arms for Apartheid; No Blood on Our Hands; Remember Sharpeville; Justice for Sisulu, for Mandela, for Mbeki, Wolpe, Motsoaledi and Mlangeni.* Strange, alien names. Characters from a story she barely knew anything about.

'So we both abandoned our Somerset parents,' Bill said. He took her hand as the people around them began to move. For a few minutes it all felt stiff and bumbling, until a chant arose from within the march and everyone's feet fell in time.

*No-o—wea-pons-for-South-Africa!*
*No-o-African-blood-on-our-hands!*
Now they were part of something.

Elsewhere in the same crowd, Tess and Jimmy were also marching. Tess added her voice to the rest, and after only a few repetitions, the chant had become automatic to her, part of walking. She half forgot she was doing it.

Almost everyone here was white, she thought. Which seemed wrong, somehow, though she struggled to pinpoint quite why. And she realised she probably wouldn't have noticed, except that there were a few black people scattered among the crowd. There was one, an elderly man marching just behind Jimmy, who was on her left. To her right were a couple with one child in a pushchair, and another on his father's shoulders. Across the whole row just ahead of them a group of veteran campaigners wearing trade union and CND badges held up a wide banner on which was painted the yin and yang insignia of the Anti-Apartheid Movement.

The mood of the marchers, which she had expected to be sombre and angry, surprised her. It was wrong of them to be so happy, she thought; although at the same time she was glad to see Jimmy's eyes looking brighter than they'd been in weeks.

The Anti-Apartheid Movement seemed to suit him. After taking Bill Shearsby's leaflet that night in the Gaudi Club, he had discovered the Camden branch of the society. On the same Sunday afternoon Tess had taken her trip to Fenfield, he'd gone to a meeting at the Secular Hall.

'I knew it was bad over there, just not *how* bad. What you see on the news is just a tenth of it,' he'd told her afterwards. 'The British government are nothing more than gun runners. I'm definitely going on that march now. You have to come as well, Tess. You said you would.'

Well, she *had* said something about wanting to find out more about the march, even if at the time she hadn't particularly meant it. More importantly, Jimmy was her friend, so she went along with this new enthusiasm of his. He gave her pamphlets, rough documents produced on Photostat machines and spirit duplicators, and once she'd read them, she couldn't pretend this wasn't important. One document he'd given her described the massacre at Sharpeville – how sixty-nine people had died that day, just for demonstrating. They'd been shot by the white police for trying to do the same thing she and Jimmy and all these others were doing now. The language of the pamphlet was simple and unemotional. Its anonymous authors had understood that all that was necessary was to list the facts. Fifty-one men killed. Eight women killed. Ten children killed. Shot with British Sten guns and British Lee-Enfields by police sitting safely in Saracen armoured cars built in Coventry.

She'd known, of course, that such things happened. Before, she had avoided looking at them. Now she couldn't look away. One fragment in particular she could not shift from her thoughts: 'Shot in the back as they ran for safety'. So Tess was right to raise her voice for them today, here where it was safe to protest; where the policemen surveying the march carried neither rifles nor sub-machine guns, did not sit inside armoured cars.

A few tourists had stopped to watch this Interesting Example of British Culture. Most of the other passers-by ignored the march entirely. Further up the road, a group of young men started berating the protestors.

'Who pays for your bleeding student grants?' one of them yelled. 'Me, that's who! My bleeding taxes!'

'Cheap price to buy yourself a conscience,' Jimmy shouted back.

'Up yours, Duffelcoat!' the man replied, acknowledging neither Jimmy's debating point nor the green anorak he had put on to distinguish himself from the other marchers, but Jimmy kept grinning anyway.

'Are you all right?' he asked Tess.

'I'm fine.'

She wasn't sure there was any point to what they were doing, but that mattered less than she had thought. Setting off for the march, she'd believed she'd be demonstrating against power, against money, against factories, armies, secret police; against the kind of self-belief that took centuries of privilege to build. Now she understood, she and power were not enemies. Enmity required both sides to be engaged in the fight.

Power did not care about their march, did not even notice it. Power allowed it, in fact. Encouraged it. What they did today would trouble the conscience of no businessman, and no politician. They would not prevent the sale of a single Lee-Enfield rifle, of a single Sten sub-machine gun, of a single Saracen armoured car. They would not prevent the manufacture of a single bullet.

And if oppression and injustice were ever to end in that part of the world, it would merely move somewhere else, continue making money there. Such things would keep going forever. Protesters would always be silenced, beaten and tortured. The innocent would always be shot in the back as they ran for safety. Understanding this, she saw why the march was not sombre but joyous. She felt it too now. She was on the right side, though all the power in the world disdained her one small voice. Because it did.

The marchers filed into Trafalgar Square, and became first a crowd, then an audience. Barbara Castle spoke, then Harold Wilson, then Duma Nokwe, the exiled secretary-general of the African National Congress. Fairly quickly, Tess found herself only half listening to the speeches, hearing the rhythms of their rhetoric, but little of the detail. Occasionally she became aware of a sentence or two, and was reassured nobody was saying anything she hadn't already read in one of Jimmy's pamphlets. For the most part, she played follow-my-leader. She clapped when others clapped, cheered when others cheered; she booed the names of Tory politicians, booed the names of arms manufacturers and booed the name of Charles Robberts 'Blackie' Swart, the South African president.

Then it was over and the crowd began to thin as the demonstrators dispersed towards Tube stations, buses and pubs. Banners were rolled up and packed away. Tess saw the woman with the pushchair break her own placard in four so she could squeeze it into a waste paper bin.

'Over there,' Jimmy said, pointing through what was left of the crowd at the broad steps up to the National Gallery. 'That's Mr Shearsby, isn't it? I wondered if we'd see him today. And look who's with him.'

Interesting, Tess thought. Shearsby and Delia were heading for the gallery's entrance. 'Shall we go over and say hello?' she said.

'I don't think they want company, Tess. Looks like they're here together – you know.'

'Mr Shearsby invited us to this demonstration. I'm sure he'll be pleased to see we came along.'

She barged her way through the thinning crowd. No longer bothering to object, Jimmy followed in her wake. By the time she'd almost caught up with them, Delia and Shearsby were talking in the gallery foyer. Jimmy put a hand on Tess's upper arm and muttered, 'Let them be, Tess.'

She stopped, realising she had no idea why she'd been so determined to force this encounter.

'You're right,' she said. 'Let's go.'

But Delia had spotted them, and Shearsby, who must have noticed his companion's reaction, turned around. There was no trace of the other night's irascibility in his smile.

'Hello,' he said. 'You're my son's friends, aren't you? I assume Marius isn't with you though.'

Jimmy said, 'No, he's not. But Tess and I did the whole thing. Marched here from Portland Square.' His face flushed.

'I thought Mr Nokwe was a very powerful speaker,' Tess said, just before the ensuing silence became unbearable.

Shearsby nodded. 'I'm always impressed by how hopeful Duma is, after everything he's been through. Barbara was good too. Harold less so. He knows how to give a speech. I mean, I believe him, but I don't always believe *in* him, if you understand me.'

Tess noticed the way he used these people's first names, as if unintentionally or habitually, and she wondered if it was really either of those things.

'Must be good for the cause,' she said, 'to have such well-known politicians speaking for it. And it looks as if Mr Wilson has a chance of being the next prime minister.'

'If he *is* elected I suppose we'll see whether he's got the courage to place human rights before business interests.'

'I suppose so.' Tess was already at the limits of anything she could confidently add to a political discussion. Fortunately, Shearsby wasn't interested in testing her.

'Are you two here to see anything in particular?' he asked.

'The gallery?' Tess said. 'No. We just wanted to say thanks – for telling us about the march.' She turned to Delia. 'There was something else, actually – I wonder, is there any chance I could visit you again next week – to do some more work?'

'Tess came out to Fenfield to do some sketches of me last week,' Delia said.

'Really?' Shearsby said. 'I'd be interested in seeing those.'

'I've really only started. I do think the work might be worth looking at eventually, though. When it's more – realised, perhaps. It'll be my end of first year project for college, and there's an art dealer on the exam panel, so it's important we do something that'll get her attention.'

Jimmy bridled unexpectedly. 'I thought you weren't both-ered about any of that.'

His reaction annoyed her. Surely he could understand that she was only keeping the conversation going. Whether or not she really cared about the opinions of this mystery dealer didn't matter in the slightest. She ignored him and turned back to Delia. 'So, could I come back?'

'If you can make it tomorrow, there's something I think you'll like seeing.'

'I have classes, but I can probably get around that.'

'Then get to my flat for ten. Don't bring your painting stuff, though. And wear something ordinary, so you won't stand out.'

'Will you be – working?' That seemed an exciting prospect as well as an unnerving one.

Delia shook her head. 'This is something else.'

Jimmy was quiet all the way back to Camden. By the time they came out of the Tube and separated to head for their own houses, Tess had long since given up trying to engage him in conversation. Then, just before they parted, he said, 'Are you really thinking about trying to impress that dealer?'

The question revived her irritation at him. 'It was just some-thing to say, Jimmy. You'd made things so uncomfortable, I thought I needed to keep talking.'

'Sorry,' he said, looking neither contrite nor convinced. 'So you're telling me Garvey didn't change your mind the other day, when he came to Roger's class?'

'Oh. I'd forgotten about that. What do you mean, change my mind? He only wanted to make sure I understood I hadn't fooled him with that hitch-hiking stuff at my interview.'

'It's more than that, Tess. He thinks you have something. And that dealer does too. She's already bought one of your pictures, after all.'

Now she saw. It was envy that had made Jimmy so stupid and sullen, so unlike himself – and all because she'd sold a picture; because Garvey thought she might *have something*; because Bill Shearsby had been interested in her work; because she might be about to do something good for once. Maybe because, unlike Jimmy, *she* hadn't wrecked things for herself by having sex with a Moncourt tutor.

'Well, I'm looking forward to finding out what this mysterious business of Delia's might be,' she said, trying to change the subject. 'Can you cover for me at college tomorrow?'

He gave a sharp, intolerant sigh. 'You're going back to Fenfield? I don't think it's sensible, Tess. You've no idea what that woman might get you involved in.'

'I'll be careful. So, can you tell them I'm ill?'

Jimmy looked down at the ground and said, almost to himself, 'I don't know if I should. I mean, if you were hurt or something, and I'd helped—'

What remained of her patience with him broke. 'Then tell them what you like, or don't bother. I'm going anyway.'

'Nous voudrions assises loin de la fenêtre, s'il vous plaît,' Bill said to the waiter.

They were in a bistro on a side street off Shaftesbury Avenue, a tiny place with tables packed uncomfortably close to each other. If it had been busy, Delia thought, she'd have found it difficult to talk, but it was almost empty tonight. Just one other couple.

Bill had suggested they come here. It was a favourite of his. For some reason, ignoring the waiter's excellent English, he insisted on speaking to him in French, and although Delia didn't understand the language, it seemed to her it often took a lot of repetition and rephrasing from Bill before the waiter grasped what he was saying. Perhaps it was the Somerset accent.

'The other night at the Gaudi,' he said, layering butter on a chunk of thick-crusted bread. 'I don't remember that girl saying anything about painting your picture.'

Delia could hardly explain that Finlay had sent her back to find out more about Bill's son's friends. She took a mouthful of the house red. It had tasted harsh and sour at first, but the second glass seemed much smoother.

'Tess, you mean? She came up to me at the bar after you left. Said she thought I'd make a good subject.'

Bill dipped his bread into the cassoulet. 'I can see her point.'

Delia ignored the threshold he'd just crossed. 'I wasn't sure about letting her come back – what people in Fenfield might think of that. But I don't think it's me she's interested in, so much as the life of crime.'

'Le demi monde,' he said, smiling. 'Typical middle-class bohemian.'

'I wouldn't know,' she said. 'Anyway, that's what I'm taking her to see tomorrow. A crime.'

Once again, he understood that she wasn't going to tell him more, and he didn't ask her to. She liked that about him, his instinctiveness.

After the meal, they walked together past the theatres. Delia could go to his house, he said, if she wanted, or he'd go to hers if she preferred. She was tempted, but Stella knew she'd been with him today, and would have eyes on Delia's door. There was also the arrangement she'd made for Tess to come to Fenfield the next morning. Wisest to return home alone tonight, she decided.

'Tomorrow,' she said, and gave him her address. 'Come late, after midnight, and wear dark clothes. Take a taxi, but not all the way. Get out on Spendlove Road and walk the rest. Not too quick, not too slow. Keep your head down. Don't whistle or anything like that.'

'Jesus, Delia. Is there anything else? A password? Should I bring a gun?'

'Have you got one?'

'No, I—' He realised she was joking.

'I'm not allowed men where I live,' she said. 'Just being discreet, that's all.'

He accepted the explanation, but she could see he knew there was more, that he would likely push for it later. She'd need to be ready. She waved down a cab and left him there on the street. She'd no illusions. This wouldn't last. But he stood on the street and watched the taxi carry her home. Her secret man, half-melancholy, half-joyous, who would soon enough be heading towards her bed.

# 10

On Monday morning, conscious of her instructions, Tess set out for Doddington Road carrying only a small sketchbook and pencil, both hidden in her handbag. She'd been uncertain what 'wear something ordinary' meant, but had borrowed a beige jacket from one of the house-sharing secretaries, to which she'd added her dullest pinafore dress and a pair of flat shoes.

Delia came down to the front door ready to leave. She was almost unrecognisably dowdy in a long black coat and maroon headscarf.

'You'll do, for a librarian,' she said, straightening Tess's jacket collar. 'Ever seen a robbery?'

Tess shook her head.

'Well that's what we're doing today, watching a robbery. A gentleman acquaintance of mine is going to rob a butcher's shop. I thought you might find that interesting.'

Tess agreed. She certainly would find it interesting.

'Good. A friend's going to take us to where it's happening. Well, she's more a colleague actually – her name's Rita. And just so you know, I've told her you're thinking of learning the business, maybe becoming a hoister yourself. Can't tell Rita you're an artist – she wouldn't understand that at all. Wouldn't like it. So I've said you're my cousin from up north. Can you remember all that?'

'Yes. I'm your cousin from up north. I want to learn how to shopl— to hoist.'

'And you're called Julie. Don't think I'd have a cousin Tess. Doesn't ring right.'

Tess was unconvinced by the explanation. It seemed to her that Delia had set out purposely to make her day difficult, to put her through a sort of exam, and she was just going to have to pass it.

At a bus stop outside a pub, they met the friend-or-colleague: a slender woman whose fashionable bleached-blonde hairstyle framed a hard, thin-lipped face.

'This your niece, then?' Rita said to Delia.

'Cousin. Her name's Julie,' Delia said. 'Down from Yorkshire.'

Tess had recognised Rita immediately. She recalled the chirpy astringency of her voice cutting through the noise of the Les Jensen Trio at the Gaudi, telling some kind of story, Tess remembered, about animals in a forest. That night, Rita had looked a good deal more glamorous. Today in a dark grey mackintosh, she appeared as drab as Delia. She gave the new-comer a judgemental look.

'Never been in London before, girl?'

'Never.'

'Funny. You look familiar.'

'There's an actress a lot of people say I look like,' Tess replied. 'Perhaps that's who you're thinking of?'

'Oo's that then?'

'Susan something or other. She's on television, I think. Mainly does comedies.'

Rita peered at Tess. 'Must be who I'm thinking of, I s'pose. Can't have seen you in Yorkshire, that's for sure. I ain't never been north of Fulham. What's it like up there, then?'

Tess paused to give the impression she was considering the question carefully, then said, 'S'all right.'

'Christ! Proper chatterbox, this one, Dee. Can't shut her up, can you?' Rita directed her attention towards the approaching bus. 'Here we are. Number fourteen. All aboard, girls.'

## Finer Things

After they disembarked on Ealing Broadway, Rita led the way through a series of back alleys until they emerged onto an affluent shopping street. They stopped outside a florist's. Pretending interest in a bucket of white roses, Rita tilted her head to indicate a butcher's on the opposite side of the road.

'That's the one,' she said.

A few shoppers, mainly housewives and pensioners, ambled up and down the street. There was a bank here, Tess noticed. A jeweller's too. Butchers had money, she supposed, like the one who had bought the picture from her fellow student in Leeds. She focused her attention on the details of the shop. It was called *Faraday and Son, Family Butchers*. In the window a grinning automaton in a striped apron raised and lowered his cleaver again and again. The motto *Pleased to Meet You: Meat to Please You* had been painted in white along the bottom of the glass.

She could see clearly what was happening inside the shop. The proprietor (a young man, more likely 'son' than Faraday) reached into the window display, lifted out a string of grey-skinned sausages and carried them to his scales. On the other side of the counter a queue of customers waited patiently: all well-to-do women, some accompanied by children, some not. Doctors' wives, accountants' wives. Professional wives. Before the war, they would have kept servants to do their shopping and cooking for them. Now they were fending for themselves.

'Here he comes,' Delia said.

'Tommy the Spade.' Rita spoke the name under her breath, but it was an announcement.

'Tommy the—?' Before Tess finished her question, she saw the answer – in the form of the person heading up the road towards them on an old delivery bicycle. Tommy the Spade was heavy and swarthy: a massive man of the type in whom muscle and fat were indistinguishable from each other, and he was too big for the bike. He rode standing on the pedals, rocking from side to side. Sweat ran liberally down his face. He carried two large empty shoulder bags with their straps crossed over his chest. Along the top of the handlebars, he held a garden spade, reminding Tess of a tightrope act.

'Look at him go!' Rita cackled with delight and clapped her hands as Tommy the Spade jumped his bicycle up the kerb and onto the pavement, scattering a few pedestrians from his path. An old man in a tweed suit stomped furiously towards him. Tommy turned his back and leaned the bike against the butcher's window.

Though physically tiny, the old man seemed used to the deference of others. He drew himself to his fullest height, and reached up to tap Tommy on the shoulder. Tess thought he might be a retired army officer, or perhaps just a lifelong bully.

'Young fellow—' he began.

Tommy spun around, swung the spade above his head like a war hammer and let out a hideous bellow.

How swiftly the world could be overturned. Tommy's roar and that upward sweep of his spade changed the meaning of everything. Passers-by became witnesses. A garden tool became a murder weapon. Everything froze into testimony. This awful thing was about to happen in front of these people, in front of their children, and nothing would prevent it. Tess knew with absolute certainty that she was about to see a human head smashed open with a garden spade; hear the wet crunch of steel through bone. Yet she neither shut her eyes, nor put her hands over her ears.

After that moment, events lurched for a while in strange discontinuity, from one completed tableau to another.

Now the terrified old man hadn't been killed after all. He had landed on his backside, and sat on the pavement, his skull unexpectedly intact.

Now Tommy was inside the shop, directing the butcher to empty the cash register into one bag, pointing out all the cuts of meat he wanted to go into the other.

Now Rita said, 'I asked him to get me some nice pork chops. I hope he remembers.'

Now, exiting the butcher's, Tommy stepped gently over the still-dazed old man and remounted his bike.

Now he dropped his spade to the pavement, and as the clang it made died away, Tess became aware of the bells of distant police cars.

Now Tommy, spadeless, dangerously imbalanced by the two stuffed bags he carried, wobbled away on his bicycle.

Now Delia was no longer by Tess's side. She was helping the old man back to his feet.

Now she was back with Tess and Rita. 'Poor sod's in a right state,' she said. 'I bet that'll give him nightmares for months.'

And time began running normally again. Bystanders unfroze. Someone from the bank brought out a chair for the old man, and he sat on it. A woman brought him a cup of tea, and he sipped at it. The butcher came out of his shop and stood staring at the spade on the pavement, as if it could provide some explanation of what had just happened. The injury Tommy had inflicted on this place had already begun to heal over.

'Time to go,' Rita said.

As the women escaped into the same side street by which they had arrived, three police cars drew up outside the butcher's.

Rita was sulky on the walk back to Ealing Broadway.

'Could've got us all caught, Dee, going over to help that old sod,' she said when they were on the bus back to Fenfield.

'Sorry. I wasn't thinking.'

Rita addressed Tess in a tone of the highest seriousness. 'If you want to keep out of the nick, girl, you got to learn how to blend in. What Delia done there means someone might remember her afterwards, and that's the last thing you want.

Course, sometimes you can't help being noticed. That's when you've got to make sure it's for the wrong thing.'

'Misdirection, you mean?' Tess said.

A quizzical expression crossed Rita's face. Delia interjected immediately, 'Grammar school girl. Likes her big words.'

'Oh yeah? Don't remember you mentioning *that* before, Dee.' Rita looked out of the window and said, 'You got qualifications and all that, Julie?' Her tone was breezy, but not to be trusted.

'No,' Tess said. 'Spent too much time hanging around with boys. Ended up failing all my exams.'

'Shame. You got a job, now then?'

She remembered something Jimmy had told her about his late mother. 'I'm a canteen girl in a shoe factory,' she said. 'Been there since I left school. Five years.'

'What's that like?'

'Stinks.'

'The shoes or the food?'

'Both. And the men who work there. You can smell the place for miles around. You ever been in a tannery?'

Rita gave her a supercilious look. 'What do you think, Julie?'

'It's revolting,' Tess said. 'It takes all sorts of horrible stuff to turn the skins into leather. Great big tanks of piss and shit and bile. You can't get the smell off your skin. You can't wash it out of your hair. I've had enough of it.'

Rita looked down at the boots she was wearing and swung her toes back and forth. 'It's like the pie factory, ain't it? You don't want to ask what goes on there.'

Delia said they could go to a local pub later to watch Tommy selling off the stolen meat. Rita went off in advance, to make sure she got the pork chops he'd promised her, and Delia took Tess back to her flat. Tess wondered if William Shearsby had stayed here last night. If so, there was no sign of him now.

She sat and drew pictures of the robbery in the little sketch-book she'd brought with her. With thick, brutal lines she outlined the spade, ready to smash down into the old man's brains.

'Would he have done it?' she asked.

'No,' Delia said, looking over Tess's shoulder at the drawing. 'He'll do an assault, but not a battery. Menaces, it's called. If he gets caught, that's not such a long sentence as violence against the person. And if you kill someone in the commission of a robbery, they can hang you for it. You got to take all that into account, course you do, but Tommy wouldn't want it on his conscience either. Doing that to some old bloke who's just come out to post a letter. Not that there aren't some round here who'd have bashed his brains in, for fun.'

'He made it look so real. I genuinely thought it was going to happen.'

'That's part of the job. It's just acting. Were you scared?'

'Not at all,' Tess said, putting the drawing aside for now. 'If you'd asked me before we went, I'm sure I'd have expected to be terrified, but when it came to it, I was just waiting to see what would happen next.'

Delia laughed. 'You're a hard case, aren't you?'

'I was worried about Rita, though. I kept thinking she might remember me from the Gaudi.'

'I wouldn't have brought you along if I'd thought there was a chance of that. She was half-cut the other night, and I doubt she even noticed you. I must say, though, you can't half spin a yarn. Was that true – what you said about how they make the leather?'

'Maybe.' Tess vaguely recalled reading somewhere that the Ancient Romans used to tan animal hides in a solution of dog faeces and human urine. Perhaps that was still how it was done. 'I've no idea, really.'

'I could believe it, though,' Delia said. 'Most of what people do has something disgusting about it.'

There was something unexpectedly vulnerable in the way she said that. On an impulse, Tess scribbled her address on the back of the drawing and ripped the page out of her sketchbook.

'Listen Delia,' she said. 'If you ever need somewhere to go, somewhere away from here. This is where I live.'

Word must have spread quickly. By the time Tess and Delia arrived at the pub, which was called The Three Acorns, the queue reached out of the door. Inside, they found Tommy standing behind a stall of two tables pushed together, covered with lino, on which he had set out his produce. No longer playing the berserker of the robbery, he dealt amiably and patiently with each customer, negotiated prices, pointed out the excellent qualities of his goods, and praised the skill of the man who had cut the joints and stuffed the sausages. Tess was impressed to note that in the heat of the robbery Tommy must have had the foresight to make the butcher give him a sheaf of wrapping paper and a ball of string, so he could now close each deal by assembling and handing over a trim, white parcel.

When he spotted Delia's neighbour, Maureen, waiting near the back, he waved and called her forward. A couple of pensioners began grumbling volubly, until they saw the look Tommy was giving them and immediately shut up.

After she'd been to see Tommy, Maureen came to join Delia and Tess, and laid the package he'd given her on the table.

'He didn't charge me nothing for it,' she said, through her broken grin. 'There's bacon in there and black pudding. I'll make us breakfast tomorrow if you want, Dee.'

'That'll be lovely,' Delia said.

'I got eggs too. Not off Tommy. Stella gave me them yesterday. Do 'em scrambled, shall I?'

'Nice. And I'll go down the bakery first thing, get us a fresh loaf.'

They continued watching Tommy make deals until the last of the meat was sold. Then Maureen left.

'In case you're wondering,' Delia said after Maureen left. 'She got beat up in the nick.'

Tess had indeed been wondering, and had not known how to broach the subject. 'By other prisoners?'

'Couple of screws. Guards. The bastards broke her jaw and her cheekbone. Knocked out four of her teeth. Smashed her arm too.'

'God. That's awful.'

'And they left her in her cell afterwards. Didn't tell anyone. It was a night and a day before another screw come looking for her and got her to the hospital. Doctors did their best, but none of it set right. That's why Maureen looks the way she does. Luckily, she doesn't remember much about it.'

Since the march, Tess thought often of Sharpeville, trying to work out how anyone could do what those policemen had done. She'd concluded it must have been necessary for them to believe they were on the right side, to imagine they were protecting themselves and their families against some terrible threat. And on top of that they were following orders, obeying authority. It was not their choice. So when a white policeman squeezed his trigger, the consequences were distant from him. He was only a step in his bullet's journey, no more responsible for its consequences than the Birmingham factory worker who had packed it, the sailors who had shipped it. When it reached its final destination in the soft back of a running child, they all shared the blame.

So how could she comprehend what had happened to Maureen? This act of intimate personal hatred. As they'd pounded the girl with their fists and boots, those two borstal guards would have felt her bones give way. Her blood would have been on their hands, not metaphorically but actually. They would have had to wash it off themselves before going home to their families. And what story could they have told to make sense of this terrible act against someone as obviously harmless as Maureen? They would have needed to work hard to find reasons to hate her, to pretend she was their enemy. And because they had wanted to, they had worked hard. Because they wanted to license themselves.

She said, 'Do you think she'd like to sit for me? For a portrait.'

'Because she already looks like one of those Picassos, is it?' Delia said acidly. 'Save you a bit of work?'

'Look, if you don't think it's a good idea—'

'Not for me to say, is it? She's her own person. Ask her if you like.'

'I wouldn't want to hurt her. Honestly.'

'Up to you.' Delia looked at her watch. 'I should think you'll need to get back soon.'

Tess realised she'd made an error. This felt exactly like that awful conversation with Jimmy after the march.

'Look, Delia, I'm really sorry if I've upset you. It was obviously the wrong thing to say. But I wasn't thinking of how Maureen looks. A portrait's never just about showing the outside of a person. Not if it's any good.'

Delia softened. She told Tess about the stolen car the girl had got into, how her parents had cut her off, how she'd lost her job at the hairdresser's, how she'd got herself caught on her very first hoisting lesson, and how all that had led to her going to the borstal where she'd received her injuries. 'She's unlucky, that girl,' Delia said. 'She's on an unlucky path. That's why you shouldn't paint her picture. You can finish mine, though, if you want to come back on Sunday.'

Just after midnight, Delia waited outside her front door. Doddington Road was quiet and dark, with dead bulbs in half the street lights. She felt fearful and stupid, tried to hope Bill wouldn't come tonight after all. Anyone might spot him. The information would get back to Stella. Even if that didn't happen, sooner or later he was bound to lose interest, cause her hurt. Or if he didn't, she'd have to betray someone. If only the Imps would give her some indication of the right thing to do. She had no idea what they thought about it, what they wanted. And now here he came, so that meant she was committed.

He was doing as he'd been told. In dark clothes, a cap, on foot, not whistling.

'I look like a bloody burglar,' he said, his voice cutting through the night air, alarmingly clear.

'Shh. Come in. Get off the street.'

He stepped inside and she closed the door. They stood together, hidden from sight now, at the bottom of the narrow staircase.

'I got out on Spendlove Road, like you told me,' he whispered. His breath against her ear.

She led the way up, stepping as lightly as she could. 'Put your weight on the banister,' she told him, 'not on your feet.'

Her precautions must baffle him, she thought. Because who could possibly care what two people in—

How easy it was to slip *that* word in. If you weren't careful.

She'd left her flat door unlocked, so she could just push it open, no fiddling and scratching around with the key. She dropped the catch noiselessly behind them. Then they went to her single bed, where his urgency and selfishness surprised her. She reached above her head to stuff the pillow between the top of the bed and the wall, to stop it banging. Twice she had to silence him with a hand over his mouth.

'Sorry I was so rough,' he said afterwards.

Delia raised herself on one arm. 'Are you now, Bill? Genuinely sorry?'

He laughed. 'Maybe not sorry, exactly. But I haven't let go like that for— I mean I'd been looking forward to seeing you all day, and—'

She kissed him.

'I was going to offer myself to you again,' he said. 'Only I'm not sure I'd quite have it in me. Maybe in the morning.'

'There won't be time.' She rested her head on his chest, listened to his heart, his breathing. They stayed that way for a while, both awake.

'What does this open?' he asked, lifting up the small key she kept on a silver chain around her neck.

'Nothing any more,' she said. 'There was a little money box I had when I was a girl. I left it behind when I was evacuated, and it got destroyed in the Blitz. Just keep the key for sentiment, I suppose. Daft, aren't I?'

Sliding her knee across his leg, feeling the scrape of coarse male body hair against the inside of her thigh, Delia wondered if this intimacy was only forced on them by the smallness of the bed. If they'd room to escape each other, would either of them have taken it? Would she have moved away from him into her normal sleeping position, curled into herself, arms wrapped around her knees?

Perhaps Bill was thinking something similar, because he said, 'I've a double bed at my place. None of the neighbours give a stuff who comes and goes.'

'Sounds wonderful. Next time, maybe.' She reached for her bedside clock and set the alarm for three, thinking she'd send him on his way before the milkmen started their rounds. Soon afterwards she felt him drop into unconsciousness and she was free then to fall asleep herself.

When the alarm went off, Bill tried to rise almost immediately, but Delia caught his shoulder, and rolled on top.

'We'll need to be quick,' she whispered, guiding him into her.

Later, on his way out of the flat, he paused in the doorway and said, 'All this secrecy. I'm not— I mean, I know I've no right to ask. And you don't have to— It's just—'

'Can't answer a question you won't ask, Bill,' she said.

'Is it another man?'

She laughed at that.

'Seriously,' he said. 'If there *is* someone, we ought to talk about it.'

'No, it's not another man,' she said. 'You're the first bloke I've been with that way for more than a year.'

'Good,' he said.

She was surprised it should be important to him. Such a trivial measure of her honesty. What, she wondered, if he had asked the right question? If he had, she might have told him everything: Stella, Finlay, the spying, the lying. Maybe it mattered less than she feared it did.

She returned to bed, and lay for a couple of hours in a half-dreaming state of wakefulness, trying to make sense of what her life ought to be. It couldn't stay like this. Too much was out of her control.

# 11

Usually, Jimmy boarded the bus three stops after Tess and sat with her for the rest of the journey. On Tuesday morning, he didn't appear. He must still be angry, she thought, had obviously caught an earlier service to avoid her – a childish act that absolved her of any responsibility for Sunday's argument. After all, she'd only gone on that South Africa march to please him. If he hadn't dragged her into it, none of the rest would have happened. Now, because Jimmy had probably not covered for her the previous day, she needed to speak to the administrator, Mr Newbolt, about her absence.

The counter in Newbolt's office was unattended, but she could make out a blurred human shape through the frosted window of the back room, so she pressed the button marked *Ring for Service*, triggering the sound of a distant and melodious electric bell. The shape did not respond. There was a clock on the wall. Tess watched its sweep hand tick round three full circuits then she rang the bell once more. This time the blur rose to its feet, the door to the office opened and out swept a fortyish man, bald, long-legged, with a disproportionately short body and arms. The proportions of a flamingo, Tess thought. His shirtsleeves were rolled to the elbow. The fountain pen in his top pocket had leaked a little, making a circular blue stain over his heart.

'I'm not deaf, young lady,' Newbolt snapped. 'There's no need to keep hammering on that button.'

'Sorry,' Tess said. 'I don't want to be late for class.'

'Then you should have come earlier. What do you want?'

'I was absent yesterday. Unwell.'

Newbolt reached under the counter and brought out a foolscap sheet on which various Moncourt tutors had scrawled the names of the previous day's absentees.

'You're meant to telephone if you can't come in. Did you telephone?'

'Sorry, I was ill. I couldn't get out. The phone in our house is set to incoming calls only.'

He groaned with boredom, and plucked the fountain pen from his pocket. 'Very well. What's your name?'

'Tess Green. Theresa. I asked my friend to report me absent yesterday. James Nichols. Did he—?'

'No. Roger Dunbar put your name on the list, though. Something of a miracle *he* could be bothered. Look here.' He pointed out one inscrutable name among a batch of four. Upside down, Dunbar's cavalier scrawl looked like Arabic. 'Why didn't you come in?'

'As I said, I was ill.' Never having missed a day before, Tess hadn't anticipated she'd need much in the way of a story. 'It's personal,' she said, lamely. 'I'd rather not go into details.'

Newbolt's pen was poised over the space next to her name on the form. It dropped a splash of ink, and he tutted. 'I'll need something specific,' he said. '*Ill* won't wash. What was this sickness that made you so ill yesterday you couldn't manage to struggle to a phone box, yet leaves you so apparently hale and hearty this morning?'

'Stomach ache.'

'Stomach ache? That's the best you can do?'

'I had a stomach ache,' she said determinedly. 'I'm not making it up.'

'I'll put *women's troubles*. Nobody ever questions that. Then we can all get on with our business.'

'Fine. Put that,' she said. Like she had any choice.

Against the squiggle she supposed must be her name, Newbolt added six distinct capital letters: *PERIOD*. He replaced the cap of his pen and slid it back into his shirt pocket. There was, she noticed now, a single long hair growing out of his nose.

'James Nichols?' he said.

'I beg your pardon?'

'This person who was supposed to come in and lie for you. His name is James Nichols?'

She could only just be bothered to challenge the accusation, for the sake of form. 'I didn't ask him to lie for me,' she said. 'I asked him to report to you that I was ill.'

'Yes, well, be that as it may,' Newbolt said. 'I was asking if this honest broker of yours is called James Nichols?' The nose hair drifted back and forth as he spoke. She felt a strong desire to reach over the counter and pluck it out.

'Jimmy Nichols. Yes, that's him. Why?'

'Seems he was absent yesterday too. Here's his name right above yours. And *he* didn't telephone either. Perhaps he caught whatever it was you had.'

Jimmy didn't return to college the next day, nor for the rest of that week. To distract herself, Tess worked on all the things she'd witnessed during her two visits to Fenfield. She made drawings, colour studies, paintings – recorded the robbery's vicious surrealism, Tommy's cheery meat sale in the pub, Delia's unpredictability, Rita's coarseness. The cat attacking her outside the Nissen hut. None of it satisfied her. The images were competent, but not good enough, not right.

On Friday she laid all her pictures out on the studio floor, right across the space where Jimmy would normally work, and she tried to see them as one, to figure out how to pull them together and make something large enough, powerful enough, to encompass her baffled purpose. Maureen, she decided, had to be the key. So she drew Maureen's ruined face in the upstairs window; Maureen's arm that didn't bend quite right. Maureen on the floor of a borstal cell for all those hours, waiting to see if she'd live or die. But that was where it always stopped. Inevitably, she would half see the possibility of the final idea, the artwork she ought to be making. It shimmered there, teasing her, and the longer it stayed just out of reach, the more she both believed in and doubted its existence.

It might have helped her to talk things through with Jimmy, she thought. Surely he'd be back after the weekend. But he wasn't. The following Monday Tess rode the bus alone to college, worked alone in the studio, and ate alone in the refectory. On his way to the staff table with his tray of meat pudding and spotted dick, Benedict Garvey paused to speak to her.

'Theresa, isn't it?'

For a moment, she had the idea he was wearing his patch on the wrong eye. But no, everything was normal. She was tired. Hadn't slept enough.

'Work going well?' he said.

'I don't know,' was all she could think of.

'I see,' he said. 'Well, that's often a good sign.'

This struck her as nonsense. 'Is that what you really believe, Mr Garvey?'

He had been about to move away, but he stopped. 'I have to say, Miss Green, you're not the most compliant of students.'

'Sorry.'

'No, it's an unusual quality. A strength. And you're right. One says that sort of thing automatically, not because it's true, but to ease a student's concerns.'

Tess pushed on. She thought she might as well now. 'And to ease yourself out of the conversation?'

'Either way, I look to have failed, don't I?' He looked across the refectory to where the rest of the first years were braying and laughing. 'It'll get better,' he said, in a way that made it unclear whether he was talking about Tess's work or about life in general. Whichever he had meant, she was no closer to it by the end of the day, and she had decided it was time to find out what was happening with Jimmy.

To do so required a little detective work with the directory that hung on the wall next to Moncourt's payphone. She had never visited Jimmy's lodgings, but she knew he rented a room from a retired academic couple. They were called Woodrow, she remembered, and the old man was a professor. The phone book listed only one Prof. C. Woodrow in Camden.

That evening, even with the address and her *A–Z*, it took her some time to find the house, which turned out to be a spindly three-storey place out on its own off an alleyway at the end of a cul-de-sac. It was surrounded by a high-walled garden with iron gates, on which hung a *Beware of the Dog* sign in blue enamel. She could see three skylight windows in the roof. Remembering that Jimmy had told her his was an attic room, she looked up and waved, hoping perhaps he might be looking out of one of them right now, and would come down to let her in.

When that didn't happen, she peered through the bars of the gate and called 'Hello?' twice, before opening it. There probably wasn't a dog, she thought: the sign was a rust-spotted antique. Nevertheless, she left her exit clear and approached the house warily. A few minutes after she rang the bell, the door opened to reveal a tall, wiry old man, his mouth nearly invisible behind an enormous grey moustache.

'Hello,' she said. 'I'm here to see—'

But he was peering over her shoulder at the open gate. 'Sorry. Would you mind popping back and closing that? Don't want the hound getting out.'

She did as he asked.

'Thank you,' he said when she returned. 'She might run off, you see. Our last one did that. Little Westie, name of Hamish. Never came back.' He squinted at the gate, 'You did put the catch in properly, didn't you?'

'Yes. I was very careful. I'm sorry I left it open in the first place.'

'Always the chance the dog might run off, you see.'

'I understand,' Tess said, and tried moving away from the subject of dogs and gates. 'I'm here to see Jimmy.'

'Jimmy?'

'James Nichols.'

'James what?'

'Nichols. James Nichols.'

The old man shook his head, not confidently, but as if he was digging around in his memory for an especially tricky concept. 'No,' he said. 'Nobody of that name here. We do have a lodger. Nice young fellow. Jewish, but not exactly religious, if you know what I mean. Works at King's College. Leon, he's called. That's not your chap, is it?'

'No. Jimmy's an art student at Moncourt.' She had been sure she had the correct address, but it was possible, she supposed, that some kind of error had been made. 'I understand he rents a room from a Professor Woodrow and his wife.'

'Well, Woodrow's my name, yes. Charles Woodrow. And I am a professor. So you've got all that right.'

Perhaps she had misremembered the name and her detective work had brought her to entirely the wrong house. Could it have been something else: Woodville? Woodford? Woodhouse? She was sure she had it right. The bizarre thought came to her that Jimmy had been living here under an assumed identity, as Leon the Jewish lodger. But why on earth would he be doing that?

Meanwhile, the old man was continuing, 'Strictly speaking, I'm an emeritus professor – which is to say, I'm retired now.

Still do the odd lecture, of course. I've got one coming up on the Rockingham Whigs. Oh. You did close the gate, didn't you?'

'I— yes. A minute ago. You watched me do it.'

A woman in a gardening smock appeared from behind the corner of the house. She was perhaps a decade younger than Professor Woodrow. Taking off her dirty gloves as she stepped towards Tess, she said, 'Hello. Is my husband helping you?'

'I'm looking for Jimmy Nichols,' Tess said. 'I thought he lived here.'

'I see. Yes, that's right. Jimmy's our lodger.' She turned to her husband. 'Why don't you go back indoors, Charlie? I'll look after this young lady.'

'Would you check the gate, please Val?'

'Before I come in. Yes, of course.'

'We don't want the dog running off again, do we?'

'I'll make sure it's fastened, Charlie.'

After a final concerned glance up the path, Professor Woodrow said to Tess, 'Delighted to meet you. I do hope you can track down this boyfriend of yours.' And he retreated into the depths of the house.

'Jimmy's not my boyfriend,' Tess said.

Mrs Woodrow clapped her gardening gloves together, making a little cloud of dried soil. 'Of course he isn't,' she said. 'Sorry. We weren't expecting anyone. I usually try to get to the door before Charlie, but I was busy in the greenhouse just now, and I had the radio on so I didn't hear the bell. You'll perhaps have worked out that my husband isn't as sharp as he was. Our last dog died six years ago. And anyone can tell Jimmy's not the *girlfriends* type.'

Everyone seemed to spot that immediately, Tess thought, except her.

'Is he in?' she asked. And because it felt like there needed to be a proper explanation for her presence here, she added, 'He hasn't been to Moncourt for a couple of days. Nobody's heard anything from him. I was worried he might be ill.'

A look of sympathy crossed Mrs Woodrow's face. 'Didn't you know, dear? He's at home. That is, home-home, rather than home-here. He went back to Kent last week.'

'Oh—' To her shame and astonishment, Tess burst into tears, and found she couldn't stop.

'I think you'd better come inside,' Mrs Woodrow said. Still sobbing uncontrollably, Tess followed her into the house.

For ten minutes, she sat at the kitchen table trying to bring her choking and snivelling to some kind of dignified conclusion. Meanwhile Mrs Woodrow busied herself with chores, discreetly ignoring her guest. Tess had just about calmed down when an agitated Professor Woodrow appeared at the door. 'Of course! You're here to see Jimmy, aren't you?' he exclaimed. 'That other chap I mentioned was years ago! Don't know what I was thinking.'

'Thank you,' Tess said. 'Your wife explained about all that.'

'Well. Things to do. I'm giving a lecture on the Rockingham Whigs next Thursday. Have to write the blessed thing.' And he beetled off again. Smiling indulgently, Mrs Woodrow watched him go, then took a seat opposite Tess.

'You'll be relieved to hear he's not giving any lecture,' she said. Tess could see that not far beneath the brisk practicality she was quite exhausted. 'Jimmy's wonderful with him, you know – far more patient than I am. Takes him out for long walks, listens to all his muddled-up nonsense, doesn't mind being mistaken for Maurice – that's Charlie's older brother. Late older brother. He died of exactly the same thing, though it took him rather differently. They say it exaggerates the strongest aspect of a person's character, don't they? Maurice was always a bit of a monster.'

Tess nodded mutely, still on the edge of tears. This kind young man she was hearing about was a stranger to her. She

realised how little she actually knew about her so-called closest friend, how she'd never thought to ask Jimmy anything
much about his life away from Moncourt.

'Anyway, we've never said anything to him outright,' Mrs
Woodrow continued, 'but Charlie and I aren't at all bothered by
his inclinations. It doesn't matter at all to us whom a person
chooses to go to bed with. I suppose we've hoped he would
understand—' She stopped and frowned. 'Forgive me. It isn't *we*
anymore, obviously. Charlie's still perfectly sweet and decent, but
these days he can't— that is, we've always done things together,
and it's rather difficult for me to stop thinking that way.'

'Do you know why Jimmy decided to go home?' Tess asked.

'Not precisely. I assumed it was something to do with men.
Or a man. I could be wrong, though. He certainly didn't say
anything, and one doesn't want to intrude. Really, sex is such a
lot of nonsense, isn't it!'

'I suppose so.' Tess did her best to impersonate someone
accustomed to hearing this sort of pronouncement from elderly
women all the time.

Mrs Woodrow gave her a shrewd look. 'Ah.'

'We had an argument on the way back from the march. A
stupid disagreement, about nothing. I was worried that might
have been why—'

'Oh, I doubt that. You've probably noticed Jimmy's been
unhappier than usual for a while.'

'Didn't he speak to you at all before he went?'

'We were out. I'd taken Charlie to the doctor's. He left a
note, though – here—' From a drawer in the kitchen table she
produced a page torn from a sketchbook, folded in half, which
she laid on the table for Tess to read.

*Dear Val,*

    *I've decided to go to my dad's for a while. I don't know how
long I'll be, but I'm certainly not going to stay there forever, so*

*please don't let my room out to anyone else! If I'm not back by the end of the month, I promise to post the rent. There's no reason to worry, honestly. I just have to think about a few things, and I can't do that in London.*

*Give my best to Charlie.*

> *Love,*
> *Jimmy*
>
> *PS*

The rest of the message lay out of sight, folded underneath.

'What does the PS say?' Tess asked, wishing she could be rude enough to snatch the paper before Mrs Woodrow had a chance to answer.

'Just his address in Trencham so I can forward any post. And his aunt's telephone number, in case of emergencies.'

'I don't suppose you could let me copy the address down? I'd like to write to him.'

Mrs Woodrow gave an apologetic smile as she scooped up the note and deposited it back in the drawer. 'I think that would be betraying a confidence. But I'm sure he'll be in touch when he's ready.'

# 12

The Sunday after the robbery the girl Tess didn't come back to Fenfield. Maybe she'd lost interest. Thinking about it, Delia supposed they hadn't exactly made an arrangement. And what with the added complication of Bill two or three secret nights a week now, perhaps it was a good thing not to have to deal with Tess too. Even so, Delia held on to all the drawings she'd given her, including the one with the girl's address on the back, but she moved them to her secret place. It wasn't safe to leave such things lying around her flat.

Making the right next choice was such a puzzle. So many people, promises, responsibilities; so much truth and lies, and they all needed to be squared off. Nevertheless, Delia had kept faith with the Imps, certain that if she waited long enough for a sign, one would eventually be delivered. And she was right – though when it came she soon discovered that receiving a sign from the Imps might be all well and good, but working out what it *meant* was something else entirely.

Maureen brought it to her. One morning she knocked at Delia's door, desperate to pass on the gossip she'd picked up the previous night.

'I heard it from Kathy,' she said. 'You know how Pete is when the itch gets bad. You can't look at him wrong, even.'

People who didn't understand Pete Yates's itching thought it was funny. Actually it wasn't at all. It was relentless, something untreatable in his nerves, and it had turned him vicious.

When he was a kid, his nickname had been Fleabite, but by the time he left school, everyone knew never to call him that. Not to his face. Not if you knew what was good for you. These days, he got skin cream and tablets from the doctor, which mostly made the condition bearable, though he was still nasty to be around, never in a good mood, always scratching; and there were times once in a while when the medication failed – then you were wise to keep out of his way. Delia guessed that was what had happened last night.

'He was at this bar up town somewhere, trying to drink himself out of it,' Maureen said. 'Everyone was leaving him alone. And, you know he's not supposed to scratch at all, 'cause it just makes the itch worse.'

Delia murmured an acknowledgement. A really bad bout of itching brought out a fury in Pete that would find whatever target it could.

'Anyway,' Maureen continued. 'He's at this bar, scratching and scratching, and a bloke sits down next to him.' She stopped to mull over this element of her story. 'I suppose the geezer mustn't have noticed to begin with. Otherwise, why would you go near Pete when he's in that sort of a state? But once this bloke's there – you know how it is if you see someone else scratching. Makes you feel like you've got an itch yourself. So the bloke – not much, just a bit – starts to scratch too. He's trying to do it without Pete seeing, and he thinks he's got away with it. But then maybe he gets the idea whatever Pete has is catching, because he gets up and leaves the bar, without even having a drink.'

'And I suppose Pete *did* see him after all?'

Maureen applied her lipstick before finishing the story. 'Went out after him. Bloke stopped outside the door to tie his shoelace, so Pete comes up from behind and shoves him on his face, out onto the road, right under a car.'

'Christ—'

'Car was going pretty fast too. Didn't kill the bloke, but he's in a right mess, apparently. All sorts of broken bones. Cracked skull. Ain't woken up yet neither.'

'So – what's happening with Pete now?'

'Hiding out. There was a few people around on the street when it happened, witnesses. It was down the West End somewhere, I think. All tourists and that. I heard he's gone to his sister's in Brighton.'

Delia was worried. This didn't sound like the kind of situation Stella could contain. Most likely, the police would come knocking on Pete's sister's door in Brighton, and he'd end up in jail for GBH, or worse. A victim still unconscious in hospital could die, and that would make it manslaughter – or even murder. The ripples from that could affect everyone in Stella's gang. One thing causing another causing another.

*This is it*, whispered the Imps. Something needed to be done to wipe the slate. Something needed to be fixed at the root. Delia began to think she understood.

'You know what?' she said. 'It's time I went back into Barkers. I think I'll take a walk around there tomorrow.'

'God, Dee, you sure?'

Maureen looked appalled. But Delia knew it was necessary. Why, and even if, it was connected with what Itchy Pete had done to some stranger, or what it might have to do with Bill, or with Tess, she couldn't say yet, but at last things were coming back into focus again. After ten months, she had to face up to the jinx Maureen's capture had caused. Straighten her own mind. Let the poison out. Start paying off her debts.

The first thing she noticed when she arrived at the store was that they'd done something new with the window displays. Each now contained a scene assembled from various departments: a story of how one might live a Barkers life.

## Finer Things

In the first window, a Doris Dayish mannequin loaded children's clothes (Pierre Cardin, second floor) into a washing machine (Hotpoint, fourth floor), while her Rock Hudsonesque husband (suit by Tristan Johns, first floor) read his newspaper at the kitchen table (Harrison Interiors, fourth floor), and a girl of seven or so shook a rattle for her little brother, a baby in a highchair (Cosco, second floor).

Delia walked along the store front, past three more dumb shows: the same family at different times of the day, in different clothing, demonstrating different products. Here they were taking a picnic lunch against a painted backdrop of hills; here watching television together in a lounge; and finally, here they were at bedtime, both in pyjamas, Doris reading in bed, Rock brushing his teeth in the en suite bathroom. She supposed she was meant to wish this life were hers, but she'd turn down a decade of sexless luxury with Rock for five minutes with Bill in her single bed.

It was good to be back at Barkers. As she entered the revolving door, she found herself imagining what fun it would be to saunter out this afternoon with a few hundred pounds' worth of stock under her clothes. But she wasn't here to hoist, not today. She was going to feel her way back in, look for a way to placate the Imps, and that was all.

Straight away she recognised a shopwalker: a squint-eyed woman wearing a tweed dress, pretending to try out the Chanel testers in the perfumes department. This one had been working at Barkers for a couple of years, and before that Harrods, and before that House of Fraser.

Delia took a slow walk around the store, checking for other shopwalkers, and everywhere was reassured to find familiar faces in familiar locations. It looked like the system hadn't changed at all in the intervening months. Finally, she headed for Lingerie to look for the fat man who'd caught Maureen. He was mooching around the bras and panties, the same as last time.

Now she saw he was nothing to be afraid of. She'd built him up in her mind, turned him into an embodiment of terror, but he was only an ordinary shopwalker, as predictable as all the rest of them, and quite a bit slower than most. She remembered Maureen stamping on his foot, how absurd he'd been, how easy it had been to walk away from him that day. And she decided what she had to do. To set things right again she'd need to steal from *him*; from somewhere along his route, something expensive. Maybe even steal the very thing that Maureen had tried to take for herself, that ridiculous fur hat, if it was still here.

Once more, the temptation to act right away was strong. But she held herself back. For now she would only shadow him for a while, be careful. It had been carelessness that had caused the problem last time, and she wouldn't make that mistake again.

Taking a position at the far side of the department and pretending to examine a basque, she kept the fat shopwalker in her peripheral vision. He wouldn't recognise her, she was sure, after so long. He'd only seen her briefly, and she'd been careful today to make sure she looked different from last time, in a black wig and fake spectacles.

There were no other customers in the underwear department, only an assistant busy putting baby-doll nighties out on hangers. After a few minutes, she went off somewhere, leaving Delia and the shopwalker alone together.

'Excuse me – Miss.'

Forced to look directly at him, she saw he had a bra in his hands.

'I wonder, could you help me?' he said. 'I don't know a lot about this sort of thing.' He held up the bra and ran a pudgy thumb around the interior of one cup. 'Do these come in different sizes? I mean, obviously the ones for women do, but what about these?'

What did he mean, 'the ones for women'? Looking more carefully, Delia realised he was holding a training bra, one designed for pubescent girls.

'You should ask an assistant,' she said, turning away from him. This felt dangerous. She got ready to abandon her plans, started looking for a way to escape.

He took a step closer. 'It's for my daughter. She's only eleven, but I've noticed she's started to – I can't think of the word for it – not *bud*? That's more poetic, isn't it? There's a scientific term—'

She saw a sly eagerness in the shopwalker's face. He had recognised her after all. He was cleverer than she'd thought. He knew, and he knew she knew he knew. Still, Delia played it suburban, disapproving.

'Perhaps you could ask your wife to deal with this.'

'Ah,' he said. 'Sad story. Wife died last year. Just me and my little girl now.'

'Do you have a relative?' she said. 'A *female* relative.'

The shopwalker abandoned all deception. He wheeled around, brandishing an enormous pair of red silk knickers. 'These would have fitted my missus when she was alive,' he said. 'Great big arse, she had. You'd need quite a small pair, I imagine. Although, isn't that where you lot all hide what you've taken? Great big bloomers under your skirts?'

It was a wild attempt to break down her guard. All she could do now was stay in character. 'You're being most offensive. I'm going to speak to someone.'

His voice was thick and glottal, choked by the fat in his neck. 'Come off it. I remember you, darling. You were working with that girl I caught trying to nick a fur hat. I took you for a proper customer, remember? Asked you to make a statement. Then the other one stamped on my foot, and off you went, fast as you could go.'

He was trying to make her reckless, and he was succeeding. In a sudden fury, Delia almost wanted him to drag her into the back of the shop. He'd find she'd stolen nothing today. She could keep up her bourgeois persona. Insist on calling in the manager, demand a dressing-down for this bastard. Sacking, perhaps. Maybe this was *it*. Maybe the Imps had sent her in here today to defeat the shopwalker.

But she knew that was all fantasy. If he wanted to find something stolen on her, he'd make sure he did. It'd be his word against hers then, and once the coppers were here they'd soon find out her real identity. Her Fenfield address alone would prove to them that she was a criminal. Then she'd have no defence. Stella wouldn't protect her either. Like Maureen, she'd be on her own.

'You're confusing me with someone else,' she said.

He shook his head and peered at her. 'Your hair was different. Dyed it, have you? Or is that a wig? It's a wig, isn't it?'

The longer she stood here, the more control she gave him, but she couldn't find a way out.

'You know, we lost a nice fox coat the same day,' he continued. 'That girl didn't nick it. I worked it out afterwards: she must have had an accomplice.'

Finally, the Imps released her. Oh, it was simple. They'd punished her enough for now. *Just turn and walk away*, they said. So she did.

From behind her, the shopwalker called, 'I hear she went to borstal.'

She continued walking, tried not to listen.

He kept going. Needling her. 'Her name's Maureen, ain't it? Not much of a shoplifter either. She was wearing ordinary knickers when I caught her.'

Out of the underwear section, onto the escalator. How did he know, she thought, how could he know what kind of knickers Maureen had been wearing?

Halfway down now. Legs shaking, heat prickling her face. She had to get out. It was fine. She just had to reach the street, but the escalator was slow, slow, slow. Everything in her wanted to break into a run, and that would be a victory for him, so she kept her feet planted, breathed in through her nose, out through her mouth, to calm herself, remind herself there was nothing to fear, no reason to look back at him; while he stood at the top, flushed and sweating from having pursued her that far, and shouted down.

'Ordinary ones, she was wearing. I know. I had to search her. Thoroughly.'

Outside the shop, on the other side of the revolving doors, Delia leant against the store's wall until the shaking subsided. A fine, indeterminate rain, halfway to mist, had begun. There was the Doris Day mannequin, still in the window display, still frozen on the cusp of loading her Hotpoint, still smiling just as emptily as before. Nothing had changed for her. Rock's newspaper, Delia noticed now, was today's *Times*. It must be someone's duty to replace it each day. Strange that anyone should think that necessary.

Now she was calm again, she could consider how the Imps had tricked her. They had always loved Delia, always kept her safe, but now something had changed, and there were warnings everywhere of their anger. First Maureen getting caught, then Albie falling on that spike, then Itchy Pete pushing some bloke under a car, and now this. Was it Bill? Had they seen where things were going with him even before Delia had realised it for herself? Was all this their way of saying, *we won't share you*?

That must be it, she thought. The fat shopwalker was only a message. Not an actual danger, but a signal that danger was always there. He wasn't even real, just a ghost of yet-to-come; to remind her she survived only at the Imps' whim. They were telling her she could choose Bill or she could choose this life, but not both, and maybe she still had time to keep Stella on her side.

❧

The thin rain that had met her when she exited Barkers seemed to have covered the entire city. She sat at home all that afternoon, prepared herself to talk to Stella, and watched it fall, soft, cool and melancholy, outside her windows. It was still waiting for her in the evening when she set out for the Lamplighters.

She saw Lulu approaching from the opposite direction, and readied herself for a few minutes of unwanted chatter, but perhaps on account of the weather, perhaps because she too had somewhere important to be, Lulu hurried past with barely an acknowledgement.

Tommy the Spade was standing on the street outside the Lamplighters' front door, miserably pulling on a soggy Woodbine. Stella must have posted him on guard duty. That sort of public gesture was out of character, and it must mean something had shaken her pretty badly: something worse than the police, maybe; some consequence of this business with Itchy Pete pushing a bloke under a car. Whatever it was, Delia thought, it could be a good development. In the circumstances, the boss might be grateful for any support, might be less picky than usual about the details.

Almost certainly Delia would have to give her Bill Shearsby as a token of loyalty, and, after the shopwalker that morning, she was ready to do it. The most important thing now was to edge herself back into good terms with the Imps, to save herself with Stella, to re-engage the cogs of the world's clockwork and get it all running right again.

'Pub's shut,' Tommy said as she approached.

She looked at her watch. 'It's gone opening time.'

A black Humber drove by. Tommy's eyes tracked it to the end of the street. 'Pub's shut,' he repeated absently, still looking at the corner where the Humber had turned off and gone out of sight. 'Stella ain't opening tonight.'

'Why's that, Tommy? Is something wrong?'

'Flu, that's all. You'd best go home, Delia.'

'I need to talk to her.'

'Like I said, she ain't well. And it's catching.'

He fixed his eyes on the road, trying to indicate with his silence that the conversation was over. Maybe the police already had Pete in custody, Delia thought. They'd keep his skin medicine away from him. In a few hours he'd be desperate. Some detective could be grinding away right now at his resolve, trying to convince him it was in his best interests to grass up as many of his friends as possible. Pete scratching and itching and scratching, more and more desperate. He was going down anyway. And if that bloke he'd pushed under that car should happen to die—

Stella was meticulous. Surely Pete couldn't tell the police anything that could do her too much harm. But if he couldn't lead them to her, could he lead them to anyone else? To Teddy and Tommy maybe – to the jobs they did on the side. To Stella's girls. To Delia. Once this all started falling down, it could land on anyone. Even so, there had to be more to this than the coppers. More and more, it seemed essential to get through this door, to find out.

She gave Tommy one last try. 'Can't you ask her if I can go in? I've got something I need to tell her.'

'What's that, then?'

There it was. Her persistence had opened a little crack of possibility.

'It's to do with Finlay,' she said.

'What about Finlay? You tell me and I'll tell Stella. I promise.'

'Can't do that. She'd want to hear it from me.'

They both knew now he'd have to let her in. Anything to do with Finlay could be important. Still, he kept plodding on through the motions. 'Tell me and I'll tell her right now,' he said. 'That's all I can do for you. Honestly, Dee, she won't see nobody.'

Delia turned as if to go. 'Just have to leave it until tomorrow, I suppose. Stell's not going to be happy when she finds out. But if you can't disturb her—'

He gave in. 'Wait here,' he said, pulling a bunch of long brass keys from his pocket.

The pub door was fastened with two mortice locks: one at the top, one at the bottom. As Tommy undid them he kept a careful eye on the street. Once inside, he closed the door on Delia and did up the locks behind him.

While she waited another car drove by, a red Hillman this time. A few minutes later, she heard the keys turn once more, and Tommy reappeared.

'Can't be sure,' she told him, 'but I reckon that same car just went past again.'

'Humber, was it?' he asked. 'Black one?'

'Think so. It was black, but I can't tell one sort from another.'

He stepped out of the doorway to let her through. 'Thanks. In you go then.'

Stella sat on a tall stool behind the bar in the otherwise empty pub, drink in hand. Delia took a seat opposite her. Stella sloshed down the contents of her glass, then carelessly refilled it with two more measures from a gin bottle. In the process, she spilt a little on the bar and didn't bother to wipe it up.

'I am not in the habit of partaking, as you know,' she said with the punctilious, almost scripted, care of a person pretending to be either less drunk or drunker than she really was. 'But this has been a very trying day, and I do believe I have earned a dose of the old mother's ruin.'

'You all right?' Delia asked. Before Stella could reply, the door at the rear of the bar opened and in slunk Teddy.

He gave Delia a suspicious look. 'What's *she* doing here?'

Stella rolled her eyes. 'I told you where to be, Teddy. Get back there.'

'What's the point? Ain't nobody going to come that way. You'd have to climb over half a dozen garden walls. Most of 'em's got broken glass cemented on top.'

'Just go and do as I asked.' There was a snappish, exhausted quality in place of Stella's usual imperious calm. Teddy did as he was told and left, presumably on his way to stand outside in the rain and guard the back door.

'Fuckin' weakling,' Stella muttered, loud enough for her brother to hear.

Delia waited until she was sure Teddy was gone before she spoke. 'I wanted to let you know I've decided to go further with Bill Shearsby.'

Stella squinted at her over the bar. 'You what?'

'I've thought about what you and Finlay wanted me to do. I know I said I wouldn't, but—'

'Oh.' Stella knocked back half the contents of her glass. 'That.'

'Can I have one of those?' Delia said. She didn't much like gin, but it seemed a good idea to join Stella. To be women drinking together. 'I'll pay for it.'

'No, no. You're my guest, ain't you?' She took a second glass from the back of the bar and filled it for Delia. 'Won't even put it in The Book.'

'Cheers.' Delia sipped a little. The gin tasted worse than she remembered. Smelt like perfume, burned her throat.

Stella tipped the rest of hers into her mouth, and immediately refilled her glass. 'I don't know why you're telling me this now, Dee. Ain't you had that old bastard round yours four times in the last fortnight; fucking him? Dirty cow. You think I wouldn't know? Sneaking him in. Well there ain't nothing goes on around here I don't hear about. Nothing.'

'I wasn't keeping it from you, Stella,' Delia said, glad she'd been cautious. 'Course I wasn't. I'm here telling you now, ain't I? And you asked me to do it, you and Finlay. I was doing like you asked.'

'Liar. You done it because you fancied it. You don't never do nothing for anyone apart from yourself, Dee. Most likely you've worked out I probably knew, so you've come over here to try and get yourself out of trouble.' Stella grinned viciously. 'You're in *love* with him, ain't you? You think he's going to take you away from all this.'

'Course not,' Delia said, quickly but without conviction. She was beginning to realise she'd got it wrong. The Imps didn't want her back with Stella after all. Stella's world was falling down. Whatever had happened here had to be something far worse than Itchy Pete pushing some stranger under a car.

'Well,' sneered Stella. 'Lucky for you, it don't matter now. None of it. Bill Shearsby, the fucking Richardsons, Finn-fucking-Leeee. So if you've nothing useful to tell me, you can piss off.'

Stella's authority had always been an illusion. Now she looked as if she'd stopped believing in it herself, was desperately trying to hide her vulnerability behind this cruelty. It was important for Delia to stay calm, to collect as much information as she could.

'What do you mean, Stell? What's wrong?'

'Oh, you ain't telling me nobody's told you what Pete done?'

'Maureen said he pushed some bloke in front of a car last night 'cause he was itchy.'

Stella snorted. 'Since when did Maureen know anything? It weren't just some bloke. It was fucking *Finlay*. Pete pushed Finlay in front of a car last night. And he didn't do it 'cause he was fucking itchy. He done it for the Krays.'

When Delia left the Lamplighters, the rain had finally stopped. It was dark now. Tommy grunted something at her as she passed, then busied himself with securing the door again. That night she slept well. It had been a tiring day and still nothing was certain. Maybe Bill was meant to be her way out after all. Anyway, Fenfield wasn't safe for her now. She'd leave tomorrow.

# 13

Penny had evolved with startling rapidity from the perfect model of an art student into the perfect model of a private school art mistress. In preparation for a job starting after the summer, she'd swapped her mannish workwear and eighteenth-century make-up for flimsy dresses, mid-heeled shoes and bright, flirtatious colours: thoroughly modern, thoroughly conventional and thoroughly marriageable.

'It worked rather well,' she told Tess after her interview at the school in Hampshire. 'The headmaster just stared at my tits the whole time. No pretence about it. When he offered me the job, he told me there was no need for me to finish my DipAD if I didn't want to.'

Nevertheless, she had decided she would stay the course at the Slade. There were only a few months to go, she said, and one never knew, the diploma might be useful sometime in the future. On the other hand, she'd be lucky to scrape a pass so while it was certainly disgusting that a young woman's education should matter less than how she presented her bosom, she had to admit that in some ways it was also a bit of a relief.

Tess couldn't decide what she disapproved of more: the headmaster's lechery or her friend's pragmatism. She also suspected that Penny's main reason for staying in London was not to finish her diploma but to secure her future as Marius Shearsby's Tory wife. Having given up all her bohemian friends, and the bars and cafes she used to haunt with them, Penny now accompanied him to his Conservative Club twice a week. 'It's terribly boring, but surprisingly unpolitical,' she claimed. 'All about business contacts, really.'

As if that made it any better, Tess thought. Naturally, however, Marius was delighted with the metamorphosis. He'd always known there was a 'proper girl under all that nonsense', he said, proving once again what an idiot he was, how little comprehension he had of beauty.

Tess had been struggling with her monthly letter to her parents. Everything that actually mattered to her was too personal, too painful or too incomprehensible to share with them, and all that remained was drab repetition and dissembling. Her housemate's arrival at her bedroom door came as a welcome distraction.

'Fancy walking to a church?' Penny said. 'I've found a good one.'

The school in Hampshire was denominationally C of E, and Penny was expected to replace her careless, orthodox atheism with equally uncommitted faith. So far unable to face attending an actual service, she had decided to work up to it by purchasing *A Guide to London's Historic Churches* by Mrs Josephine Winstanley and visiting all the locations it described. This, she thought, should help her 'get used to the religious atmosphere'. Tess was normally happy to join her on these excursions. With Jimmy away, and still no word from him, they suited her mood.

An hour after Tess abandoned her letter home, she and Penny stood under a violet sky in the graveyard at St Pancras Old Church, looking at the Hardy Tree. According to Mrs Winstanley, hundreds of gravestones had been disinterred here in the 1860s to make way for the new railway line. As a young architecture student, Thomas Hardy had supervised their relocation into a pile around the roots of an ash tree. The sculpture they had formed after a century of erosion reminded Tess of puppies crawling over each other to get at their mother's teat.

An explosion of noise interrupted her thoughts. In the tree above them, four magpies were raucously attacking a blackbird nest. Two of the predators drew off the parents, while another pair swooped in to grab the chicks. At first, the adult blackbirds darted anxiously back and forth, their instincts divided between protecting their young and their own self-preservation. Then, accepting it was hopeless, they flew off disconsolately into the evening, leaving the marauders to divide their winnings.

Tess thought she might draw the blackbirds' return later that night, to sit a silent vigil over their bloodstained nest: a final scene from a gory nursery rhyme. It wasn't a bad idea, but she hadn't tried seriously to make any kind of picture since her visit to the Woodrows' house. For the last fortnight she'd turned up day after day at Moncourt to do nothing more than doodle. As for the Fenfield project that she'd once found so inspiring, it had simply drifted out of sight. After Jimmy's disappearance she hadn't felt like a third visit to Delia, and she hadn't gone. So that was the end of that, most likely.

'Conventicle,' Penny said.

'I beg your pardon?'

'I've been trying to remember the collective noun for magpies. I'm sure it's *conventicle*. Because they look like nuns, I suppose. Ugh. Look at that. How horrible.'

Two of the magpies perched on a gravestone and pulled at a half-dead chick in a tug of war.

'I don't think a conventicle has anything to do with convents,' Tess said. 'It means a sort of secret protestant religious group.' She was certain that was right, though she couldn't place the source of the knowledge – history at school, perhaps, or some book she'd read.

'Well, that isn't as good as nuns.'

The chick came apart. They watched the magpies gobble up half each and fly away into the dusk.

'I might leave Moncourt,' Tess said. She was just trying the idea out, seeing how it sounded if she said it aloud. It was more believable than she had expected. 'I can make a decent enough living as a graphic artist. Benedict Garvey said that at my interview. Maybe he was right. And like your headmaster said, a *girl* doesn't need qualifications.'

'Oh, I'm no sort of an example, Tess. Anyway, you're not like me. You've got genuine talent. You need to be a real artist.'

What right did Penny have to say that? To spout nonsense about duty to one's talent? Surely she should understand how it felt for Tess to turn up each day to classes she had no interest in; to make picture after picture, unable to care any longer that none of them were any good. Two weeks since Jimmy had gone, and she'd still not heard from him. Her friend, who had kept almost everything from her. Whom she would never have expected to miss so much.

The next day, following yet another unproductive morning, she considered walking down to Ginelli's for lunch, but settled as usual for a solo meal in the refectory. A group of her fellow first years at the next table were chattering with infuriating enthusiasm about the possibility of a mystery dealer on the exam panel. How ridiculous they were, how vain, to imagine themselves of interest.

She finished her meal quickly and silently. As she left, she heard Olivia Rackham mention the name *Veronica Wilding*. It seemed Jimmy's guess had been right: the mystery dealer really was the same woman who had bought Tess's picture that day by the Thames. Well, nothing had come of that, had it? Only fifteen pounds spent long ago on paint and pencils, used up in empty, valueless work.

It was still the middle of the lunch hour when she returned to the studio. Roger Dunbar was alone there, eating sandwiches from a paper bag. Everyone knew his wife had thrown him out. Now with nobody to iron his shirts or dry-clean his suits, he had grown ragged, his breath so rancid that when he could be bothered to lean over your work and offer you advice you had to turn your head away. Tess would have felt sympathetic, except he was at least in part to blame for whatever it was that had driven Jimmy from Moncourt.

As soon as she entered the studio, Roger grabbed up a piece of paper from his desk. 'I've received this memorandum from Mr Newbolt,' he declared. Bizarrely he spoke over the top of her, as if he were addressing a full room, and not just one person. 'It seems a large number of student pigeonholes are over-full, leaving no room for important college communications. All students, therefore, are instructed to check and empty their student pigeonholes immediately.'

She looked blankly at him. The words, delivered in the manner of a pneumatic drill, had not made any sense to her.

'Well,' he said. 'Why don't you go to your pigeonhole and see if you can sort it out to Mr Newbolt's satisfaction? Take your time, by all means. Make sure you do a proper job.'

The first-year pigeonholes were kept in a basement with mousetraps around its skirting and a smell like someone had recently lifted the lid of a neglected biscuit tin. To reach it, Tess had to walk to the far end of the college and down a narrow concrete staircase. There was nobody else there.

Like all the other students, she had checked her pigeonhole quite regularly during her first fortnight at Moncourt, and then, like all the other students, she had entirely forgotten its existence. They were all now so jammed with paper it would have been impossible to squeeze in another page. Much of the blockage in hers, she found, was formed of copies of *The Moncourt Review*, a sixteen-page magazine produced once a fortnight by a couple of third years with ambitions in journalism. Christ only knew what they filled it with, and Tess certainly had no wish to find out.

After a couple of minutes' pushing and pulling, she managed to unplug the pigeonhole. Then, resisting her first impulse to dump the whole lot in the bin without further investigation, she transported the stack of documents to the woodwormy table in the middle of the room and began unenthusiastically rifling through. There was, she supposed, a possibility she might find something here of actual importance.

Between back issues of the *Review*, and sometimes buried in their pages, were countless bits of communication, all meaningless. Overdue notices for books she'd long since returned to the library, circulars from half a dozen student societies she'd joined and lost interest in, reminders about events she'd already missed. This, she thought, might be the story of a parallel Theresa Green: one who had held on to the ideas she'd brought to Moncourt, one who still believed she could become an artist.

Then she found something unexpected: an envelope, addressed to her in Jimmy's handwriting, c/o Moncourt Institute. Postmarked Trencham, Kent. It was dated three weeks ago; the day after he'd left. The words *IMPORTANT* and *PRIVATE* had been scored deeply in black capitals on both sides.

Inside she found four sheets of paper torn from a sketch-book – just like the note Valerie Woodrow had shown her. Both sides of each page were covered in Jimmy's tiny, wobbly scrawl.

*Dear Tess,*

*Excuse the handwriting: I'm doing this on the train, and I'm in a bit of a state, as you'll understand once I've explained myself.*

*I'm on my way back to my dad's house in Kent now, to take some time to think about everything. Whether I come back to*

# Finer Things

*Moncourt or not is just one aspect of it. Of course, Moncourt may not even <u>take</u> me back. The way things are, that's just a risk I have to accept.*

*It's hard to know where to start explaining. There's so much I haven't told you about myself. I hope you aren't feeling personally responsible for my having run away from everything like this. I feel bad about our silly little disagreement yesterday. I acted like a child. Please don't take anything I said to heart. I had other things on my mind.*

*It started that night at the Gaudi, when we met William Shearsby.*

# 14

When Tess had first tried to persuade Jimmy he should join her and Penny for a night out in Soho with Marius Shearsby, he'd told her the idea didn't appeal to him in the slightest. She kept on wheedling. Francis Bacon might be there, she said, and Lucien Freud and Marius's writer father, whose name she didn't recall.

'Bound to be some awful old Tory journalist,' Jimmy said.

'No. He's a playwright. Used to be one of the Angry Young Men.'

That was when he made the connection. 'Hold on. Are you talking about *William* Shearsby?'

'Yes. I think so. He left Marius's mother years ago.'

'Find out, Tess. If it really is him, I'll come along.'

William Shearsby was an important name to Jimmy. Two years previously, his sixth-form art teacher had recommended a touring production of a play she'd seen during its original London run. He'd never heard of either the play or its writer, but he trusted this teacher's opinions, so he travelled alone to Margate to see *Consider This Your Notice*, for himself, in a half-empty theatre.

The play told the story of an elderly woman, sacked after a lifetime working in a laundry. At first it was confusing, because scenes kept alternating between the protagonist's final day of employment and events from earlier in her life. But once Jimmy had grasped the pattern, he saw how each juxta-position of the present-day with the past illustrated some way in which modern people failed to see the value of the past or learn the lessons of history. It was bleak and upsetting, and unlike anything he had ever experienced. When he returned to school the day afterwards, he talked excitedly about it with his art teacher, and she, an old socialist who had, in her twenties, marched with the Jarrow Crusade, suggested he go to the public library and take out a couple of Shearsby's other playscripts.

He'd read three of them. Perhaps it was because they were words intended for performance and seemed dead without actors to speak them, but none had moved him in the same way as *Consider This Your Notice*. He had half forgotten the play, until that conversation with Tess when, with a shock of recognition, he recalled how utterly that night in the theatre had seemed to change his perceptions of the world. And so when he saw her the next day and she confirmed that Marius really was, astonishingly, the son of William Shearsby, Jimmy agreed to go.

At first, he told himself he could approach it all quite dispassionately. But as the night approached, making a good impression on the playwright, and finding an opportunity to talk about *Consider This Your Notice* seemed more and more important to him. Consequently, by the time he set out for that evening in Soho, he'd become terrified by the certainty that he was going to make a fool of himself.

And he was right. Things had gone disastrously. In Jimmy's attic bedroom, the luminous hands of his alarm clock clicked into place at 5 a.m. and the horror was still circling his mind. William Shearsby had thought he was an idiot, or, worse, had barely noticed him at all. Picking that fight with Marius afterwards had gone some way to improving Jimmy's state of mind, but now he was alone in the dark it all grew worse and worse to him.

Looking up at the ceiling window, out at the moon, cold and silent and very far away, he recalled how, the day she showed him around the house, he had told Val Woodrow his main interest in this room was the light.

'It's perfect for an art student,' he had said.

Then Val had told him how the previous occupant had set up a telescope under the skylight. He had been an astronomy PhD student at King's College, and this telescope of his was so huge there was only just room to squeeze his head between the eyepiece and the floor.

'He'd lie there on his back for hours,' she said, 'scowling up at the stars, getting splinters in the back of his head.'

Jimmy thought now of that astronomer, and of all the other lodgers who had sweated and cried into this mattress, who had lain under the same bone-faced moon, masturbating with a slow, cautious hand to keep the bed frame from creaking. All of them had bathed in the same bath, all had shat in the same lavatory. And each of these young men was a chapter in Charlie's decline from brilliance to incoherence. Where were they now? He knew Val kept in touch with some of them. Cards at Christmas. The rest might be dead for all she knew.

Just before Christmas, one ex-tenant had turned up with his wife and two young children for a nostalgic tour of the premises. He'd been there a decade previously, and Val clearly struggled to recall his name until the man's wife, spotting the awkward way she was avoiding it, said pointedly, '*Theo* always speaks very fondly of you and the professor.'

'Would it be all right if we went up to your room for a few minutes?' asked the man who they all now knew was called Theo. And Jimmy had thought no it wouldn't be all right, really, but there did not seem to be any way to say that.

'I did English at University College,' Theo said, while his wife waited awkwardly in the doorway, and the two children sat, bored and fractious, on Jimmy's bed. 'You're an art student, aren't you?'

'That's right.'

'You must really love the light through this window.'

'I do,' Jimmy had said.

But the truth was he'd never done much painting or drawing here, and the real attraction of the skylight had been neither the stars nor the light. It was access. He'd seen it as soon as he stepped through the Woodrows' gate for the first time. Someone could clamber out through that window, onto the tall, dangerous roof, and jump off. He, Jimmy Nichols, could. The excitement of that secret idea had flipped around inside him like a dying fish. He had taken the room because of it.

After he moved in, he'd discovered he should have looked more closely. The window frame had been painted shut. But, he told himself, it wasn't as if he'd been planning anything seriously. Anyway, the light *was* good in there, and London offered plenty of other ways to kill yourself. You might leap in front of a speeding Tube train, pick a fight with some hard-case in a pub. Drop quietly at midnight into the filth of the Thames. So many opportunities in the city. It was just a matter of choosing.

Now, however, kept awake by the shame of last night at the Gaudi, it seemed to him that the roof was the right way after all.

He raised himself from the bed and stepped quietly across the uncarpeted floor, taking care to keep his footsteps light because Val and Charlie slept in the room directly below. Here on his desk lay a folding knife: keen and practical for sharpening pencils, useful for holding against the edge of a steel ruler and slicing around pictures when a composition needed to be reshaped. The blade was tucked away inside the wooden handle. Just enough metal showed to let him grip it between two fingernails and pull against the spring inside until he felt the simple mechanism click into the open position. It was frighteningly sharp. Once, whilst using it to peel an orange, he had accidentally sliced across the pad of his own thumb, deep into the meat. The trail of Japanese flags he had splashed onto the floorboards was faded now, but still visible all the way to the bathroom sink, and the scar on his hand would remain with him for as long as he lived. That orange juice had stung too, he recalled, with an almost sexual pleasure.

He pressed the blunt side of the knife against his wrist. How would he feel if he were to flip it over, he wondered, if he should saw it back and forth and let the keen edge bite into his blood vessels? But instead he reached up and pushed the knifetip into the corner where the window frame met the casement. The skin of paint yielded and split under the lightest pressure. He dragged the blade down and across, easily unsealing the join all the way around, then he closed the knife and placed it on the sill. It was no trouble now to swing the window open, letting in a gulp of cold early morning air.

Best not to think about the end point until later, he thought. Stage one had been cutting the window free. That alone was a statement of intent. Stage two would be climbing onto the roof. He lifted himself through and swung his feet out onto the tiles. Then he sat in his pyjamas and slippers on the steep slope and looked out across the city. Dawn was not far off. The sky, still densely black at its core, had started to lighten at the edges. Silhouettes of TV aerials stuck up from a few chimneys.

Of course it would be absurd to jump off a roof over William Shearsby's opinion of him. But it was not absurd to be sick to death of being the sort of person who could *care* about a thing like that, who could let it bother him into insomnia. There were so many problems in the world that actually mattered: civil rights in America; prison camps in Russia; the Congo Crisis. South African apartheid. Yet those horrors bothered him less than a meaningless snub from a man he'd met only once.

He would not throw himself off the roof because he'd failed to impress William Shearsby. He'd do it because letting himself be devastated by something so trivial was clear proof that he didn't deserve to live.

His motivation having been arrived at logically, he moved on to practical matters. He'd need to choose his position carefully, find a spot from which he could more or less guarantee success. If he landed on the lawn, he might do no more than break a leg, or his back, and have to lie in agony and humiliation until the milkman found him an hour or two later.

Between the window where he currently sat and the edge of the roof lay a long, steep slope of tiles. Stage three, therefore, was to make his way down to the gutter and find the point directly above the flagstone path. A head-first dive ought to do the trick. Arms tight against his sides.

*It had been raining,* his letter to Tess said, *and there was moss on the tiles, so the roof was wet and slippery. I started edging my way down.*

The next morning, surprised still to be alive, he asked Val about local doctors' surgeries.

'Are you unwell?' she asked.

'I just thought I should get myself registered.'

She left it at that, probably imagining he'd contracted something embarrassing – or shameful. Perhaps she was right, he thought. She gave him the address of a group practice nearby, and on his way home from Moncourt that evening, he went in to sign up. Once he'd filled in his form, he asked how soon he might see someone. If he was willing to wait for half an hour, the receptionist told him, there was a new doctor at the practice who had an appointment free.

Jimmy didn't like doctors. Professional men in general he found high-handed, overly keen to require from him an unearned deference – or was that just *men*? Dr Malvern, however, seemed different. At the start of the consultation, he squeezed out from behind his desk to shake Jimmy's hand: a clumsy, endearing gesture. He was older than Jimmy had expected, gruff-voiced, poorly shaven, with an air of generous-spirited disorganisation.

'Quite refreshing to have a patient of my own,' he said, wheezing a little as he made his way back to the chair behind his desk. 'Only been here a couple of months myself, and the regulars all want their usual blokes. They'll take me on sufferance, as a last resort. It's understandable – now, what's the problem, James?'

Never having told anyone before, Jimmy had wondered how he could broach this. There seemed no indirect route.

'I've been feeling suicidal,' he said. This was already quite a relief, he thought. Just sharing the burden with a kind stranger. It might be enough on its own.

'I see.' Dr Malvern's professional concern seemed utterly ordinary, as if Jimmy had just told him he'd developed a rash on his neck. 'And how long has this been going on, exactly?'

'Forever.'

There were biscuit crumbs on Malvern's shirt front. He noticed them and brushed them off. 'Can you be more precise, James? For example, can you pin down your earliest memory of a suicidal idea?'

Of course he could. He'd thought about this enough times, unarchiving his own past to try and untangle the mess of his emotions. 'Do you know *Tom Sawyer*?'

The doctor nodded and smiled, 'I suppose you're talking about the part where they all think Tom's dead, and he gets to see his own funeral?'

Warm relief flooded through Jimmy. This man *understood*. 'I'd have been eight or nine, I suppose. I never wanted to be Tom, though. I wanted to be Huck Finn.'

## Finer Things

Malvern looked puzzled by this. 'If I remember right, Tom's the one they're all so sad about.'

'That's right. Nobody cares about Huck. It's like he's not even there. He only gets the funeral because they all think Tom's dead too, and when they come back it's only Tom they're pleased to see. Obviously that's meant to be awful for Huck, but I envied him for it.'

Jimmy looked down at his hands and imagined the book in them. He'd read it countless times, knew almost by touch the cover picture of Tom tricking Ben Rogers into whitewashing the fence. It was a children's edition, simplified and abridged, on coarse, cheap paper embedded with the odd chip of flat, unpulped wood. He recalled the way the print's edges blurred where the ink had soaked in and spread.

'I'd think about it all the time. How nice it would be to escape into silence and darkness. While most of my friends were getting stuck into their wet dreams about the chemistry teacher, mine were all about how I could vanish from the world.'

'Are you saying there was a . . . sexual element to your thoughts of death?'

Jimmy noticed that despite the studious objectivity of his tone, Malvern's cheeks had coloured a little.

'Sorry, no. That was a joke. I should stick to the facts, shouldn't I?'

'It's fine. Only – forgive me for asking – was it just the death fantasies, or did you also have an interest in this chemistry mistress?'

At Jimmy's secondary modern there had been both schoolmasters and schoolmistresses. He had said 'chemistry teacher' on purpose.

'Yes. That sort of thing went on in my head too. All the time.'

'What was it about her you liked?'

Tidy, kind Mr Knox in his crisp, white lab coat. Jimmy hadn't thought about him for years. Trying to recall his face now, he conjured an image of a man who looked rather like Roger Dunbar. Bloody hell, he thought, did he have a *type*?

'I'm not sure. It was a long time ago now.'

'But you'd describe any sexual feelings you had as a teenager as normal?'

'I think so.' *Normal* could mean *regular*, couldn't it? *Usual*?

Thankfully, Malvern dropped this line of enquiry. 'And when you think of suicide, what stops you?'

'Mostly other people,' Jimmy replied. 'The thought of what it would do to my dad, for example – how I'd feel if I actually *could* see him at my funeral, how destroyed he'd be. That's held me back more than once. But I think, if the conditions are right, I'll probably end up going through with it someday.'

It was interesting that Malvern obviously felt a lot more comfortable talking about suicide than about sex. 'Can you explain why?' he said.

This was easy. It was as if all his life Jimmy had been waiting for this opportunity to explain himself. 'For me it's the logical solution to more or less any problem. When my work isn't going well, or I'm feeling miserable, or embarrassed or ashamed, the first thing I always consider is killing myself. It's a constant companion. I try to keep myself ready for when the time comes. Have plenty of options available. For example, when I came in here today, my first thought was, what if you were to prescribe me some pills? Could I use *them*?' He laughed. 'It isn't rational, is it?'

'You have a disease, that's all,' Dr Malvern said. 'It's called depression. You're lucky you came to me, though. A lot of GPs have no idea how to deal with psychological problems. I'm not an expert, but I've had some training, and I can tell you I won't be giving you any pills today.'

Despite himself, Jimmy felt disappointed at this news. Perhaps if he hadn't talked about overdosing the doctor might have sent him home with a bottle of Drinamyl. Others had done so before. He liked Drinamyl.

'Are you saying it's not curable?'

'It can be cured if we can get to the causes. It might take a specialist. But I think I can already see a possible approach.'

'Really?'

'Let's not rush into this, though. Perhaps we can build up a little more information? Could you tell me why you decided to come here today in particular?'

*So I told him about the roof.*

'It was steep up there, and pretty slippery – wet moss all over the place. Also, some of the slates were loose. I was in my pyjamas and slippers, making my way down to the edge quite gingerly, but at the same time, feeling more and more committed to what I was going to do. I'd told myself if I could get all the way there and stand up, I wouldn't have the option of chickening out.'

'Why not?'

'Because I'd be there. Of course, I can't say for sure now if I'd actually have had the guts to go through with it. Probably not. Anyway, about a third of the way down, I lost my footing, and found myself sliding out of control towards the edge. It's funny how your intentions can change.'

'How so?'

'It wasn't a decision anymore. At first I didn't want it happening by accident, then I didn't want it happening at all. When I'd crawled out I'd been dead set on chucking myself down at the ground, trying to smash my head in on the flag-stones. Now I was flailing around, trying to grab at anything that would save me. I'd realised I didn't actually want to die.'

'And you managed to stop yourself. Obviously.'

'That's right. When I got to the bottom I rammed my heels into the gutter. The metal came away from the wall a bit, and that sort of dampened the impact, brought me to a stop. I lay there for a while, on my back, crying. Glad to be alive, miserable I wasn't dead. Then, once I'd calmed down, I turned over and crawled back up to my window. That was pretty terrifying in itself. I scrambled back into my bedroom. Next morning, I was feeling a lot more sensible, and I decided I needed some sort of help. Which is why I'm here.'

Dr Malvern smiled generously. His confidence made it seem almost possible Jimmy really could feel better. After all these years.

'I'm very glad you came here today,' Malvern said.

'You think you can—'

'Perhaps. Yes. I know of several treatments that have had efficacy in cases of this sort. The trick is to get at the root cause.'

*He stopped talking and waited. But something about that phrase 'the root cause' seemed wrong to me. It set off an alarm in my head, almost too late.*

*'It's your impulses making you unhappy,' he said. 'You need to understand that suicide is an unnatural desire, and one unnatural desire is usually connected to another.'*

*Unnatural desire. That was what he saw in me. I'd fallen for what I'd thought was his kindness, but he was just a slippery evangelist, luring me in, building my trust, trying to win me over. And with people of that sort, there always comes the moment when they have to show their true colours. Thank Christ he'd mistimed his!*

*He kept talking, even though he must have seen in my face how horrified I was. I suppose he thought he might as well make sure I got the message.*

*'I think you understand what I'm referring to,' he said. 'It's not just a moral issue, it's a legal one. As a doctor, I have a responsibility to help you correct yourself.'*

# Finer Things

He didn't say, because he wouldn't want to spook me, but I knew what he had in mind. It's a kind of treatment they call 'aversion therapy'. Electric shocks to the testicles every time you get an erection, hallucinogenic drugs, sleep deprivation, starvation and so on. I've met men who've had it. If you get caught importuning in a gents' lavatory the judge sometimes gives you the choice – imprisonment or therapy. Given the sort of thing that happens to queers in jail, I can see why any alternative might look better. Also, I suppose, the idea of becoming 'normal' could be attractive to some.

In case you're wondering, the torture treatment doesn't work. At best, you end up a self-hating homosexual, and I'm already pretty good at all that. I don't hate the homosexual part of me. I'm just a homosexual who also happens to be exceptionally gifted in the self-hating department. Malvern's big mistake was trying to make a connection between those aspects of my character.

I let him finish what he was saying and told him I'd give it some thought. Then I left, shaking with fear and cursing myself for my stupidity. If only I'd given a false name and address at the surgery! Like a bloody idiot, I'd sat and confessed to a suicide attempt. At least that's not grounds for prosecution in itself anymore. But I'd still given that man all the evidence he needed to certify me mentally unfit.

I looked it up in a law book afterwards. Once a doctor's given you the label of 'lunatic' you've no rights at all. They can lock you up for as long as they like, and subject you to whatever treatment they see fit. My 'perversion' can be classified as a psychological illness, of course, and with the admission of a suicide attempt on top . . .

After that things got a bit deranged. More than likely, the man forgot about me as soon as I left his office – also he had no proof of anything I'd told him, and the part about my inclinations was all just guesswork as far as he was concerned. But I became obsessed with the idea that he was now *determined to track me down and have me dragged off to an asylum. I spent those days in a kind of terrified fog, expecting the men in white coats to turn up at any moment.*

*Perversely, the anti-apartheid stuff helped a lot: going to meetings, reading all those grim pamphlets and newspaper stories. It gave me something to focus on other than myself. And then, when we were on the march itself, I felt joyous. I expect I looked quite the fanatic out there. I was drunk on it. Honestly, I can't remember a time when I've been happier.*

*Then, of course, we had to run into Shearsby. I didn't want to go anywhere near him, but you insisted. It was just awful. It brought back that night at the Gaudi, and everything that followed it. You and I had that stupid argument afterwards, of course, which I think was more to do with my feeling there was nothing to look forward to now the march was over. Anyway, by the time I got home to my digs I knew I needed to go back to my dad's for a while.*

*My train's pulling in to Trencham station now. So I'll leave this, except to say I'm feeling a great deal better already, and I'm sure that getting out of the hothouse of Moncourt for a while is the right decision.*

*Before I sign off, I want you to know that, apart from the old couple I live with, you're about the only person in London I really trust. You're my truest friend, Tess, and I don't want to lose you. I'm so very sorry I haven't talked about any of this before. If I've been difficult recently I hope you can understand why.*

*What an idiot I am! I've just realised, I don't know your address in Camden. I'll have to send this letter to you care of Moncourt and hope they pass it on to you.*

*Please write back if you get this.*                    *J.*

After she finished the letter, it occurred to Tess that in the three weeks since Jimmy had posted it, he might have tried writing to her again. She checked carefully through the pile of papers, lifting up each copy of *The Moncourt Review* by its front cover and shaking it in case anything should have been trapped between its pages. There was nothing more.

Footfalls and chatter approached from outside. Lunchtime was over. As soon as the rest of the class had arrived back at the studio, Roger must have sent them all on the same errand as her. Now they were on their way down towards the pigeon-holes. She put Jimmy's letter in a trouser pocket and dumped everything else from her pigeonhole in the bin.

She found the stairwell choked with a noisy queue of her classmates. It was difficult shoving her way back up through the crowd. At the top, she squeezed out between two of them into the corridor, and stood for a few moments listening to the retreating hubbub, then, rather than returning to the studio, she headed directly for Benedict Garvey's office.

# 15

Delia stood in the bedroom she used as her walk-in wardrobe, surrounded by rails of coats and dresses, by uncountable shoes, by boxes and boxes of underwear. Most of it, she hadn't touched for years. She wondered why she'd bothered. There were only a few of these things she could even remember hoisting.

She had already dragged her suitcase out from under her bed, and found it heavier than expected, being already full of enough neatly folded clothes for several days. She must have packed it long ago, thinking that one day she'd have to be ready to go quickly and leave everything else behind. Now that day had arrived.

Last night, before Delia had left the Lamplighters, Stella told her the rest of the story. The driver of the car that ran Finlay over had not stopped to find out what harm he'd done, but had vanished into the night, and so had Pete. The police found the vehicle next morning, abandoned near Charing Cross, its radiator grille still covered in blood, and they had tracked down its owner from the registration. It had been stolen eight weeks previously from the driveway of a Bexhill bank manager. Pete's whereabouts, however, remained mysterious.

The Krays, who had been behind the whole thing, were twin brothers from Hoxton. For the last couple of years, they'd been doing well in protection and other criminal enterprises around the Mile End area, and now it seemed they had ambitions in Soho. Kray men had taken over all three of Finlay's clubs before his ambulance even reached the hospital. The Richardsons, to whom he had been coughing up protection money all those years, hadn't got there in time to do anything about it.

There probably wouldn't be a war. Not yet, anyway. One was going to be inevitable eventually, but not over Finlay. Delia's guess was that the two sides would reach some kind of settlement that saved either of them from losing face. If Finlay had died, things would have been simpler. As it stood, the reputation the Richardsons were building for themselves would demand they provide him with the protection he'd been paying for, and take action to return his property to him. There would need to be revenge too. Scapegoats and sacrifices. Itchy Pete would be tidied away soon, if it hadn't happened already.

That was why Stella was frightened. Pete had been one of her boys, so the Richardsons would assume she'd been involved in the plan. She'd been in business with Finlay, so the Krays would consider her a danger. Whoever won this, Stella was likely to lose, and anyone connected with her was at risk too. That was why Lulu had been striding so determinedly away from the Lamplighters last night. The old bird knew it was time to disappear. She'd done it plenty of times before.

Thinking she should at least say goodbye to Maureen, Delia went and knocked at her neighbour's door. When she saw the suitcase, the damage to the girl's face amplified her obvious despondency.

'You're going, ain't you, Dee?'

'It's not safe.'

'Everyone's leaving,' Maureen said miserably. 'I heard Maggie Chisholm got her kids back off her sister and took them to the seaside somewhere. Rita and all that lot have scarpered as well.'

'I'm going to try and stay with a friend in Clapham,' Delia said.

'Do you mean that writer bloke you've been seeing?'

'Jesus. Does everyone know? Yes. You should leave too.'

'Ain't got anywhere, Dee. I'm not going back to my mum and dad.'

'Just get a room.'

'Haven't got any money for rent.'

'If you come with me, I can give you some,' Delia said. 'I've got plenty put away.'

'Thanks, but I'll be all right here. Anyway, I owe Stella for looking after me.'

Something about Maureen's implacable loyalty filled Delia with anger. 'Don't be an idiot, girl,' she snapped. 'Stella couldn't give a shit about you. You're a lightning rod, that's all. We kept you around so all the bad luck would fall your way instead of ours. And it turns out you haven't even managed that, have you?'

The girl's lower lip began to tremble. Delia didn't have time to try and make her feel better. She softened her tone, though there was no taking back what she'd said.

'Listen, Maureen. You mustn't stay around here. I don't know much about these Krays and Richardsons, but I've seen how Stella is. If she's scared, you should be too.'

'I've been happy here,' the girl told her, swallowing down a sob. 'I'm not going.'

To start with, as Delia headed down Doddington Road, she felt unburdened. She'd done her best for Maureen, who would just have to be responsible for herself now. But the journey from Fenfield to Clapham took four different buses, and each time she lifted her suitcase on or off a luggage rack, it seemed heavier than before, as if the further she got away the less she was leaving behind.

## Finer Things

This was how it had always been for her. During the war, on the first day of her evacuation, she'd hiked up a hill to the farm gate with a suitcase just like this one weighing her down. Later, on the day she returned to London, she had sat on that case outside a pub, waiting for her father to come out and show her where she'd be living, now their old house had been bombed out in the Blitz. To have nothing, to depend on the whims of others, that was reality. She'd spent her whole life waiting to be homeless again.

She disembarked near Clapham Common. After asking directions from an old woman who had left the bus at the same time, she found she should have stayed on for two more stops. The street she wanted was fifteen minutes away on foot.

'I should just wait here for the next one if I were you,' the woman said, with a meaningful glance at Delia's suitcase. 'They're every half an hour.' But Delia decided to walk anyway. She'd had enough of buses and enough of waiting.

Bill's street surprised her. Whenever he'd talked about where he lived, he'd implied it was a kind of artistic locale, a place where people had no time for traditional moralities or hypocrisies. So, without really thinking about it, she'd envisaged something modernist, like those new concrete blocks of flats that were springing up where the bombs had cleared the slums. She had certainly not anticipated a prissy red-brick terrace, with white-rendered curlicues framing the bay windows and mock-classical columns flanking every porch. This street had been built at the turn of the century for the aspiring middle class. Through each tiny front garden, a chess-board-tiled path led from door to gate. A reminder to the inhabitants as they left for work every morning that they were pawns en route to promotion.

Bill's was number twelve. Leaving her suitcase on the street behind the garden wall, Delia walked up to the door and rang the bell. After a minute, she saw a shape approaching on the other side of the frosted glass. Female. There was no time to run off, but at least she had a few moments to prepare herself before the door opened.

The woman was thirty or so, in a Japanese silk dressing gown – printed with splashy red chrysanthemums on a black background – under which she was obviously naked. She pulled it a little more tightly around herself and gave Delia a shrewd look.

'Can I help you?'

She was glad she had left the suitcase out of sight; that she would not have to make things any more embarrassing by having to account for it. 'My name's Delia. I'm a friend of Bill's. I just need a quick word. Would that be all right?'

'Mhm. Very well,' the woman said, and without inviting Delia in, she disappeared into the house.

A few minutes later, Bill hurried to the door, barefoot, in denim trousers and a shirt with the buttons done up wrong.

'Delia,' he said, too enthusiastically. 'It's good to see you.'

'Sorry to turn up unannounced,' Delia said. 'Actress, is she?'

He shrugged an apology, had the good grace to look ashamed. 'Zoe's a writer. We're working together on an idea for a script about Sharpeville.' He glanced over his shoulder, into the house. 'Delia. I mean, it's not like Zoe's my— That is, she's got a husband.'

'None of my business. I just came by to tell you, things have got a bit dangerous in Fenfield, so I've left for a while. Might not go back, actually. So I didn't want you going there looking for me.'

'Christ,' he said. 'I wish you'd— Do you have somewhere to stay? I can put you up here. I mean, you might need to give me half an hour to explain things to Zoe.'

She felt sorry for Bill, sorry for having caused this embarrassment. His concern was genuine, she could see that – she hadn't misjudged *everything* about him. And after all, it wasn't as if she had been entirely honest herself. He had the right to know, she decided; to forgive her or not, as he chose.

'It's all right,' she said, 'I've got a place sorted out. But there's something I need to tell you before I go. Maybe I could come inside for a while?'

He took her into the room he called his study. At one time it would have been the parlour. Now it was empty apart from a couple of office chairs and a cheap modern desk on which stood a typewriter and two orderly stacks of paper: one clean, one typed-on. Perhaps he really had been writing a script with that Zoe woman.

Delia sat by the window and told him all about Itchy Pete, about Stella and Finlay, about the Richardsons and Johannesburg. How she, Delia, had done her best to keep him, Bill, safe.

'God,' he said, when she'd finished. 'I had no idea.'

'Sorry about all the lies,' she said. She'd missed out the part where she'd tried to sell him to the boss the previous afternoon. 'I really did like you, Bill. Still do.'

But he was already distracted, rummaging in a desk drawer. 'And Stella told you this was all about a letter I sent? I wonder if she can have meant—' Then he must have realised what she'd just said, because he looked at her again, and said, 'Oh, it sounds like you only did what you had to. No need to feel guilty about it, Delia. I doubt you've done any harm.'

As he returned to his search through the drawer, Delia's attention was caught by the sound of someone carefully closing the front door. She looked out of the window and saw Zoe, now dressed, leaving the house. Bill was too busy rifling through papers to notice.

He gave a sharp little laugh 'Here it is,' he said, unfolding a piece of cut-out newsprint and handing it to Delia. '*Guardian* letters page, last year.'

# David Wharton

## *PLAYWRIGHTS AGAINST APARTHEID*

*Public Declaration: June 25th 1962*

*While not wishing to exercise any political censorship over their own or any other works of art, but feeling colour discrimination transcends the purely political, the following playwrights, after consultation with the Anti-Apartheid Movement and with South African artists and writers, as an expression of their personal repugnance to the policies of apartheid and their sympathy with those writers and others in the Republic of South Africa now suffering under evil legislation, have instructed their Agents to insert a clause in all future contracts automatically refusing performing rights in any theatre where discrimination is made among audiences on grounds of colour:*

*Arthur Adamov, Janet Allen, John Antrobus, John Arden, Mary Hayley Bell, John Barton, Samuel Beckett, Robert Bolt, Ray Cooney, Clemence Dane, Paul Dehn, Shelagh Delaney, Daphne Du Maurier, Ronald Duncan, Charles Dyer, Graham Greene, Robert Gore-Browne, Elizabeth Hart, Lillian Hellman, Frank Hilton, N. C. Hunter, Stephen King-Hall, Bernard Kops, Hugh Leonard, Benn Levy, Henry Livings, Miles Malleson, Alan Melville, Bernard Miles, Ronald Millar, Arthur Miller, Jonathan Miller, Spike Milligan, John Mortimer, Robert Muller, Iris Murdoch, John Osborne, Harold Pinter, J. B. Priestley, J. D. Rudkin, James Saunders, Gerald Savory, Murray Schisgal, Peter Shaffer, William Shearsby, Dodie Smith, C. P. Snow, Muriel Spark, Lesley Storm, Gwyn Thomas, Arthur Watkyn, Fred Watson, Arnold Wesker, Angus Wilson, Tennessee Williams.*

'I don't understand,' Delia said, handing the cutting back to Bill. 'Why would the Richardsons' business friends care about this?'

Bill was enjoying the drama now, the discovery that he had been unwittingly caught up in some kind of conspiracy. He was making a story out of it, Delia thought.

'You can't separate business from politics,' he said. 'And this is public criticism of their regime. The South Africans really don't like that.' He took a notebook and pen from the drawer. 'Do you mind if I write a few things down?'

It didn't seem as if he needed her to answer. He scribbled for almost a minute, then said, 'You know what? I bet they aren't businessmen. Or not *just* businessmen, anyway. Have you ever heard of the *Broederbond* – the Brother Band?'

Delia shook her head.

'It's an Afrikaner secret society. Sort of a cross between the Masons and the Nazis. Deeply unpleasant people, and highly influential over there. It wouldn't be the first time they'd tried to get their claws into the Anti-Apartheid Movement.'

Thinking back to that night in Stella's kitchen, Delia recalled Teddy's shiftiness. That unsettling figure outside in the garden – might he have been one of these sinister Broederbond men? Yet she still couldn't see why Bill would be of any interest to such a person.

'Are you involved in anything else to do with South Africa?' she said.

He seemed disappointed she wasn't more impressed. 'Apart from my name being on that letter? I suppose it *is* quite a long way down the list, but that's only because it's alphabetical.' He paused to assess his contributions to the movement. 'Well, I'm treasurer of the Clapham branch, and I do quite a bit all over South London – handing out leaflets, speaking at events and so on.'

'I suppose all that *could* be what they were looking into,' she said, sure it was not, and sure too that he knew that. She had heard his conviction drain away as he spoke.

He studied the pattern of the carpet. 'On the other hand,' he murmured, 'it's possible I might have overstated my influence. Encouraged a few people in the Gaudi to think I was involved at the top level of the British Anti-Apartheid Movement.'

'Well,' Delia said. 'That's the impression you gave me too. Was there no truth in it, then?'

Though obviously abashed, he was ready to admit his foolishness. 'Not a great deal of truth, no. I've *met* Barbara Castle and Harold Wilson quite a few times, at events, rallies, marches; Duma Nokwe too; but the fact is, I'm just an insignificant old scribbler trying to sound like he's more important than he is. Embarrassing, isn't it? Christ! Have I put myself in danger, do you think?'

Delia understood: a falsehood always expanded in the retelling. Someone had listened to Bill's fibs in the Gaudi and taken them for sale to Finlay. Finlay had sold them on to the Richardsons, and the Richardsons had traded them for friendship with their South African associates. At every stage, something had been added to give the information a little more value, to make it worth passing along. Who knew what nonsense the Broederbond had heard about him in the end? Whatever it was, it meant a message had returned to Finlay: *keep an eye on that writer, get one of Stella's girls to lead him on*. All the time there had been nothing more to it than the usual blagging and boasting. Bill was right to look ashamed of himself. Delia knew how to lie to get herself out of trouble, of course, but what sort of idiot would lie to get *into* it?

'You're probably safe enough,' she said, remembering how uninterested Stella had been last night in news of Shearsby. 'Finlay's in a coma, and there's more urgent things for the Richardsons to worry about. Most likely they'll all forget about you. I'd keep out of Soho for a good while, though.'

She stood, readying herself to leave. He remained in his seat, but caught her hand between his.

'Are you sure you won't stay? There's a spare bedroom if that's what you'd prefer. Please don't turn the offer down just because you're angry at me.'

'I'm not angry at you, Bill.' She was surprised to discover she meant it. Whatever passion she had felt for him had evaporated. Perhaps it had never been there; perhaps she'd rid herself of it yesterday when she'd decided to betray him to Stella; perhaps it was just that he was only another liar, no different from the rest. 'I'm fine, I've got a bed at a friend's place for a few days, then I'll look for somewhere on my own. Would you mind calling for a taxi? I need to get to Paddington Station.'

'Off somewhere nice?' the driver asked as the cab pulled away.

'Don't know,' Delia said.

After her encounter with the fat shopwalker in Barkers yesterday, she had imagined she knew how to fix her life; believed that she'd worked out what she needed to do to appease the Imps. Now it seemed all that had just been the start of this series of trials they were putting her through. They hadn't wanted her to give up Bill for Stella. They hadn't wanted her to run to him either. So she had to unpick the pattern of her life, look for other threads to follow. Sooner or later she'd find the right one.

Bill had insisted on coming out to pay the man in advance. After finding Delia's suitcase where she had left it by the gate, he had loaded it into the boot without remark.

'I hope they remember you,' was the last thing he said to her, through the taxi's open window. He had guessed her reason for going to Paddington must be to make a trip out to Somerset, in search of the old couple who had taken her in during the war, and she had allowed him that nostalgic fiction, even though Reg and Janet Lander were probably dead. They'd both been in their sixties twenty years ago, and as she remembered it, Reg had some kind of heart condition.

Delia had no intention of leaving London at all. It was time to go forward, not back, and surely there couldn't be many more wrong choices left for her to make. At the station, she went straight to the left-luggage lockers. She undid the chain around her neck and took the key from it, thinking of how she had once told Bill it belonged to some long-lost money box. Well, that was true in a way. She opened up her locker and took out one of the half-dozen account books inside. Here also were those two sketches Tess had given her after her first visit to Fenfield. Delia pushed them to the side of the locker so they would not be damaged when she slid in the suitcase. She would leave it here while she went to collect some of her savings.

Many of Stella's hoisters hid cash around their rooms, under loose floorboards, taped to the backs of drawers or in other obvious places. Delia took more care. She knew that while the girls were out at work Teddy liked to prowl around his sister's properties with his spare key, nicking whatever he took a shine to, and doing Christ knew what else besides.

Delia had saved everything she could, and she'd kept the cash books here in her locker at Paddington, close to the stores where she did her hoisting. Over the years she'd built up a decent amount, distributed between six accounts under six different names.

At the Chelsea Building Society on Spring Street she took out enough to support herself for the next fortnight. She also asked the cashier to make out a cheque for the amount Bill had given the cab driver, which she posted to him on her way back to the station. Then she returned the savings book to the locker with the rest, collected her suitcase and hailed another taxi.

Half an hour later she arrived at a shabby townhouse in Camden. No front garden this time, just a door directly onto the street.

'Can you wait, please?' she asked the driver. 'I don't know how long I'll be.'

Always someone waiting behind her with the meter running. Door after door to knock on, and no idea what might be behind any of them.

With her bare legs and light summer frock, the young woman who answered this time was unsettlingly reminiscent of the Doris Day mannequins in Barkers' window. She was holding a livid green apple, into which she had obviously bitten just before she'd opened the door, and though she looked very different from that time at the Gaudi, Delia recognised her.

'You're Penny, aren't you? I don't know if you remember me. My name's Delia.'

The young woman swallowed the mouthful of apple. 'It's Penelope, not Penny. I'm going by the full thing now. I suppose you're looking for Tess?'

'She gave me this address. I was thinking if she wanted to finish the portrait she started, I could pay her for it.' Delia had concocted this excuse in the cab on the way here. It didn't matter that it wasn't especially convincing. It was just a way in. She needed somewhere to leave her suitcase, and maybe a floor to sleep on. That could come later.

'You've come to the right place,' Penny said, 'but I'm afraid Tess's out of town. Remember her friend Jimmy from the Gaudi that night? He hasn't been well. She went this morning to see him at his father's place in Kent. But she'll be home tomorrow afternoon if you want to come back then.'

Delia sighed involuntarily. Another test, then. 'I suppose so. If you wouldn't mind, could you let her know I stopped by?'

'Hold on,' said Penelope, stretching her neck to look over Delia's shoulder at the waiting taxi. 'Have you travelled all the way here from Fenfield? You must be exhausted. Why don't you come in for a cup of tea?'

'Thanks. But I've just moved out of the place I've been living. I need to find a guest house or something for tonight.'

Penelope swept past her and tossed away the half-eaten apple. 'That's easy enough,' she declared, as the apple bounced along the pavement a couple of times and rolled into the gutter. 'You can sleep in Tess's room, at least until she gets back. I'm sure she won't mind. Shall I just tell this taxi chap he can go?'

# 16

After reading Jimmy's letter, Tess had marched from the pigeonholes directly to Garvey's office, convinced she was going to persuade the head of department to take her friend back onto the course.

All the necessary arguments ran through her mind. She would overwhelm Garvey with them swiftly, leave him no room to refuse. She stamped in without knocking, stood opposite him. And language deserted her.

For nearly a minute he looked up at her from behind his desk, seemingly untroubled by this silence, willing to let it continue forever if necessary. All her sense of advantage ebbed away. Now she could only think of the insult Garvey had once, long ago, levelled at Penelope. It had no bearing on why she was here, but all she could do was say it anyway.

'You once called my housemate a talentless – sapphist.'

His evident amusement at this declaration caused his eyepatch to lift slightly. Tess thought she saw some scarring just below its edges.

'Who is this housemate of yours?' he said.

'Penelope Hoxworth. You taught her at the Slade.'

'Can't recall the name, sorry. It's two years since I left the Slade, though.' His tone was disconcertingly kind. 'Now why not take a seat and tell me what you actually want to discuss?'

'It's about Jimmy Nichols. He's gone home because of an illness. Look, this is completely private—' Still unable to think of a way to explain, she handed him Jimmy's letter. He read it twice, gave it back and watched her replace it in the envelope.

'How long has he been missing from classes?' he said.

'Just over three weeks.'

'In that case, Mr Newbolt will have been in touch with him to say he's no longer to consider himself a Moncourt student.' Before Tess could interrupt him, he raised a hand and said, 'Don't worry, you can tell Nichols to ignore it. We send those letters to frighten idlers out of their beds and back to college, that's all. It's not as if we're going to draw a line through his name on the register.'

'So if I can get Jimmy to come back, he'll still be on the course?'

'His final project's the only thing that counts. As long as he hands something in for that, he'll pass the first year. Shouldn't be too difficult. The standard isn't all that high.'

Tess's relief was mixed with disappointment. She'd expected a fight, not this easy accommodation. And presented with a standard that *wasn't all that high* she would almost have preferred Jimmy to have been thrown out. 'I'll let him know,' she said.

'Nichols is one of our most gifted first-year students, after all,' Garvey said. 'I'd be sorry to see him drop out. Why not tell him *that*? If it'll help, you can suggest I've made a special effort to challenge nasty Mr Newbolt on his behalf.'

'Thank you.'

'It's come back to me,' he said as she stood up to leave. 'I do recall your friend from when I taught at the Slade. Quite a distinctively dressed person?'

'That's Penny – Penelope – yes.'

'Although sapphist seems a bit mealy mouthed for me. Was the word I used not *bulldyker*?'

Tess nodded.

'Then, yes, you're right. I did say that. I don't understand why she should be so upset about it, though.'

'I suppose, for a start, because she isn't one.'

'A sapphist, you mean? Isn't she? Well, that was a misapprehension on my part. Understandable, though, wouldn't you say? She certainly liked to create the impression she was giving it a try.' He gave Tess a sly look. 'I notice you haven't challenged my calling her talentless.'

'I doubt she'd have got into the Slade if she had no talent.'

'That's an assumption I could easily disprove. But fine, I'll admit she's neither a bulldyker nor completely talentless. You know, it's all the same thing, Theresa. Take you, for example: you're unusually talented, but that's nothing to be proud of. It's in your genes or your upbringing – you didn't make yourself that way through virtue. Equally, your friend the non-bulldyker isn't so talented, but that's no reason for her to feel ashamed.'

'She isn't ashamed,' Tess said. 'Just the opposite, in fact.'

'Good for her. Talentless or talented, attracted to women, attracted to men. These are just ways a person *is*. Just descriptions – like tall, short, ugly, pretty, cheerful, miserable. You can't be insulted by facts, can you?'

'I suppose not.' Tess saw how impressed he was with himself. He was already weighing the idea's potential, storing it for later expansion into some television lecture or book chapter.

'Even so,' he said, 'do pass on my apologies, won't you? Tell her if I had the time again, I'd describe her accurately. As a heterosexual woman with a modicum of artistic ability.'

'Perhaps I will,' she said. Though she was certain Penelope would rather stick with the *talentless bulldyker* version than let go of a useful anecdote.

The next day, at about the time Delia was arriving at the house in Camden, Tess's train pulled into Trencham. Like Delia, she had started her journey with no idea how it would end. Now, overnight bag in hand, she stepped out of the railway station into the gloomy streets of a Kent mining village, and she felt no uncertainty, only relief.

It took her half an hour, and several requests for directions, to find the place: number 130 in a terrace of tiny houses that continued to 200 at least. Jimmy's father answered the door, and brought her into the room he called the parlour. Tess could see no obvious similarity between this slight, courteous man and his larger, pricklier son. Perhaps Jimmy took after his mother, she thought.

'Jim's down in his shed. I'll go fetch him. Take yourself a seat.' Mr Nichols paused by the door before he left, scrutinising this young woman whose arrival, she could see, had baffled him a little.

'What was the name again?'

'Theresa Green. Tess.'

'And he isn't expecting you?'

'No.'

'Won't be a minute, then, Miss Green.'

All year she'd believed her own ordinariness had prevented her from fitting in at middle-class Moncourt. Here in Mr Nichols' parlour, she wondered if she'd ever really known what 'ordinary' was.

Her parents' home in Dewsbury had no parlour, but both a living room and a lounge instead. Asked what the difference was, her father would invariably reply, 'Simple. The lounge is where we lounge around; the living room's where we show people what kind of a living I make.' This remark, which had started out as a joke had, over the years, calcified into simple fact. By contrast with the soft, homely lounge, the living room was self-consciously formal. Its stiff chairs were upholstered in slippery leather; its bookcases were full of unread hardbacks; it contained no television set. The living room was only for visitors, which meant not friends or close relatives, but another grade of person – distant aunts, colleagues from her father's work, members of her school's parent-teacher association. It was where these visitors came to share stilted small talk over scones and tea served on the good china. As a child, Tess had dreaded being called into there, to show her pictures or talk about her glowing reports, or to reprise unaccompanied the song she had sung at the Christmas Concert.

In its way Mr Nichols' parlour was formal too, but Tess liked it better. There was a generous melancholy in its hulking old coffinwood furniture; in the way its tiny, net-curtained windows kept the room embalmed in permanent evening, warmed by the glow from the coal fire. Mr Nichols must have been listening to the Light Programme when she had knocked. He had lowered the volume on the antique wireless so that the announcer's voice still churned away, almost inaudible and treacle-brown as the patina on the sideboard. Every surface bore its cargo of silver-framed photographs – not grinning Kodak snaps like those that littered her parents' house, but stiff-backed studio portraits going back three or four generations.

She got up to inspect the photos on the mantelpiece more closely, looking for evidence of genealogy, trying to spot Jimmy's features in the solemn faces of his Sunday-best ancestors. A wedding picture caught her eye – young Mr Nichols with a full head of hair back then. Neither the dressmaker nor the photographer had been unable to disguise the bride's pregnancy.

Tess spotted a much older portrait. *Here you are*, she thought. Because the man in this photograph might have been Jimmy himself, trying on the fashions of half a century ago – a moustache, a checked cloth cap, a high single collar, a three-piece suit and a watch chain. Was it only that the features were similar, she wondered, or could she see the same critical eye peering warily at the camera? The same discomfort in the world? The same capacity for self-damage? She thought she could.

'That's my great uncle Terence. Dad's father's brother. One of our family's famous lifelong bachelors.'

She turned around. Jimmy looked well, standing next to his father. Better than she had anticipated, though he obviously hadn't been for a haircut or used a comb in a while. Nor had he ironed any of his clothes. He came past her and picked up the photograph she'd been looking at.

'Poor bugger took a bullet in the face at Verdun when he was thirty-five. Didn't kill him, but it left a nasty mess. I suppose he wasn't so marriageable after that, even if he'd wanted to be. Looks kind of like me in this picture, doesn't he? Everyone's always saying so. And he had the old family curse too.'

'Ain't no curse,' Mr Nichols added quickly. 'Terry was a lovely feller. Nobody round here had a word to say against him. How a bloke is – you can't blame him for that.'

Jimmy kissed the top of his father's bald head. 'Dad's taken to defending me against everyone. Myself especially.'

Mr Nichols blushed as he lowered himself onto the settee. 'My missus is passed on, and I've only got the one son. Don't see no use driving him away. Would you mind turning my wireless up, Theresa?'

'What Dad means,' Jimmy explained, 'is "would you two kindly go somewhere else, and leave me in peace to listen to *Dick Barton, Special Agent*?"'

'No I don't,' Mr Nichols said. 'That hasn't been on for years. It's *Send for Paul Temple*, if you want to know.'

They walked out to Jimmy's shed at the end of the back garden. He was carrying a paint-spattered old dining chair he'd rescued from the under-stairs cupboard, and he kept up a steady stream of information with a buoyancy Tess didn't entirely trust.

'The coal company built these streets. This whole village, really, for miners to live in. All the houses have vegetable gardens, and everyone got a shed, for potting out and so on.'

Looking up and down the row of gardens Tess saw there was a similar squat brick building right at the end of each. 'Potting out?' she said. 'What's that?'

Jimmy laughed. 'No idea. Anyway, Mum and Dad let me have this one right from when I was a kid. They must have realised my need for a hideout was greater than Dad's. I never told them how rough it was at school, but—'

'I got your letter,' Tess interrupted. 'It was in my pigeonhole for three weeks before I found it.'

He opened the door. 'Here we are. It'll be a bit cold right now, but I've got my Aladdin.'

Whoever had furnished the interior of Jimmy's shed had not been a carpenter. He (Tess assumed it must have been a man) had taken assorted roughly sawn hunks of wood and grafted them onto what looked like old kitchen cupboards to form inelegant shelves and work surfaces, all painted the same powdery duck egg blue.

The shelves were covered in junk: souvenir figures made of glued-together seashells; toy cars; a broken piggy bank. Around the walls, Jimmy had pinned perhaps forty pages from a child's colouring book. All the pictures showed cartoons of animals behaving like humans. Rabbits in tweed jackets carried wicker baskets of vegetables; a cat and a donkey in trilby hats played cards; a dog as a cobbler, hammered nails into the sole of a boot. All these images had been meticulously and correctly coloured-in. Blue skies, green grass, yellow daffodils. The clothing and fur or feathers of each character was of a sensible shade. They seemed recently done.

Jimmy set down the paint-spattered chair next to a similar one that was already in there. They each took a seat. There was a triangular paraffin heater on the floor. He leant forward to light it.

'This is my Aladdin,' he said, holding a match against the wick. The small yellow flame metamorphosed into a larger blue one, and the shed filled with a camphorated burning smell. 'It's good to see you, Tess. I wondered if you'd written me off as a bad job.' He picked up a puppet from one of the shelves – a boxer, scarred and crop-haired, mounted on the end of a stick. 'Do you remember that doorman from the Gaudi Club? The one who saved Marius from having to fight me? Could be him, couldn't it?' He pulled a trigger at the bottom of the stick to make the puppet throw a left then a right. 'Two peas in a pod. Like me and Great Uncle Terence.'

'Are you coming back to Moncourt, Jimmy?'

Another left, another right. 'Pity I don't know that doorman's name. I've had to call this bloke Biffer.'

She waited for an answer.

'Let's not talk about Moncourt,' he said.

'Haven't you done enough not talking, Jimmy? Isn't that why you're in this state?'

'Well, I'm not in a state now. And if you remember, it was telling someone how I felt that got me in trouble in the first place.'

'Nonsense. You said it yourself. That doctor gave you a scare, but there was never any real danger he'd lock you up, was there?'

Jimmy held the mechanical boxer up so it was facing him. 'You hear that, Biffer? She's turned my own words against me.' He pulled the trigger again and the toy landed a punch on his nose. 'Technical knockout!'

'So?'

'All that's academic, Tess. It's not my choice to make.' He put down the puppet and picked up a sheet of typed foolscap from another shelf. 'This is a letter from that awful Newbolt man. Due to my long period of unexplained absence, blah, blah, blah.'

'I know about that. It doesn't matter.'

'Of course it matters. They've thrown me out, Tess.'

'No. They haven't. I went to see Benedict Garvey. He says you can have as long off as you need. As long as you submit a final piece, you'll qualify for the second year.'

'Why would Benedict Garvey decide to be so generous? What did you tell him?'

He was suspicious, ready to be angry. If she didn't handle the next few minutes correctly, she thought, she'd lose him. 'I explained you'd gone home because you were ill,' she said. 'I'm sorry if that was breaching a confidence, I didn't know what else to do.'

'You told him I was ill? That's all?'

'Obviously, he realised you hadn't gone off with a bout of measles. He's not stupid. But he didn't ask for details about what was wrong.' Hoping Jimmy wouldn't notice she hadn't exactly answered his question, she continued, 'I'm to let you know you're to ignore any letter you might have received from Mr Newbolt. Garvey told me you're one of the most gifted artists this year. He'd prefer to keep you at Moncourt if he can.'

'Bloody hell,' Jimmy murmured.

That did it. He'd come back now for sure.

Later Jimmy suggested they go for a walk. The sun was almost down when they left the house.

'It's a bit of a risk, letting myself be seen around,' he said. 'But you'll protect me, won't you Tess?'

There was a council playground in the centre of the village green – a climbing frame, some swings and a roundabout – around which a cluster of children were playing tag. A girl of nine or so spotted Jimmy, and her clear, high voice sang out across the dusk.

'Nine-bob Mary!'

'Here we go,' Jimmy said, as the other kids picked up the song. Its tune was vaguely familiar, a variant on some simple folk melody.

*'Don't bend down when Mary's around,*
*Or you'll get a nine-bob SAUSAGE UP YOUR BUM!'*

After their final rhythmic flourish, the children scattered into the growing darkness, giggling excitedly.

'They probably have no idea what any of that means,' Tess said.

She and Jimmy walked over to the freshly vacated playground. She sat on the teapot-lid roundabout and he spun it for her, timing his pushes to build up her momentum.

'Actually, I'm not sure what it means either,' she said after she'd been round the third time. 'Why *nine bob*?'

'From the common simile "queer as a nine-bob note". Witty, isn't it? A girl in my class called Freda Mason wrote that song especially for me. It had twelve verses originally – most people only know the chorus now, though.'

Tess gripped the bar tight, pushed herself inwards, opposing the centrifugal force. Something in her belly tingled with a kind of pleasure she hadn't felt since childhood.

'Twelve verses. That's a lot of work,' she said.

'Isn't it? I saw her recently, bumped into her in the village shop. She was completely nice about it. Said she'd just enjoyed fitting the words together and finding all the rhymes. She writes poetry now, dreadful stuff, once a week for the local paper. She did one about me, by way of apology.'

Still keeping the roundabout going, he recited the poem to her. Each line was a rotation, each first stressed syllable marked with a push.

'We *bull*ied you and made you cry.
Now *I* am older and I wonder why

## Finer Things

Young *chil*dren do such dreadful things
To *clip* each other's growing wings
When *all* we all desire is to fly?
I *hope* now you are free and bold as I.'

He stopped pushing, let the roundabout slow down.

'God,' Tess said. 'That really is poor.'

'She's made her mark, though. I reckon the kids of this village are going to be singing *Nine-Bob Sausage* at each other for generations, long after Freda and I are both forgotten.'

Tess stepped off the roundabout while it was still turning, misjudged its speed and stumbled into Jimmy. Instinctively he caught her around the waist. Before he could let go of her, she landed a kiss on his cheek. He released his grip and stepped back. Darkness had fallen, and the moon was lost behind the clouds. There were no street lights here, only the glow from the windows of a jumble of village houses around the green. In the distance, the pub had come to life, and above the noise from within, the cracked sound of an old woman's singing drifted faintly to them.

*Fresh aaaare the dayeezeezzz, I've cuuuulled from the gaaaaaarden* . . .

They walked on in silence. The kiss had been an error, a transgression. Tess had meant it as a gesture of friendly solidarity, but she had tasted a teardrop on his cheek.

Outside the pub door two male shapes were pushing each other around, halfway between playfulness and a fight. There was a crash of breaking glass. Someone called Joe was a stupid cunt, and fucking owed someone else another fucking beer. Joe was sorry, but it had been an accident, and someone called Denny needed to watch his fucking mouth.

'Let's not go by there,' Jimmy said. He turned and vanished into the black space between two cottages. Tess followed him into a lightless alleyway. Although she could see nothing at all, she heard him striding ahead with native confidence, and, assuming that must mean it was safe, she made her own way forwards. There was no path here. Underfoot it was soft and slippery, with the damp-mud odour of ground that never quite dried out. Soon her eyes acclimatised to what had at first seemed like a uniform darkness, and she began to make out vague shapes – just in time to avoid walking into the side of a coal bunker. The alleyway ahead of her opened out into a brighter space, lit by a thin wash of moonlight from behind the clouds. She saw a narrow path with a low hedgerow running along one side, and fields rising into the hills beyond. Jimmy was waiting for her.

'If either of those two had spotted me they'd've put their differences to one side while they kicked my head in,' he said. 'Hope you don't think less of me for avoiding them.'

It seemed the problem of the kiss had passed now. They would just not mention it again, and that would be fine. A flight of ducks passed high overhead, breaking the quiet with chaotic quacks and wingbeats.

'I was wondering about all those colouring-in pictures,' she said.

'Oh yes. I'm rather proud of all those. Just after I came back, I found the book lying around at my aunt's house. It belonged to her daughter, my cousin. She'd had a half-hearted try at the first picture, then got bored with the whole idea. So I borrowed it. I thought it would be soothing for me. Then it got to be a bit of a habit.'

He set off along the path, and she walked with him.

'And have you done any actual work, Jimmy? Any painting or drawing of your own?'

'Honestly, I've been afraid to let my imagination off the leash. Safer just keeping inside the lines, you know? And actually I'm beginning to think there might be something more I can do with those pictures.' There was a gap in the hedge. He led her through it onto a scrubby field. 'Look how far you can see, even in the dark. That's something I missed when I was in the city.'

She followed his gaze, past a glum-looking pony tethered to a fence, beyond which she saw hills beyond hills, rising away and darkening in the distance so she couldn't quite make out where the land finished and the sky began. 'It's the same in Yorkshire,' she said. The air was cold here, out of the shelter of the path. It occurred to her that maybe the kiss had meant more to her than she'd realised. She moved closer to Jimmy.

'Tess,' he muttered. 'You know I'm not—'

She was quietly insistent. 'We're friends, though, aren't we – best friends?'

He pulled away from her. Even in the dim light, the outrage was evident in his face. 'What are you up to, Tess? Christ! You don't honestly think all I need to set me right is a *woman*, do you?'

She turned and strode away across the field. She had no idea where she was going; the ground here was uneven, rutted by tractor wheels, and she couldn't move over it nearly as fast as she would have liked. As she picked her way from trough to peak, she yelled back, 'Why do you imagine everything's always about *you*, Jimmy Nichols?'

By the wall at the far side, she could see a rough shelter, built so farmworkers could hide from the worst of the weather. By the time she reached it Jimmy had caught up with her.

'All right,' he said. 'If that's what you want. I've no idea why, though.'

He was cross, defensive and fragile. If it were to happen now it would be awful, just another step in an argument. What on earth had she been thinking of? She looked around at the hard, chilly stone of the shelter, smelled its old animal stink, and thought of her long-abandoned fantasy: the sleeping poet, the attic room. Such romanticism was far behind her now. Even so, this wouldn't do. She was ashamed of herself for having thought of it.

'Let's go back to the house,' she said. Then, seeing his reaction, she added hurriedly, 'Oh, not for *that*. I was just being silly. It's getting cold out here, that's all.'

They talked about other things on the way home, to put what had almost happened behind them. Tess told Jimmy about how Penny (Penelope now) had changed. He wasn't surprised. When they got back inside, she went to the kitchen to pour herself a glass of water and Jimmy found his father in the parlour, sitting upright on the settee, fast asleep. The BBC having long since finished for the night, the wireless now hissed quietly away to itself. Gently, he touched the old man's shoulder.

'I was worried,' Dad said, when he woke up. 'I didn't know where you'd gone.'

'We took a walk around the village and down by the backs.'

'Any trouble?'

'Kids on the green taking the mickey, that's all. And Joe and Denny Briggs were laying into each other outside the Star. Seemed sensible to keep out of their way.'

Tess came back into the parlour. Dad looked around at her. 'Well, Miss. Have you persuaded my son to go back to your college?'

'I hope so, Mr Nichols. It's where he ought to be.'

'I think I will,' Jimmy said. 'Not straight away, though. I'm not quite ready yet. But Tess says they'll take me back.'

He gave her his bedroom, and said he would sleep in the parlour. His father gave him a pair of stale-smelling blankets, still warm from the airing cupboard where they had been stored. Once he was left alone, he sat with a book for an hour, until the fire was nearly dead and, finding himself in the middle of the same paragraph for the eighth time, finally conceded it was time for sleep. The settee was too short to let him stretch out comfortably, so he laid its cushions on the floor in front of the hearth, with one of the blankets rolled into a pad between them. This made a bed that almost matched his outstretched body length, and the remaining blanket seemed to be just about enough to keep him warm.

For a couple of hours he slipped back and forth between violent dreams and bouts of wakefulness. Then an animal howl startled him out of all possibility of sleep. His watch said it was two in the morning. He lay on his back, fully conscious, listening, trying to determine whether the howl had come from outside the house or inside a dream, and gradually he recognised the sharp cold of the air around him. His own breath, hot in his nostrils and across his lips, told him how far the temperature had dropped. The fire was out completely. Returning to sleep in these conditions would be impossible.

He decided to fetch his paraffin heater from the shed. He got up, went out into the hallway and switched on the light. His dead mother was sitting on the stairs wearing her pink candlewick dressing gown. Presumably, then, he was still asleep after all, still dreaming.

'I heard something screeching outside the house,' Mother said. 'It woke me up.'

'Foxes most likely,' he said. 'I heard it too. But I've barely slept at all – it's absolutely frozen in there. I was just going out for my Aladdin.'

'I suppose this must have been your mum's,' said his mother – who was, he saw now, Tess.

He was awake after all. 'It didn't half give me a jump seeing you in it,' he told her, and he went off to the shed to get the heater.

When he came back, Tess was in the parlour, sitting on the makeshift bed. She had put on a jumper borrowed from one of his bedroom drawers.

'Sorry about the dressing gown,' she said. 'I found it on a hook behind the bathroom door. I've hung it back up there now.'

'It doesn't matter. I just forgot she was dead for a moment. Funny, Dad having kept it there all this time. I never really thought about that until now. I'd just stopped seeing it.' He set a match to the heater. His skin tingled with pleasure at the immediate blast of warmth.

Beneath her borrowed jumper, Tess's nightdress formed a flimsy kind of skirt. Her pale, thin legs stuck out in front of her. She reached forward with both hands to rub her bare feet. Her toes, he noticed, were turning a little blue from the cold. They were long and slender, almost apelike. It occurred to him that he had never seen them before. She looked up at him, top-heavy in the thick, black sweater, and that was when they both knew he could do it after all, the thing she'd wanted from him.

'It'll only be this once,' he said.

'I know. That's all I need.'

He'd thought things might be difficult afterwards, uncomfortable. But he and Tess lay in each other's arms and they talked more easily and more honestly than they had in months. She told him about her visit to the Woodrows' house.

'You kept them secret from me,' she said.

'Not at all. I just didn't say much, and you didn't ask much.'

'I like them.'

Her hair tickled his shoulder. He brushed it away. 'Charlie's difficult, of course, and Val's sadder about it than she lets on. Most of their old friends seem to stay away too. It's quite a lonely life for her.'

'She's worried about you, I think.'

'Maternal, isn't she, underneath? Even though they never wanted kids of their own. I suppose she's guessed—'

'About your disposition? Yes.'

'Everyone does.'

'*I* didn't. Not until you told me.'

'No.' It seemed wrong, given what had just happened between them, to say what he thought. But then she said it for him.

'Perhaps I had my own reasons for not noticing, though.'

They were quiet for a while, until he said, 'Did you mean it? Is once really enough?'

'Yes,' she said. 'Once with *you* is enough. I don't know how I'll feel about anyone else in future. It was just something I needed to do for now.'

'Well, I'm glad to have been of use.'

'Sorry. I hope it wasn't too awful.'

'Not at all. It was—' There really should be a better word than this, but there wasn't. 'It was nice. But I don't think you've cured my— Oh Christ!' he sat up in alarm what he'd suddenly realised. 'We didn't use any protection!'

She remained where she was, untroubled. He had a sense that she'd been wondering when this would finally occur to him.

'It's fine, Jimmy.'

'What a bloody idiot I am. I didn't even think of it.'

'Well, I suppose you don't, in your world. I did, though. We'll be fine.'

He wasn't entirely naïve about heterosexual practices. There was a pill women could take, he was sure, and other ways they could prepare themselves. It was a relief Tess had done something, even if it now seemed this was less of a spontaneous event for her than she'd led him to believe.

'You're certain?' He lay back down again.

'Yes.'

They slept for a while. Later, disentangling himself from her, he said, 'You'd better go back upstairs. Wouldn't want Dad finding us like this in the morning.'

# MARCH – MAY 1963

# 17

Tess stayed two more nights with Jimmy. They did not have sex again. There was no need. It had only been a sort of experiment after all, and they had found out everything they needed from it. On the third day, he walked with her to the station to say goodbye. He'd be back at Moncourt, he said, as soon as he felt ready.

She arrived in Camden at one o'clock. Putting down her bags in the hallway, she felt a strangeness about the house, as though she had been away for much longer. Objects appeared larger or smaller than she remembered, spaces lighter or darker, and she could smell a shared-house aroma, of which she was normally unaware: tinned stew and steamed fish; undusted surfaces; sinks nobody ever cleaned. Altogether, it pleased her to be here again.

Someone upstairs was playing a pop record. Or perhaps the sound was coming through the walls from next door. Of the four young women who shared the house, only Penelope owned a record player, given to her by her parents in a vain effort to encourage an interest in classical music. As far as Tess could tell, the sole record Penelope owned was a copy of Janáček's *Sinfonietta*, which she would play very loud when Marius was in her room. *Ba-ba-ba ba-ba baaa-baaa ba-ba ba-pa-baaa-ba-pa baaa-baaa ba-pa baaaa-baaaa* not always disguising the sounds of Marius's enthusiastic lovemaking.

Tess was about to climb the stairs when Penelope appeared above her, leaning over the bannister.

'Your friend from Fenfield's in your room. That's her music you can hear.'

It took Tess a moment to realise what that meant. 'Delia? Why?'

'She turned up the day you left. I thought she was obviously in some kind of trouble, so I told her she could have your bed until you came home. You don't mind, do you?'

'No, I—'

'Thought so. Of course you don't,' Penelope said, cheerfully imperious as ever. She retreated from the landing, and from the consequences of her own actions, to vanish back into her room.

Tess left her bags in the hall and headed upstairs. The music coming through her bedroom door was interesting. She liked the way its melody jerked by turns from maudlin waltz to bombastic common time. For a minute, she stood outside, wondering what she was going to say when she went in, considering whether she ought to knock first. And actually, she thought, she *did* mind. This was typical of Penelope – to presume on behalf of someone else, when Delia wasn't even someone she knew all that well.

She opened the door quietly. Inside she found Delia lying on the bed, eyes closed, apparently unaware that she was no longer alone. There was an open suitcase on the floor, half-full of clothes, and on the desk a blue Dansette record player, the source of the music.

The singer crooned something about 'the honey and you', then the song ended. The Dansette's needle crackled its way across empty vinyl for a few seconds before a mouth organ and two harmonising voices burst in. This new piece sounded jollier than the previous one, though as usual in pop songs, the chirpiness of the music belied the desolation in the words, which were all about escaping the misery of the real world into the false comforts of memory and imagination.

Delia opened her eyes, saw that Tess had arrived and sat up. Serenely, as if there were nothing at all unusual going on here, she reached across to stop the record.

'I bought the Dansette yesterday, and the man in the shop threw in a few LPs for free. I like this one best. It's the Beatles.'

'I've heard of them,' Tess said, noncommittally. She still wasn't sure how to deal with the reappearance of this woman, whom she had come to consider no more than a slightly dissatisfying episode, just another example of this year's relentless string of failures and almosts.

Delia ruffled her own hair in the manner of a person who had just woken up. 'The record player's a present for you, to say thanks for the room. I know you didn't exactly *choose* to let me stay, but I'm grateful.' She told Tess the whole story. About Stella and Finlay. About what had happened with Bill Shearsby. How she had arrived in Camden. 'That Penelope's nicer than she seems, isn't she? After she let me in, I just dragged my suitcase upstairs, fell on the bed, and that was me till lunchtime the next day. I don't think I've slept as well as that for years.'

Tess felt ashamed of her self-absorption, of having again seen everything through the lens of her own petty feelings. Delia had been in serious trouble, had arrived at her door broken and exhausted, and Penelope – selfish, superficial Penelope – had been there to take care of her; had done the decent thing.

'I'm sure we can work something out if you need to stay longer.'

Delia got up from the bed and knelt down to close the suitcase on the floor. 'Thanks, but I'm sorted out now. I've found myself a bedsit a couple of streets away from here. Unfurnished, so I've been shopping in Camden this morning – real shopping, with money, don't worry – all the hoisting's over for me now. I've got a proper job too. Barmaid in a pub in Chalk

Farm – near that big old train shed they're turning into a theatre.'

'Things can change so quickly,' Tess said. 'It's hard to make sense of it sometimes.'

'You have to find your luck, that's all. Mine's been off for a while, but I think I've got it back now.' She snapped down the catches on the suitcase. 'I'll need to get going. My new furniture's arriving at three. I only wanted to wait here until you got home – explain things and say thank you. How did your trip go? Kent, wasn't it?'

Briefly, Tess considered telling Delia everything. But she decided there had been enough narrative for one afternoon.

'It was good to see Jimmy,' she said. 'He's had a hard time too. He's better now. I think he'll be back quite soon.'

The next day, on her way home from Moncourt, she stopped by the Woodrows' house. When she arrived at the gate she found Val struggling to push a battered old rotary mower around the lawn.

'I can't find anyone to sharpen this thing,' Val said. 'There used to be an old man who came by once a year, but I haven't seen him since fifty-eight. I suppose he must be dead. Don't forget to shut the gate on your way in, or you'll have Charlie panicking about his imaginary dog getting out.'

Uncertain she wanted to accept such an ambiguous invitation, Tess stayed where she was.

'I came because I thought you might like to know I've been to see Jimmy.'

'I've been making lemonade. It's sour, but you're welcome to a glass.'

In the end, it was more than a month before Jimmy returned. He decided it would be easiest to come back when nearly everyone was away. Tess was staying over Easter to catch up too. Moncourt was still open. They could use the studio to work on their end-of-year projects, due three weeks after the end of the holidays. And so, on the first morning of the break, he boarded the bus three stops after her and came to sit next to her, just as he always had before. He looked thinner, physically flimsier than when she had last seen him in Kent. The bus's rough suspension was no match for the uneven roads and he held his sketchbook close to his body all the way to Moncourt, as if afraid the juddering might bounce it out of his hands.

'Do your folks mind you not going home for the holidays?' he asked. It sounded clumsy to her, like he was making prepared conversation. He was unsettled, of course, nervous about returning to Moncourt. She supposed they'd have to get him through that together.

'They're quite upset. I've had some difficult phone calls with them – well, with my mother. Dad doesn't really talk about it. Mum can't see why I should want to hang around London when I could be in Dewsbury.' She caught herself on the verge of an unkind remark then, but held back from it, saying instead, 'It's understandable. Mum doesn't like big cities.'

An elderly caretaker sat just inside the college entrance, apparently making sure nobody would wander in who wasn't meant to. As Jimmy and Tess entered the building, he gave them a nod that looked like recognition, though neither of them could recall having ever encountered him before.

This was the first time Tess had ever been in the college during the holidays. The quietness seemed quite natural to her, like something homeless had been waiting for this opportunity to come inside. A few other students were still around, drawing or painting or sculpting in sparse rooms. They too needed to catch up on losses from term time, she supposed – or perhaps they simply had nowhere else to go. Here and there, members of teaching and administrative staff sought to occupy themselves despite the absence of anyone to teach or much to administer.

It had occurred to her that Roger Dunbar might not have gone away for the break, given his home circumstances, but to her relief, it seemed he was not here today at least. When they arrived at the first-year studio, they found it empty.

Jimmy was briskly practical. He collected a couple of easels and set them up next to each other in his usual spot. Onto one he tacked a sheet of heavy cartridge paper, onto the other a set of photographs cut out from magazines and newspapers. He opened his sketchbook and laid it on the floor. Then he fetched himself a chair.

'Do you paint sitting down now?' Tess said. He had always stood at his easel before, moving his brush with broad, confident strokes from the elbow or the shoulder.

'I'm not painting, I'm drawing. And I've given up all that sloppiness I used to go in for. No more splashing around for me. I've been practising – you should be impressed.'

He took an HH pencil and began laying down lines with a meticulousness she had never seen in him before. As he worked, he glanced restlessly between the photographs on the second easel and his sketches on the floor.

'I don't understand what you're doing,' Tess said. She could discern no relationship between his pictures in the sketchbook and the images in the photographs.

'You'll see,' he said. 'Why don't you get on with yours?'

She rifled through the pile of studies she had made during the last month. Since Delia had set up in Camden, they had spent a lot of time together, and Tess had sketched her a great deal. The pictures were fine, she thought. At least none of them were actually bad. This one of Delia pulling pints at the Enterprise had potential. There was life and activity in it, like a Degas sketch. Maybe she could develop the idea into a painting. She set up a canvas and started laying out the main shapes in charcoal.

As usual, she lost faith in the picture as soon as she started it, but she kept going anyway. They had been working quietly for over half an hour when Jimmy said, lightly, as if bringing up something entirely inconsequential, 'Val Woodrow mentioned you'd been around to the house a few times.'

Tess knew where this would lead. It seemed important to get there by making him ask properly, not just allowing him the ease of implication.

'That's right.'

'Friends with her now, are you?'

'I suppose so. Yes.'

After a few minutes more he said, 'I got the idea she might know something about – when you came to Trencham.'

'Really? Did she say something?'

'Nothing direct. But the way she spoke about you seemed – well it's hard to put my finger on it actually. I just felt like she knew more than she was telling me.' He became absorbed for a time in outlining a new figure, then he put down his pencil. 'What I'm asking is, have you told Val about what we did?'

'Yes.'

She looked at the work they had each produced so far that morning. In bold, black outline, Jimmy had drawn cartoon ducks with machine guns and armoured cars opening fire on a terrified crowd of squirrels. It was the Sharpeville massacre in the style of one of his colouring-book images. 'That's really good,' she said. 'It's so horrible and distressing. Mine isn't going very well, though, and there's something I need to talk about. Can we take a break?'

Ginelli's was half-full when they arrived, and the old woman was running the place alone. They sat at the same table where she had first met Penelope. How long ago that day seemed now, she thought, but had only been nine months previously. While they waited for the old woman to bring their coffee, Tess told Jimmy the thing she had so far only told Val Woodrow.

He seemed surprisingly calm. 'It's probably a stupid question, but if you don't mind me asking,' he said, 'are you sure?'

'I'm sure I'm pregnant, yes. Or do you mean, am I sure it's yours? Yes to that too.'

'It's just – I thought you were using some sort of contraception.'

'The pill, you mean? Only married women can get that. And it wasn't as if I'd gone out to Trencham with a plan. It just happened.'

'But I asked about it, didn't I? Afterwards. You said you were sure we were safe.'

'I thought we were.' She knew how stupid she had been, to believe the nonsense other girls at school used to say, but there it was. 'I'd just finished my period,' she said. 'And it was my first time. It turns out neither of those things is any kind of a guarantee.'

'What bad luck – for both of us, I mean,' he added hastily, as if he was afraid she might think he was trying to escape responsibility.

'Jimmy, you don't need to—'

Tess was interrupted by the arrival of the old woman, who seemed slower now, and moved with jagged discomfort. Her hands shook as she lowered the tall aluminium pot to the table, causing its lid to rattle and some of the coffee to slop over the sides.

'Can't carry everything all at once no more,' she said, and set off to fetch their cups from the counter. Tess and Jimmy continued to sit in silence, not quite looking at each other, while the old woman made a third laborious journey for the milk and sugar. This time, before she left them, she peered at Tess.

'I remember you. You came in here to change your clothes.'

'Oh yes. That's right.' Tess turned to Jimmy. 'When I came up for my Moncourt interview I wasn't dressed right. This lady let me use the loo in the cafe to put on my interview stuff.' To the old woman, she said, 'It worked. I got into the college.'

Evidently deciding no further comment was required, the old woman turned her attention to another table.

Tess was glad she had told Jimmy. At first she had thought she would find an abortionist, deal with it herself, perhaps with Val's help or Penelope's. Now she knew she was going to have it, there would be a child who was his too – whose father he would be, to whatever extent he might want.

'I'll have to leave the course, obviously,' she told him. Saying it saddened her inexplicably. A month ago, she'd wanted to abandon Moncourt. Why should she feel such regret about it now? It was only nostalgia, she supposed, brought out by their being in Ginelli's, at the same table where only a few months previously she'd sat and hoped above anything in the world that Benedict Garvey would give her a place.

Jimmy's face had a way of dimpling just below the cheekbones when he was worried. 'Why would you do that?' he said. 'It's not as if they'd have any right to kick you out, as long as you get your final project done. And honestly, I doubt they'd especially want to. Anyway, you've just dragged me back to this place. I can't say I'm too happy about you deserting me here after that.'

'It wouldn't be practical to stay. I'll need to earn a living. I'll have to look after the kid.'

'Don't rush,' he said. 'We can think about what we're going to do.'

He told her what that meant two days later, in the garden at the Woodrows'. Val, with whom, no doubt, he had prepared his strategy, had brought them some of her revolting lemonade and then gone off pointedly to take Charlie for a walk.

'Don't be an idiot,' Tess replied once he'd made his suggestion.

He pressed on. 'I thought of offering as soon as you told me about the baby, but I wanted to be certain it was a sensible idea. I've thought it through, Tess. Obviously, I couldn't be a typical husband, but I do want to try to be a good father.'

'I don't know, Jimmy. Maybe I *want* a typical husband.' She didn't, and was fairly sure he knew that, but it appeared they had entered some kind of negotiation.

'We could have a decent life, look after the baby together,' he said. 'I can get work in the evenings and at weekends. Maybe we can both sell some of our art. You'd be able to stay on at Moncourt.'

'Why would we need to be married for that?'

'We wouldn't, but it would make things easier in all sorts of practical ways. And we do love each other.'

'Except I suppose you'd still— that there would still be men? And you and I wouldn't—'

'Does that matter?'

A little, perhaps, she thought, but not enough to be a problem.

All she had to do, he reminded her, was pass, to progress into the second year. Her rough sketches and paintings were better than most of her contemporaries' finished work. She could easily throw together a collection of similarly themed pieces, allow herself this time to be merely good enough. She could be brilliant next year.

'Actually,' she said, 'I may have an idea for something better than that. Go on, then.'

'Does that mean you accept my proposal? Such as it is?'

'Such as it is, yes,' she said.

Jimmy had told his father right away, but Tess wanted to keep both the wedding and the baby secret from her parents; not forever, of course, but long enough to settle herself into the role of married young mother. The deception would be easy enough to handle, she said. Taking advantage of her mother's unwillingness to come to London, she could make any number of excuses to stay in the city while her pregnancy was visible. Maybe, when it came to it, they would never need to know. She could see Jimmy was unconvinced, but whatever misgivings he had, he kept to himself.

Val Woodrow, however, could be relied on to tell her outright that such behaviour was horribly selfish and would cause far more problems than it solved. In any case, she pointed out, there was the question of parental consent.

'You can wait until you're twenty-one to get married, or you can just get it over with,' Val said. 'Use our telephone if you like.'

Tess took a seat by the phone in the Woodrows' hallway. Four times she made it halfway through dialling the number and hung up. On the fifth attempt, she held her nerve. Her mother's response was not what Tess had expected.

'Will this young man make you happy, Theresa?' she said.

She was unsure how to reply. There would be no illusions in Jimmy and her being together. They would be honest and kind with each other. This would be sufficient.

None of that seemed like the kind of thing Mum would comprehend.

'I love him,' Tess said. 'Of course we wouldn't be doing this if I weren't pregnant, but it's what we both want.'

'Well, as long as you're sure.' There was a silence as her mother worked herself up to a delicate suggestion. 'You know there's other things you can do than getting wed, don't you? We've a fair bit of money put by for emergencies, if it's needed.'

This conversation had taken a quite different path from the one Tess had anticipated, and now she had the disconcerting impression that her mother had just offered to pay for an abortion. 'I'm certain, Mum,' she said. 'We'll just need a letter of permission from you and Dad, for the registrar. It'll be here in Camden. We've already put in our fifteen days' notice.' She didn't add that they had done so a week previously.

'It'll be in a registry office, will it? Of course it would have to be. I suppose you don't want your father and me to be there?'

The disappointment signalled that the crisis had been dealt with. Normal relations could be resumed. At last, here was a manoeuvre for which Tess had prepared herself. 'It's not going to be much of a ceremony,' she said. 'Just a bit of bureaucracy, really. So if you *are* going to come down to London, it would mean much more to me, to both of us actually, if you and Dad could be here for the end-of-year show at college. I'd love you to see my stuff and Jimmy's on display. I'm doing much more modern work now.'

Clever, she thought, after the call was over and her mother had promised to think about it. An art exhibition with *much more modern work* would be alien and unsettling to them, and they would most likely find some reason not to come.

Tess had miscalculated again. Her parents took her at her word and made arrangements to visit London for the whole week of the first-year exhibition. Dad booked the time off work. They would stay at the same bed and breakfast in Upper Norwood that Tess and her mother had used the night before her Moncourt interview. Their impending arrival was an uncomfortable prospect, but Tess supposed it had to happen sooner or later, and at least they could get the wedding out of the way beforehand.

Delia and Val had agreed to be witnesses. Jimmy wanted Professor Woodrow to be there, despite the old man's worsening condition, and Penelope's presence felt unexpectedly essential too. She was, as it turned out, a closer approximation to a good friend than Tess had thought. Unfortunately, asking her also necessitated inviting Marius, but he was no keener on being there than Tess and Jimmy were on having him, and pleaded a prior engagement.

The wedding took place on a nondescript Thursday afternoon. After meeting at the Woodrows' house, the six of them set off on foot towards Camden Register Office. They formed a peculiar group, and would have found little to say to each other had Professor Woodrow not been in such a talkative mood. All the way there he maintained an unbreakable stream of anecdotes about other weddings he had attended, holidays he had been on, famous people he had encountered. It didn't matter, Tess thought, that he never managed to get through more than half a story before drifting into a new one, or into one he had already told, or into the same one from the beginning again; at least his voice filled up what would otherwise be room for doubt. Doubt was not what she needed today.

They arrived half an hour before their appointment. On the road outside the register office, waiting for whoever was currently being married in there, was a vintage Rolls Royce.

'Isn't that pretty?' Penelope said. 'It's a Silver Ghost. From the twenties I should think.'

Tess was struck by the car's primitive glamour, by the way all its panels had so obviously been beaten into geometric shapes and fastened together with rivets. There was something magnificent about that, a kind of perfect *made-ness*. Its uniformed driver stood on the pavement by the front passenger door, enjoying his association with this beautiful machine. He seemed to believe that the car gave him status; that it belonged to him, rather than he to it. Normally, Jimmy would have had something to say about that, but he had been quiet ever since leaving the Woodrows'.

The just-married couple exited the building. They were almost as young as Tess and Jimmy. The bride wore a sharp-edged, off-white dress, and the groom had on a fashionably cut suit, with a round collar like the ones the Beatles favoured. Their two witnesses, gruff, thick-set men in overcoats, looked more like bodyguards than friends or relatives.

As soon as his passengers appeared, the driver switched from proud custodian to obsequious servant. He nipped around the Silver Ghost, opening doors for them all and gave a tiny bow to the couple as they stepped inside.

'Who were those two, I wonder?' Val said, watching the car drive off.

'Money,' Delia answered. 'Can't tell what sort though.'

'Old pal of mine had a Roller,' Professor Woodrow began. 'We used to motor around Essex in it with fishing rods stuck out the windows—'

'Hush, Charlie,' Val said.

Thinking she ought to give Jimmy a last chance to back out if he wanted it, Tess turned to him. 'How do you feel about this?'

'Fine,' he said. 'You?'

She considered her situation, this peculiar wedding party, and was reminded of something she'd recently discovered concerning Van Eyck's *Arnolfini Marriage* portrait. Tess had always assumed the bride in that painting was heavily pregnant, but apparently that was not the case. The young woman looked to modern eyes as if she was carrying a child only because of the way she held her dress. Just a misreading of fifteenth-century fashion.

For herself, Tess half wished she had waited until her pregnancy was properly, scandalously visible before arranging the ceremony. Otherwise, she had no regrets.

'I feel good about it.'

'I do too.'

They went in.

# 18

Delia stood on her old street, watching a tiny paperboy struggle with his bag of evening papers. She recognised him as the one she'd watched stealing lemon suckers from a jar at Jemima's that morning after Albie Chisholm got himself killed.

It was late on Saturday afternoon: two days after Tess and Jimmy's wedding and over eight weeks since Delia had dragged her suitcase out of Fenfield. If you'd asked her the day she left, she'd have said she'd never be back – but nothing was predictable, it seemed. At least the disruptions that had caused her departure looked to have abated now. She'd kept an eye on the papers for news of further violence or disappearances, and found none. It seemed like Stella had survived the whole Finlay business after all.

Even so, it was stupid of her to return, she knew that. As regards getting what she wanted, maybe it would be enough just to breathe this air, to feel these streets beneath her shoes. Probably not. Yes, she was moving on, and that was right, but for days the Imps had been scratching away at her, reminding her of what she had to lay to rest. Then, a week ago while she was serving behind the bar at the Enterprise, she had half thought she'd spotted Teddy Bilborough lurking in the crowd. That was when she'd decided she'd have to come back.

She headed for the newsagent's, where she found Little Maggie Chisholm sitting on the outside step reading a *Beezer*. There was a rusty brown line in the groove between the girl's nose and her mouth, and a few similarly coloured spots on the skirt of her grey dress: residues from an earlier nosebleed. She looked up at Delia with neither surprise nor interest.

'I thought your mum'd taken you to live by the seaside,' Delia said.

'That was ages ago,' Little Maggie replied. 'Weeks an' weeks. We went on holiday to Hunstanton with her. I didn't like it there much. Then Mr Finlay got out of hospital. He came to get Mum in his car, an' now we're staying with Auntie Jem again.'

'Mum too?' Delia reached into her bag for her purse. 'You want a sixpence, Maggie?'

'Ta,' the girl said, taking the money. 'Nah. Just me and me brothers.'

'Where's your mum now, then?'

'With Mr Finlay,' Little Maggie said placidly. 'Dunno where. She don't live round here no more.'

There was a *ting* from the bell above the shop door as it opened. Jemima stepped out and regarded Delia with suspicion.

'Thought that was your voice,' she said. 'What you doing back round here?'

'I've come to give Stella my keys back.'

'Shouldn't bother if I was you. She's let your place out already to some old brass. She'll have had the locks changed too, most likely.'

'Still, I ought to give them back,' Delia said.

In fact, she had posted her keys through the locked door the day she'd left but the lie had served its purpose. She knew now that Stella was still renting out her flats. That meant she must have found a way to survive the Finlay episode. And Finlay had run off somewhere to hide, taking Jemima's sister with him.

The newsagent turned her scowl on Little Maggie. 'Go upstairs and wash your face and hands, then find your brothers and tell them it's time to eat. What have you got in your hand?'

Reluctantly, the girl opened a grimy fist to reveal the sixpence. 'Delia gave it me,' she said.

'Give it back, Margaret,' Jemima told her. Little Maggie obeyed without complaint, returning the coin to Delia then squeezing past her aunt into the shop. Jemima remained where she was, barring the doorway.

'I was surprised to see Little Maggie here,' Delia said. 'Thought your sister'd taken her and her brothers away.'

'Yes, well. She came back. She's with Finlay again, and the kids are with me and Ern.'

'What about Stella's other girls?'

Jemima was clearly enjoying this chance to be the one on the inside of something for once, to be more than just a bystander. 'Ah, well. A lot of them made themselves scarce, just like you did. The only one who stayed was your little friend with the messed-up face. But none of them were gone more'n a few days. Lulu, Rita, Kathy, they all came back. Everyone did, apart from Itchy Pete and you. And we know why Pete stayed gone, don't we?'

In the unlikely event that Itchy Pete was still alive, he'd be trying his best to make sure he remained that way. Delia was perturbed to find her story lumped in with his. 'Nobody thinks I had anything to do with that, do they?'

'I don't know,' Jemima said. 'All I heard was that you were getting friendly with some funny people right before all this started. You don't want to hang around here, Dee. If I was you I'd get back sharpish wherever it is you're staying.'

Obviously, connections had been made in Delia's absence. Jemima was right: she would be wise to leave as quickly as she could.

'Listen, Jem,' she said. 'I just ran off after it happened 'cause I was scared, same as everyone else. But I've been worried about Maureen. She still living in the same place?'

Jemima nodded.

'I'll just pop round and talk to her for a few minutes, then I'll be on my way.'

Standing on the step above her, the shopkeeper was slightly taller than Delia, who now looked up at her, trying to turn this apparent position of weakness into an advantage.

'I shouldn't ask you to do this, but I shall. Don't mention I'm here, will you?'

'None of my business, is it?' Jemima said primly. 'You know I don't have anything to do with all that. If nobody asks me, I'll have no reason to tell anyone. I can't promise more'n that.'

She'd go running to the Lamplighters as soon as Delia was out of sight. No question.

When Delia got to the old flats, someone happened to be coming out of the street door onto Doddington Road. A scrawny, tired-looking old brass.

'Visiting a friend,' Delia said as she pushed past. A flicker of distrust crossed the brass's face, but she let Delia in unchallenged. Perhaps this was the woman who now lived in her old place. Maureen was inside, at the top of the stairs, her broken features full of anxiety.

'I saw you coming up the street,' she stage-whispered, beckoning urgently. 'Get in quick.'

Delia ascended quickly and quietly to Maureen's flat where, as soon as she had closed the door behind her, she found herself unexpectedly hugged.

'I'm so pleased to see you,' Maureen said once she'd released her. 'I thought you were never coming back. You oughtn't to be here, though. Rita and the rest have been saying you was working for them Krays all along. I never believed it, though.'

'What does Stella think about it all?'

'Dunno. She keeps it all to herself, don't she?'

'I think she might have sent Teddy out to where I work now, to check up on me or something.'

'Fucking Teddy. I hate that bloke. He's even worse now.'

Delia ought to say something about what Teddy had done to Maureen while he'd been delivering her to Kensington, but there wasn't time now. Someone would be on the way to get her.

'I'm sorry for what I said to you when I was leaving.'

'That's all right, Dee. I know you were just looking out for me. Thought I'd be in danger. It's been fine, though.'

There was a knock at the door, brisk and rhythmic.

'That'll be Tommy,' Delia said, 'come to take me over to see Stella.' Jemima must have got over there pretty fast, she thought. Maybe she'd had a phone installed at the shop.

'Jesus—'

'It'll be all right.' Delia wasn't sure that was true, but there was no running away from this. Before she went to let Tommy in, she said to Maureen, 'Come where we first met. Day after tomorrow. About ten in the morning. Only if you can. Don't put anything special on. Dress exactly like you are now.'

Tommy led her into the kitchen at the back of the Lamplighters. Things appeared to be just the same as always. There was a pot of tea on the table, two cups, a sugar bowl and a milk jug. Stella's smile was narrow and untrustworthy. Tommy left them there together. The boss (she was still that in Delia's mind) motioned to her to sit opposite.

'Why'd you run off, then, Delia?' she asked. There was no hint in her voice of how she might actually feel about it, or that she already knew the answer, but she couldn't have forgotten that last time in the bar of the Lamplighters, when she had been drunk and afraid. Back when it had looked like everything was coming apart.

'I was scared about the Richardsons and the Krays,' Delia said, picking her way carefully through the truth. 'Didn't know what was going to happen. Same as everyone else, far as I could tell.'

'Same as *nearly* everyone else, you mean. I didn't run, did I? Nor did Teddy or Tommy. Nor did your friend Maureen. So have you been with Bill Shearsby all this time?'

'Me and Bill are finished.'

'Oh yes. I think I heard about all that. Teddy says you're in Camden now, or thereabouts. Chalk Farm, maybe. Nice respectable barmaid at some pub. The Enterprise, isn't it?'

Delia nodded, unperturbed by the attempt to throw her off her guard, but the Imps told her that meant it *had* been Teddy that night, and coming back today had been the right decision, or at least it had been the only possible decision. Stella poured tea for them both, added milk and sugar to Delia's cup without asking. 'What's brought you back, Dee?'

She had prepared a story – a way of framing things that had enough truth in it not to be a lie, and yet would make sense in Stella's pragmatic, self-interested view of the world.

'I wanted to put things straight. I heard there's talk around here that I was involved in what happened to Finlay. So I've come to face you myself, let you know I had nothing to do with it.'

'Well, ain't that fucking *honourable*!' Stella let out a supercilious laugh. 'You know what I think, Dee? I reckon you were frightened I might send Tommy over to Camden to sort you out. Give you a good hard wallop with his spade.'

'You've always been fair, Stella. I wouldn't expect you to do a thing like that unless you were sure I deserved it.'

'So you thought you'd better come over here and smooth things over. Well you've nothing to worry about. I'd be a fool to think *you* knew anything about what Pete was up to.' She seemed to be absolving Delia of blame; nevertheless, there was still menace in her voice. 'I ain't no fool, am I?'

Delia nodded. Deferred. Won. It was all over now. In the end, the Imps had scripted everything perfectly. Soon she could be on her way, once Stella had rewritten the past, explained how nothing had really gone wrong for her after Pete pushed Finlay under the car. How she had been neither drunk nor petrified that night when she and Delia had met alone in the bar of the Lamplighters.

'Things got sorted out quick,' she said. 'There was no need for anyone to go running off. The Krays said they'd had nothing to do with what had happened, and they were just taking care of business for Finlay while he was in the hospital, out of the goodness of their hearts. Load of bullshit of course, but nobody wants a war, do they? So the Richardsons said the Krays could keep the clubs if they bought Finlay out. He took their money and fucked off to Devon with that Maggie.'

'So it's all settled, then,' Delia said, knowing it wasn't.

Stella gave her a look of contempt. 'Don't tell me what you think I want to hear, Dee. We both know there's no fucking way it's finished between the Krays and the Richardsons. Finlay's done with, that's all, lost his nerve. They offered him half what those clubs were worth, and he took it. Nobody gives a shit about him now.'

'What about you and me, Stella? Is *that* settled? I can't carry on hoisting. It ain't for me anymore. That's why I went, really. But I'm here now because I didn't want to leave things wrong between us.'

'You ain't touched your char,' Stella said, stonefaced.

Delia lifted her cup and took a drink. It was a gesture of trust, she supposed, though poison wasn't Stella's style. The tea had gone cold and it was far too sweet.

'One way or another, I'm not coming back after today, Stella. I just wanted to know if there's anything in The Book I need to clear. To ask you that to your face.'

Stella got out of her seat and came around to Delia's side of the table. 'Stand up and give me a hug,' she said.

Delia did as she was told. Her second embrace in less than an hour, but this was something very different from Maureen's uncontrolled gesture of affection, and not only because Stella's body felt so brittle and flimsy.

'You and me, we go back a long way, don't we?' Stella said.

'Since just after the war. There's only Lulu been with you longer.'

'Yeah, and she ran, didn't she? They all fucking ran when they were scared, and they all came back when they thought it was safe.' Stella paused to let the subtext sink in, then she said, 'At least you had the self-respect to stay gone, Dee. You ain't come back all apologies, pretending everything's like it was before.'

'Like I said, I'm just here this one time, to make sure we're all square.'

Stay or go, Delia had thought when she left – nothing between – and she'd been right. Only she and Maureen had made the smart decisions. The others might think they were safe, but Stella had a score to settle with each of them, sooner or later.

'Well, there's nothing in The Book for you to worry about. No debts either way.' Stella stepped back and looked Delia up and down, assessing not just the woman in front of her, but the value of the history between them. 'And you say I'll probably not be seeing you round here again?'

'Most likely not,' Delia said, entering into a contract whose terms were a great deal more precise than they sounded.

'All right then.'

Stella left the room. Delia stood where she was, waited for what would happen next. After a couple of minutes, Teddy came in. She saw right away that Maureen had been right: he was different from before. *Watch out for this one*, the Imps whispered. He had taken on the role of frightener, recently vacated by Itchy Pete.

'I'm to see you to the station, Dee,' he said.

He wore the same old greasy suit and overcoat, but Teddy's new persona was measured and dispassionate. If he had plans for you there'd be nothing personal in it. He walked behind Delia as she made her way out of the pub, and though she was almost certain Stella had decided to let her go, she remained prepared for a sudden shock of pain, a punch to the kidneys, a claw hammer to the back of her head. For the world to go dark and something very bad to begin.

But it didn't happen. Teddy was simply ensuring she knew she was never to return again, understood what would happen to her if she broke that agreement. Out on the street, he walked alongside her, on the outside by the road, an old-fashioned gentleman offering her his *protection*. She thought of the double meaning that word had around here, and she decided, the Imps being finally back with her, that there was one last risk she wanted to take.

'How's Stella doing?' she said. 'After all that with Finlay?'

Teddy's answer was a reflex. 'Stella's tough. Nothing gets to her.'

'I'm not saying she isn't,' Delia took a breath. She was about to pose a question that everybody wondered about, but nobody ever asked. 'Only I haven't seen her outside in ever such a long time. You know, now I come to think of it, not since fifty-one, actually, at the Festival of Britain—'

Teddy took hold of Delia's arm to silence her.

'You want to be careful, Dee,' he said. The street was empty, and they both knew that any witnesses would keep what they'd seen to themselves. But Delia guessed he'd been instructed to do her no harm, and she was determined to hear the truth for once. On top of which, she could see how glad Teddy would be to share the burden of his secret, even with someone he had always detested.

'I'm out of all this,' she said. 'You know that. Just tell me if I'm right, Teddy.'

'Fucking hell, Delia.' He looked around them, as if he thought Stella might be somehow listening nearby, and she remembered how, only a few months ago, Maureen had made a similar gesture on her way to Barkers. They were all afraid of Stella's omnipresence, she thought, when in reality—

'It's called agoraphobia,' Teddy said. 'She can't go two steps outside the door. Hasn't even tried for years.'

That part everyone knew really, but Delia thought she understood why.

'What happened with that army friend of yours, Teddy?'

'Me and Pete dealt with it,' he muttered. And that was all he would say.

She left him at the entrance to the station, his eyes on her back as she walked away. Most likely he'd wait until he was sure she would not reappear. Then on his way home to the Lamplighters he'd be round to see Maureen, to take her over to Stella for a little chat. But the boss wouldn't hurt her, or have her hurt. Delia was almost certain of it. The girl had been loyal, after all.

Teddy and Pete had dealt with it, he'd said. So now Delia knew for sure.

That day in 1951, Teddy was home on leave, and an army pal of his had come to stay with him: a big, confident bloke from Essex. Teddy, Pete, Stella, Delia and a few of the other girls had all gone to the festival together, on the South Bank, out Waterloo way. This soldier had come too, and he'd been particularly friendly with Stella. The pair of them got drunk out of his hip flask, wandered around the festival being vulgar and stupid, laughing at things in the exhibitions – mostly things that weren't especially funny. Delia hadn't liked him. He'd seemed like a bully to her.

She'd got a bit drunk herself. The weather was hot, and everything went a little fuzzy. Then at some point Teddy's army pal wasn't there anymore, and Stella was distraught. According to Teddy they'd run into some bloke, and this squaddie had gone off with him on an offer of work. Nobody knew the bloke's name, or what sort of work it was meant to be. That was what Teddy told the military police too, a couple of days later, after the squaddie had been found dead in a back alley, beaten and stabbed.

Two days later, waiting in Kensington Square in the morning, Delia was an image of working-class respectability – some posh household's cook on her day off, wearing her best Marks and Spencer.

Maureen arrived at ten.

'We're going back in Barkers, ain't we?' she said. 'You trying to look like a shopwalker?'

'I'm playing your mum,' Delia said.

As instructed, Maureen had on the same cotton skirt and cheap sweater as before in Fenfield.

'Does Stella know you're here?' Delia asked her

'Yes.'

'Good. Don't want you telling her any lies. She send anyone to keep an eye on you?' She wondered whether Teddy should be here, as he had been the first time. But this was about fixing the past, not reproducing it.

'Don't think so. What's this all about, Dee?'

'I've been on tramlines,' she said. 'That day you got caught, the track split off two ways, and we ended up going in the wrong direction. The right way's been pulling me back bit by bit all this time.' She put her hands on Maureen's shoulders. 'And now here you are. Stella could've told you not to come, couldn't she? But she didn't. She might not know it exactly, but she's part of all this too.'

Maureen shook her head. 'She says she just wants to know what goes on. I'm to tell her all about it when I get back.'

'Fine. That's what I'd expect.'

'*If* I get back,' Maureen said gloomily.

'Last time I only got away because of you. Maybe I'll have to return the favour, but don't worry, I'll make sure you don't get caught, whatever happens.'

A beat copper strolled in from Derry Street. It was the same man as last time, Delia was sure. Day after day, for months, he had been making this round, she thought, maybe for years. Last time, all she'd noticed about him was his uniform, his role. Now she saw a man of about her own age, dark-haired, friendly looking.

'Ladies,' he said, but not sarcastically; not like he thought they were up to anything. Of course, today they looked respectable. The worst they might be was lost.

'Constable,' Delia said, effortlessly unsuspicious. Like she belonged.

'Nice morning.'

'Beautiful.'

It was too. She hadn't even noticed. Bright spring sunshine, a light, warm breeze. The buildings somehow appeared more welcoming than they had been last time. The greenery in the square's private garden was sleek and glossy.

'I think I saw you here once before, Miss. About a year ago, maybe?'

'Yeah,' Delia said. 'That's quite likely.'

'Live round here, do you? Or visiting a friend?'

'Just out for a walk. Like you say, it's a nice morning to go strolling.'

The copper gave her a knowing smile. 'Well, some of us got no choice when it comes to going for a walk, have we? Nice morning or not.'

'I suppose that's true. Still, I bet you've got your preferences.' They were flirting now. Harmlessly passing the time.

'Oh yes, Miss. Some days it don't even feel like a job.' He smiled broadly and raised a single eyebrow, so she'd know exactly what he meant, and then he was on his way.

When he was out of earshot, Maureen said, 'I thought we were meant to be invisible.'

'Not today,' Delia told her. And she explained the plan. Her role in it. Maureen's.

This time there was to be no reconnoitring for shopwalkers, no hanging around in the Food Halls, no checking to see what the Imps thought about their chances of success, no splitting up. Delia and Maureen took the escalator together, straight to the top of the store, and headed directly for Furs. They passed through Lingerie on the way. No sign there of the fat shopwalker, but Delia was confident he must be around somewhere.

They found the Russian hat, still on display in exactly the same place. The two assistants were still working in Furs: one junior and one senior. A year ago it had not occurred to Delia that the ages of these two women more or less matched Maureen's and hers. Now the Imps drew her attention to the parallel, and they told her the shopwalker would be along soon enough. Without him things couldn't fall back into place. He was needed. He would be here.

The older assistant watched Delia and Maureen carefully. Doubtless, she remembered Maureen's capture. It was unlikely she often saw such drama here. She muttered something to her junior, who scuttled off in the direction of Electricals. Pleased by this development, Delia lifted the hat from its display pedestal, and placed it carefully on Maureen's head.

'Take a look in the mirror.'

There was a full-length one near the counter. Maureen scrutinised herself in it and giggled. The hat was ridiculous; even more so on top of her ordinary clothes.

'What do you think?' she said. 'Does it suit me?'

But she was not talking to Delia. Her question was addressed to the fat shopwalker, who now filled the mirror behind her, red-faced, panting and sweaty. He'd been fetched by the junior salesgirl, and had obviously run all the way. Maureen turned to face him. He stepped back, keeping both women in sight, recessed dots of eyes darting from one to the other.

His voice was wheezy. 'You want my advice? Try another line of work, girl. Doesn't look like this one's doing you a lot of good. State of your face.'

To emphasise his point, he reached forward, as if to put his hand to Maureen's damaged features. She jerked away from him, and the hat fell to the floor.

'Don't you touch me! You got no right!'

Delia picked up the hat and returned it to its display stand. 'You want to be careful how you talk to customers, Mister.'

'*Customers*,' he snorted. 'I caught that one a year ago trying to steal this very hat. And we both know what happened the last time I saw *you* in here.'

Delia addressed the senior sales assistant, keeping her tone deferential and decent. 'I think this gentleman's got me confused with someone else, Ma'am.' Like the cook whose character she had adopted, she pronounced it almost as *mum*. 'Today's the first time I've ever come in this store. But I'm sorry to say he's right about my Maureen here. He did catch her trying to steal from you Ma'am. She'd always been a good girl before. Then she got herself into some bad company, and she had to go to borstal for it.'

She considered choking back a sob, but that would be too much. It was enough to let a pause imply her restraint. The emotion could speak for itself.

'We were both here at the time, weren't we, Miss Chalmers?' the saleswoman said. 'I'm sure your daughter's learned her lesson.'

'Thank you both,' Delia said, glancing accusingly at the shopwalker. 'Those so-called friends of hers all got off scot-free. It was only our Maureen got locked up. She wasn't suited for it, Ma'am. All those young criminals. You can see from her face how she suffered in there.'

'Oh, the poor thing!' said Miss Chalmers.

Affecting a struggle to reassert her dignity, Delia kept an eye on the shopwalker. Obviously he didn't believe any of this, but he was puzzled enough by her game to let it continue.

'You're very kind,' she said. 'But we didn't come here today to make excuses. We came to make amends. Me and her dad've thought and thought about this, and we've decided there's only one thing we can do.' She took her purse from her handbag. 'That's the same hat my daughter tried to steal last year, I believe? We'd like to purchase it.'

As she had anticipated, both saleswomen were horrified to see this unfortunate woman reach deeply into her life's savings to buy an item for which she'd have no use whatsoever.

'There's really no need, Madam,' said the senior assistant.

'I insist,' Delia replied, opening her purse. She'd chosen the smallest one she owned and overstuffed it with far more money than it had been designed to contain. 'Sixty pounds, isn't it?'

'Sixty guineas, actually,' said Miss Chalmers.

'Oh.' In a perfect moment, Delia actually felt her face flush with shame, as if she had not known, had not constructed this misunderstanding on purpose. 'I see. Well, that would mean another three pounds, wouldn't it? I'm sure I must have that much. Would you mind if I—?' She went over to the counter, opened the change pocket of her purse and tipped its contents carefully onto the surface. There were eight silver shillings in there, a sixpence and a scattering of copper coins. Delia set about counting the money meticulously back into her purse, as if she hoped some impossible mathematics might reveal the three extra pounds she needed to pay for the hat. She made this awful process last as long as she dared, paralysing the two saleswomen into an agony of embarrassment. Once she had finally collected all the coins, she kept her eyes down and said, 'I'm afraid I'm a little short. I'll have to go the bank and come back later, if that's all right.' She turned to the junior assistant. 'Would you mind taking it off display for me, Miss? I'd hate to find someone else had bought it.'

This prompted the senior saleswoman with the idea she needed. Her voice was almost joyous, 'Ah. I was about to explain about that, Madam. I'm afraid another customer has already purchased this item. A gentleman bought it only this morning. For his wife's birthday. We were just about to wrap it up for him.'

This woman was an appallingly poor liar, Delia thought, and May was an odd time to give anyone a fur hat. But the script had unrolled according to plan, so she remained mute.

'He'll be back to collect it this afternoon,' Miss Chalmers added helpfully.

Maureen took Delia's hand in hers. 'Let's go, Mum.'

But Delia was not quite ready yet to finish. Fixing the senior assistant with a look of desperation, she said, 'You'll be ordering more of these, surely?'

'I'm afraid not, Madam. This one has been in stock for some time, and the furrier only makes them in winter.'

Delia looked around herself, as if in a daze of bafflement. 'I just thought I should— that I had to—'

'Come on, Mum,' Maureen said, tugging gently at her hand. 'I don't like it here.' She glanced in the direction of the two assistants. 'No offence.'

The fat shopwalker decided it was time for him to take charge. 'Tell you what, ladies,' he said. 'Why don't I walk you both out of the store? This isn't a place either of you wants to be, is it?'

The kindliness was a pose, of course. Still, Delia let Maureen lead her to the down escalators with the shopwalker at their side. He rode behind them, one step above, during their descent, and when they all stood on solid ground, he was his sneering self again.

'Whatever you pair of slags are up to, it isn't going to work,' he said. 'You might have fooled those two up there, but you can't fool me.'

'Is that right?' Delia said.

Discreetly, out of anyone's sight, unless they'd been watching closely, he gripped her wrist, held it just tightly enough to hurt a little.

'I'm thinking perhaps we might all go into my office for a little search,' he said.

'Oh yeah,' Maureen said. 'You going to make me strip down to my underwear again, are you?' And she whispered, 'We're not scared of you, you dirty sod.'

With his free hand, he took out a handkerchief and wiped his face. 'Maybe you ought to be scared, *Maureen*. Because you've got a record, been locked up for this sort of thing already. I'll bet I can find evidence on you two. Stuff you've got hidden in your knickers.'

'Whether anything's there or not, I'll bet,' Delia said.

His mouth compressed into a narrow smile. 'See, Maureen. Your *mum* understands.'

He shut up as a young couple went past. The husband fussed over his heavily pregnant wife, annoying her. The woman's tight black jersey emphasised her gravid belly.

'Just let me *be*, Alec,' she snapped.

'Well, sorry for trying to take care of you and our baby,' the husband said crossly. He pushed on a little ahead of her, but then stopped to let her catch up and began apologising for real.

Delia watched this little drama play itself out all the way to the exit, where the young woman finally planted a kiss of forgiveness on her husband's cheek. The shopwalker's paw was still around her wrist. She felt it growing slippery with sweat.

'Some of the girls who come pinching stuff here,' she told him, 'have employers. Businessmen.'

'Oh yes?' he said. 'Why should I care about that?'

'Because these particular businessmen have ways of dealing with things that get in the way of their business. For example, if some shopwalker turned out to be a problem to them, he'd probably wake up one morning with his fat fucking belly sliced open and his guts all over the bedroom floor.'

She'd been mimicking the sort of thing Stella might say. It seemed to work. At the very least it had surprised him. His mouth flapped open and shut several times. He let go of her wrist.

'That's a lot of rubbish,' he said eventually, but he stepped back from them. 'Piss off, the pair of you. And don't let me catch either of you in this store again.'

'Bye then, porky,' Maureen said. 'See you soon.'

They strolled unhurriedly away. About halfway to the exit, Delia stopped and looked back. The shopwalker had not moved. She picked up a cashmere scarf, held it up to the light and then wrapped it around Maureen's neck. The shopwalker stayed where he was, watching them as they continued on their way. Just before the revolving doors Maureen stopped, took off the scarf and draped it over the shoulders of a female dummy in swimwear. Then they left.

'You scared the life out of him,' Maureen said once they were out on the street. 'He won't sleep for days, probably.'

But Delia wasn't thinking of the shopwalker any more. She was looking at the window displays. There were dummies in the new season's fashions; piles of tableware; a kind of gigantic fan made of different curtain materials. The Doris Day scenes had all gone.

Some silences are easy and comfortable, some are not. As they walked together along Kensington High Street, Delia found the one that had fallen between her and Maureen was of the latter sort. She had thought she felt a kind of mother's love, had imagined herself bound by it, but now she no longer owed the girl anything, all she wanted was to escape.

After fifteen minutes they reached the Albert Memorial. A young couple were messing about on the street. It was the same pair who had pushed past them in Barkers. The pregnant wife leant against the memorial's gates, watching her husband perform a kind of unschooled tap dance on the street.

'What's he up to?' Delia said to the wife.

'Entertaining me, apparently,' she replied. 'He's still all excited.'

Jimmy stopped dancing. 'I've never done anything like that before. It was terrifying.' He didn't look terrified. He was gleeful.

'Can I see it?' Maureen asked.

Delia nodded and Tess reached up into the bottom of her jumper. She wriggled a little, undid some buttons under there, and pulled out a domed cloth pouch. She looked down at her now-flat belly, thinking perhaps of the real bump that would be there in a few months, of the real child in there, invisible for now, growing.

'It was *so* easy,' she said, handing the pouch to Delia. 'After you went down the escalator, those two assistants were gabbing about what had just happened and paying no attention to the store. They were just like you said they'd be. But then it got better. The older one went off to tell her friend in Cookware all about it, and she left the younger one on her own.'

'I distracted her while Tess did the business,' Jimmy said. A look of uncertainty crossed his face. 'We got the right thing, didn't we?'

The pouch had been made by a clever seamstress. It would retain its domed shape and look like a pregnant midriff, no matter what had been stuffed inside. Delia opened it up, pulled out the Russian hat.

'Yes,' she said. 'This is the right one.'

And they heard the boots of the Red Army marching towards them. Not metaphorically. Really. The boots of the Red Army. Because there needed to be a sign now. The Imps wanted Delia to know she'd finally got it right. They were satisfied at last.

A month previously, Tess had brought one of her paintings to Delia's bedsit. She'd unrolled it and laid it on Delia's bed so they could both step back and take a look. In the picture, two half-defined figures, a man and a woman, floated out of a vibrant, dream-coloured world and into each other's bodies, so the viewer could not separate person from person from landscape. It was, Tess explained, an attempt to render an idea into an image.

'It's Bill Shearsby and you. I wondered whether you were attracted to him because he reminded you of when you were evacuated to Somerset.'

She didn't buy that idea at all; nevertheless, the painting moved her, seemed very beautiful to her. But Delia knew that would not be enough for Tess, because nothing ever was. The girl had disappointment in her blood. It was aggravating, how she could never settle for what she had.

'I've been thinking about when we went to see Tommy the Shovel rob that butcher's shop,' Tess said as she rolled the picture up again.

'Tommy the Spade.'

'There's this American artist, Allan Kaprow. He says a work of art doesn't have to be a painting or a sculpture, or anything permanent. It can be an event – something weird or shocking. He calls them *happenings*.'

Delia laughed. 'You ain't saying Tommy's an artist, are you?'

'I am, in a way. I mean, not quite. It needs to be intended as art. Like nature can be beautiful, but it's not art until someone does something with it.'

'So if Tommy called himself an artist, rather than a criminal, he'd be making *happenings*, would he?' Delia said. 'That might be a way to keep himself out of the nick.'

Tess was working her way towards something. She said, 'I think artists and criminals are similar in a lot of ways. Especially successful ones, like you.'

'I'm not a criminal anymore.'

'No. But you *were* a success at it, weren't you?'

'Right up until when I wasn't.'

'No, but I'm saying I think what you did was very like Art.'

'Do you want to try for yourself?' Delia said. She had heard the capital 'A'.

'Why not?' Tess's quick, unthinking reply confirmed Delia's suspicion. Her choice. Still, there was a duty to warn her.

'You could get caught. You know what happened to Maureen.'

'I'm not like Maureen.'

'That's true.'

'Could Jimmy help?'

'If he wants to.'

'I'll ask him.'

'You've asked him already, haven't you?'

Delia agreed in principle. She liked the idea of a last-ever hoisting trip; liked the idea of taking Tess along to turn it into Art, but she hadn't any particular plan yet. One would come to her, though, she was sure – and two days later one did, straight after she'd spotted Teddy in the crowd at the Enterprise. It would involve Maureen, require a return to Barkers, and if it went well, it would fix everything.

# 19

There was a sound of marching boots in the distance.

Maureen put the hat on. 'What do you think?'

'It's beautiful,' Jimmy said. 'Perfect on you.'

Tess caught Jimmy's eye. He had said *beautiful* when he really meant *ridiculous*. But wonderfully, right now these two words could be synonyms.

'Do you want to keep it, Tess?' Delia said. 'You were the one who stole it.'

'We all stole it together,' Tess said. 'But you started this, Maureen. You should keep it.'

Maureen grinned, and pulled the hat down a little more firmly onto her head. At last they saw where the sound of boots had been coming from. A long single file of uniformed men marched towards them from the east of the city. They were not British Army, these invaders in crisp, dark jodhpurs, in peaked caps and high-legged boots. They might have been threatening, except there was something not precisely military about them. As they neared, Tess saw the unevenness in their physical fitness. Some were almost scrawny, some verged on the portly. Some of them smiled as they marched, with a swing that seemed a little like dancing. Theirs was the discipline not of soldiers, but of a chorus line. If she had known the word *camp*, back then, she would have seen that this was its apotheosis.

'Oh, that's perfect! Look—' Jimmy said, and he pointed across the road to the posters on display outside the Albert Hall.

## Finer Things

*ALEXANDROV ENSEMBLE* they said. *RED ARMY CHOIR WITH TRADITIONAL DANCERS.*

'Russians!' Maureen cried out. 'Like my hat!'

The four criminals cheered the Choir of the Red Army as it marched from Knightsbridge to Kensington.

**JULY 1963**

# 20

Just over a month later, on the afternoon of the first-year show, Delia stood across the road from Moncourt and watched the trickle of guests pass through the college entrance. The old man on the door barely seemed to acknowledge them; it appeared the invitation card she had kept so carefully in her handbag would be unnecessary.

She lit a cigarette to give herself some sort of purpose and tried to decide whether she would go into the exhibition or not. The Imps kept quiet about it: their job was to look after shoplifters, not barmaids, and they didn't bother much with Delia these days. If she had to guess, she'd say they were in two minds.

Here came a different kind of omen: a coat of startling pink, Harvey Nichols, most likely, making its way towards her. The young woman wearing it walked in short, rapid steps, constrained by a tight pencil skirt. Her eyes were invisible behind dark glasses, her red hair piled into a monumental beehive. It was Penelope, Tess's housemate.

'I take it you're here for the exhibition too,' she said. However her appearance might change, the voice remained unmistakable. She inclined her head towards the young man by her side. 'You remember William Shearsby's son, Marius? You met him at the Gaudi.'

'Of course,' Delia said. 'You two are engaged now, aren't you? Tess mentioned that. Congratulations.'

Marius seemed balder and stockier than when she had last seen him; duller too, if that were possible. There was an unfriendly look about him. Perhaps he was bothered by Penelope mentioning the shameful evening at the Gaudi, or perhaps he knew something about Delia's short-lived romance with his father. More likely he was just surly about being dragged to this arty nonsense.

'Shall we get on with it?' he said. He had his hands firmly in his jacket pockets, a recalcitrant schoolboy.

Delia held up her cigarette. 'I'll be a few minutes. Just finishing this.'

'Come along then, fiancé,' Penelope said, taking off her sunglasses.

Delia watched them cross the road and enter the building. She stubbed out her cigarette on the wall behind her and began to count, as she had once asked Maureen to count, slowly, taking a breath between each number and the next to mark the seconds. When she got to three hundred, she stopped counting, but she stayed where she was.

Tess waved to Jimmy, over on the far side of the studio. ('Let's not have Mr and Mrs Nichols snuggling together,' nasty Roger Dunbar had said yesterday, while deciding who should be stationed where.) Jimmy waved back and stifled a yawn. All the first years had been here long after midnight yesterday, whitewashing the studio and preparing it for the private view.

Her peers were standing sentry next to their own artworks. With her pregnancy now an acknowledged fact, Tess alone had been allowed a chair. During the quietness of the first hour, she had caught herself almost falling asleep on it several times. Now everyone's family members had turned up, and the room felt, if not quite busy, at least occupied.

Her own parents stood in front of a vast inverted crucifixion. They listened politely to its cadaverous young painter just as they had listened politely to eight other artists already that afternoon, including both Tess and Jimmy.

A woman, some other student's mother Tess supposed, stopped to look at her work. 'This is very – er – vigorous,' the woman said, craning forward to examine a street-level view of Doddington Road with Maureen looking down from the upstairs window.

'They're mainly of the East End,' Tess replied. 'Fenfield. I've taken quite a loose approach because I want to be accurate to the spirit of the place rather than its surface.' Each time she delivered this account of her work, she found herself a little less convinced. At worst it sounded like an excuse, she thought, at best like one of Benedict Garvey's weaker lectures. Once or twice with that in mind she had thrown in the phrase 'unshackling myself from bourgeois realism', but only when speaking to a person who appeared receptive to that sort of thing.

'What about this big one?' the woman asked.

'That's the Choir of the Soviet Red Army, marching past the Albert Hall.'

'Not the East End, then?'

'No, that one isn't in the East End. But see here, watching them go by, that's the same girl as in the other picture. The one looking out of the window.'

'I see,' the woman said, not listening. A charcoal drawing of Tommy the Spade had caught her attention: his weapon raised above his cowering victim. The woman's face registered distaste.

Tess decided it was time for some mischief. 'I wasn't sure whether to show that one,' she said, with studied caution. 'And I'm not really supposed to talk about it because it's what they call *sub judice*.' She looked shyly at the floor to bait the hook, then met the woman's gaze again. 'The thing is, he actually *killed* that old man. Smashed his head in.'

'Good God! Really? With a garden spade? How horrible.'

'I had to give evidence at the trial. It was terrifying. All the time I was on the stand, he was looking at me with such *hatred.* Then he started yelling all about how he'd kill me when he got out, and the judge said he had to leave the courtroom. It took four policemen to drag him off.'

The woman looked at Tess in horror, then back at the picture, as if it could add more to the story than it already had. 'But— They locked him away, surely?'

'Not yet. Well, he's in prison, but only on remand. The trial's still going on. After I gave my testimony, the prosecution barrister told me he'd almost certainly get life, so I should be safe enough. Unless he were to get off for some reason, I suppose, or escape.'

'You've been very brave.' She put her hand briefly on Tess's shoulder in a gesture of helpless sympathy. As she did so, however, a look of suspicion crossed her face, as if touching the liar had broken the spell. Tess saw the game was up.

The woman moved on without another word.

Penelope and Marius had arrived. They were talking to Jimmy. Although Tess was too far away from them to hear, she could read the progress of their conversation easily enough. Penelope was impressed by Jimmy's pictures; Marius, predictably, was not. After *Sharpeville 1960*, he had expanded his series of twentieth-century massacres to include *Chumik Shenko 1904*, *Amritsar 1919*, *Shaji 1925*, *al-Bassa 1938* and *Batang Kali 1948*. All were perpetrated on anthropomorphic colouring-book animals by other anthropomorphic colouring-book animals. Veronica Wilding loved them. She had offered, once the first-year show was done with, to put the whole set of pictures in her gallery. It was astonishingly good news: selling just a couple could solve all their current financial problems. Still, Tess wasn't sure it would be good for Jimmy in the long run.

Penelope and Marius detached themselves from Jimmy and came over. It was not a coincidence that her parents chose that moment to terminate their tour of the exhibition and join her too. Visible only to Tess, Jimmy pulled a face behind all their backs. The week-long visit from his new parents-in-law had been difficult.

'They know I'm queer,' he'd said to Tess. 'Even if they don't realise they know.'

Whether or not that was the reason, they had certainly remained unimpressed by his efforts at charm. Meanwhile, and without even trying, Penelope and Marius had beguiled them.

Jimmy gripped an imaginary rope above his head, let his tongue sag and rolled his eyes. His pretending to hang himself probably oughtn't to be funny, she thought, given the chance he might try it for real sometime, but she laughed anyway.

'What's so amusing?' Marius said.

'Oh, that woman over there just caught me out telling her an outrageous lie.'

Her mother gave her a look of disapproval and turned to Penelope. 'I didn't know you two were coming today.'

'Bad Penny, aren't I? That's why I keep turning up.' While Tess's parents chuckled at that, Penelope took the opportunity to whisper that Delia was outside. Then she exclaimed, 'Oh, isn't that Ben Garvey? Excuse me, won't you. I've something I simply must discuss with him.' With that she was gone.

Tess's mother scrutinised the picture of Tommy the Spade. 'You used to do such nice drawings before you came here. Do you think you might go back to that one day?'

'What did you think of Jimmy's work?' Tess said.

Neither her father nor Marius heard the question. Having given quite enough attention to art for one afternoon, they had fallen into conversation about a car one or the other of them was thinking of buying.

'It's not the sort of thing I understand,' her mother said. She scanned the room, obviously bewildered by all of it. 'I've tried my best.'

Tess smiled. 'I know you have, Mum.' This was their relationship: bafflement and disappointment. A mother who wished her daughter was more like Penelope and would much prefer her married to someone like Marius. She said, 'I have to go outside for a while, to speak to a friend. If anyone asks about these, just tell them I'm casting off the shackles of bourgeois realism.'

Outside the college a few minutes later, Tess crossed the road to where Delia stood, and took both her friend's hands in hers.

'Penelope told me you were here,' she said.

'I don't think I can go in,' Delia told her. It wasn't an apology, just a statement of how things were.

'Oh, you've seen all my stuff anyway. None of it's good enough.'

Tess meant it. Those paintings weren't what she'd wanted to exhibit. Right from the start, all the time they'd been arranging the robbery, she had intended to submit the fur hat as her sole exam piece. She'd envisioned it standing on a plinth, inside a box with a window: a sort of ready-made, with a caption saying *STOLEN GOODS*. It would have failed, naturally. She might even have been arrested. What a conclusion *that* would have been to this year of surprises, shocks and confusions. To this year of wonders. Instead she'd settled for the practicality of a stolid, invisible *B* grade.

Did she regret that? As they had all stood together that day, watching the Red Army Choir, it had felt like an ending. Tess had finally done one thing that actually felt like art. Like Art. At the same time, Delia had resolved her debt to Maureen, and the four of them had got away with a crime. Five, counting the foetus inside her. Since that day, the closest she had come to telling anyone what had happened was to make a painting of a marching choir whose meaning only her fellow criminals would ever understand. Now here she was, weeks later, still walking about in the world, a married woman soon to have a child, but also with another year at Moncourt, another chance to become an artist for real.

She was still holding her friend's hands. She let them go.

'Do you know what happened to that silly Russian hat in the end?' she asked.

Delia shook her head. 'Not a clue. Maybe Maureen's kept it for the winter. I hear Stella's out of the shoplifting business now.'

Of course Tess had been right to give it away, to accept the moment for what it was. There were finer things, more beautiful things, than any *exhibit*. She was fortunate, she realised, and so was Delia. They were lucky to have found each other. It was time to go.

'I left my mum to explain my paintings,' she said. 'I expect she's in a terrible panic.'

Delia looked back across the road at the doors to the college. 'What's she think about your husband, now she's finally met him?'

The word struck Tess as odd. It couldn't encompass what Jimmy meant to her, nor she to him. Yet he was *her husband* she supposed, factually speaking.

'They're getting on as well as I'd have expected,' she said.

Delia laughed at that. 'He's a decent sort. You suit each other, don't you?'

'We do. Yes.'

They paused, looking for a way to avoid a big goodbye.

'I'd better go back in,' Tess said. 'The show still has another couple of hours to run.'

'I'll head for the Tube, then. Get back to the pub in time for my shift.'

'You'll be all right?'

'I've been all right so far.'

❧

On her way to the Tube, Delia walked past Ginelli's. Tess had mentioned this place a few times, she remembered, so she stopped at the door. It was shut. A handwritten sign in the window read, RE-OPENING SOON UNDER NEW MANAGEMENT. She continued on her way to Euston. There, she descended into the Underground.

Chalk Farm, the closest station to the Enterprise, was two stops away, but Delia was going somewhere else. She'd made her decision after counting to three hundred, before Tess had appeared at the door of the college. The flat in Camden and her job in the pub were no longer what was required.

All her life she had tried to control the uncontrollable. Her Imps had only ever been a name for a lie she told herself; a pretence of order, of rules, when at heart she'd always understood the universe's messiness. Anyone's world could be upended at any moment. People fell on metal spikes, were pushed into the paths of speeding cars, had their faces ruined in prison. Delia had been born in the shadow of one world war, and she'd lived through a second. There was plenty of time for another to come along, worse than either of its predecessors. This century was barely more than half-over.

Since leaving Fenfield, she had lived entirely on what she could earn, had never once touched her savings. What was the point of that? Why, for that matter, had she bothered to amass so much money in the first place?

She stood in front of an Underground map mounted on the station wall and traced its bright tracks with her index finger. The Northern Line would take her to King's Cross, then the Circle Line to Baker Street. Finally, she'd ride the Bakerloo Line to Paddington, where she would empty her locker. She could leave London then, taking nothing with her but her bank books and the clothes she was wearing. Doubtless she'd be back sooner or later; she belonged in this city – but just for now it would be good to see how life was lived elsewhere.

# 21

Delia exits the Underground at Paddington. On her way out, she nods cheerily to the ticket collector in his wooden booth. He is an older gentleman, studiously polite. The empty left sleeve of his uniform jacket is taped across his chest. She asks him how he is today.

'Very well, thanks Ma'am,' he says.

Delia gives him a quizzical look through the window. 'I often wonder, is your whole job just sitting in this little box all day? It must get quite dull, I suppose.'

He glances behind her. There is no queue at the moment. He has time to talk. 'We do other things too, Ma'am. Ticket office, platform. They have us on what's called a rotation. Actually, though, this is my favourite part of it, everything considered. I find people very interesting. You see all sorts passing by.' He taps his wounded shoulder with his remaining hand. 'I suppose you wouldn't call it an exciting life, but I tried excitement during the last war. Can't say I miss it as much as I do my arm.'

'Well,' she says. 'I'd never have thought of it like that.'

He releases the turnstile, and off she goes. How rare these days, he thinks as the next stream of passengers arrives, for a customer even to notice there's a person inside the booth.

Half an hour later he will remember little about his encounter with this woman. Her hair might have been blonde he'll think, or black. Perhaps her age was middle-ish, and her clothes were the normal sort. All he will recall for sure is that she spoke nicely to him as he let her through the turnstile – and being a punctilious man, proud of the care he takes at his work, he would be surprised to hear he never checked her ticket.

# HISTORICAL NOTES

This is a work of fiction. I made up almost all of it. There are no such places in real life as Fenfield, the Moncourt Institute or the village of Trencham.

Some elements of the story are based in documented fact. The Thames really did freeze over in January 1963. Several characters mentioned in passing were real. None of them did any of the things I have attributed to them. The Richardsons certainly had connections in South Africa, but the extent to which they were involved in the Broederbond or in the work of the South African Secret Service here in Britain can't be known with any certainty. The notoriously savage Kray/Richardson turf war actually began in 1965. I have imagined a kind of preparatory rattling of sabres two years earlier than that.

All-women shoplifting gangs did exist in the East End of London, and regularly crossed the city to ply their trade in exclusive establishments such as Barkers of Kensington. Most significantly, the 'Forty Elephants' operated with great success from the late nineteenth century until the early 1950s. By the 1960s, however, the Forty Elephants were finished, and as far as I am aware, there was no equivalent of Stella or my fictional crew of hoisters. Later in the decade, the remarkable Shirley Pitts would take on the title 'Queen of Shoplifters'. Mrs Pitts' own account of her vivid, unusual life is presented in *Gone Shopping: The Story of Shirley Pitts – Queen of Thieves* by Lorraine Gamman.

# Finer Things

The tone of Tess and Jimmy's experiences at art school owes a great deal to Vaughan Grills' entertaining memoir, *I Brought This in Case: The 1960s, Four Art Schools and Me*, and I collected some further factual details from *Art Schools in England 1945 to 1970: An anecdotal history* by Hywel James.

Two items held in the British Anti-Apartheid Movement's archive have been included in the novel. The first page of a flyer advertising the 1963 Trafalgar Square demonstration is quoted verbatim, and the Playwrights Against Apartheid declaration is represented with some small but significant alterations. I should add that I have no idea whether this declaration was really published in the *Guardian*. Seems likely, though. The archive is held at the Bodleian Library, and its material can be accessed online at https://www.aamarchives.org.

My description of Soho at this time was inspired above all by Wolf Suschitzky's sublime camerawork in Ken Hughes' 1963 production *The Small World of Sammy Lee*, and by Richard Dacre's documentary tour of that film's locations, included as an extra on the British Film Institute's Blu-ray release.

For Jimmy's brush with the threat of aversion therapy, a profoundly damaging experience that many gay men underwent in this period, I drew on the *British Medical Journal* article 'Treatments of homosexuality in Britain since the 1950s – an oral history: the experience of patients' by Glenn Smith, Annie Bartlett and Michael King.

Other texts from which I have extracted the odd point of reference or inspiration include *Alice Diamond and the Forty Elephants: Britain's First Female Crime Syndicate* by Brian McDonald, *The Profession of Violence: The Rise and Fall of the Kray Twins* by John Pearson, and *The Last Gangster: My Final Confession* by Charlie Richardson.

# ACKNOWLEDGEMENTS

For permission to use and/or adapt copyright material, I am grateful to the Estate of Allan Kaprow and to the AAM Archives Committee.

Thanks to everyone at Sandstone Press, but especially: Moira Forsyth, Alice Laing (without whom this book would have no title) and my marvellous, judicious and tactful editor, Kay Farrell.

I've been a while getting here. For kindness and support along the way, thanks to Jeremy Grant, Emma Matthews, Alan Murray, Dr Jenny Stewart, Ben Suri, Oscar Wharton, Jade Walsh, Damien G Walter, Sheila Dennis, Lisa Eaton, Mahsuda Snaith, Jonathan Taylor.

A special mention for Tim Jones, who has given sage advice on more drafts of more of my fiction than any living human.

Thanks to Harry Whitehead for teaching me how to write novels – anything wrong with this one is still your fault, Harry.

Thanks, and best wishes for the future, to Leicester Vaughan College and everyone there.

Frances Rippin: I doubt I'll ever pay off my debt to you, but I'll keep clearing the vig.